REMNANTS OF THE GUILTY

ASHLYNN

FOREWORD

This book is a standalone in an interconnected series. It does not end with a cliffhanger but a Happy For Now. This story takes place 18+ years after the Kings of Chaos and Mayhem series ends. This is a glimpse into the future for those characters as it does crossover. You do not have to read anything prior to this book, but it may intrigue you to dive into that world.

Please read the full content warning list. Your mental health is important to me as this book contains very triggering subject matter.

*Trigger Warnings *

MF

Dark/Horror Romance

Brothers Best Friend

- Street Racing Crew of Killers

- College-Aged

- Multi-POV

- Graphic Explicit Murders

- Mentions of (Inc3$t)

- Detectives

- Bad Boy MC

- Sassy FMC

- Hand Necklaces

- Light Voyeurism/Exhibitionism

- Graphic Explicit Sex

- Dirty Talk

- Angst

- HFN

- Standalone

- Edging

- FF

- MM (not with MMC)

- Grape(on page) & Forced Rape

- Video Recordings

- Crawling

- Forced Orgasms

- Sexual & Physical Assault(on page)

- Spitting

- Knife play/ Blood play

- Gunplay

- Toyplay

- Squirting

- Drugging/drinking/partying

- Very light off page bullying

- Crossover 18+ years after Anarchy

- Pregnancy(not FMC)

- Fighting

- OW/OM Drama

- Degradation/Praise

- Snowballing

- Secrets. Lies. Betrayal. Blackmail.

- Kidnapping

- Family Secrets

- Selling of Children through Contracts

- Hallucinations

- Pegging

DEDICATION

To the girls who always wanted to be railed by the
bad boy next-door neighbor.....
Crawl to me & gag on Daddy's cock.
-Easton.

PROLOGUE

DETECTIVE ELEANA ST. JAMES

Walking down the flower lined walkway beyond the white picket fence like I do every night, only this time I am not supposed to be here. I was kicked off this case and assigned elsewhere because I couldn't get the job done. A new detective that I fucking despise is taking over. I'm supposed to be on a plane halfway across the world chasing a ghost, but something in my gut was telling me to get home.

Dylan hasn't answered any of my texts in the last six hours. I was horrible to her yesterday afternoon before she stormed the house. The tears that pooled in her eyes as I said all those mean things to her, was enough for me to pick up on the clues that I was hurting her, but I didn't stop. I was too enraged with all the murders, all the secrets and lies hitting the surface. I refused to see what was going on right in front of me. Just putting the problems in a suitcase and zipping it up for another day. It's a hard pill to swallow knowing that I wasn't the only one keeping dark secrets.

She was so fucking upset, but I kept pushing her for answers without giving her any of my own. She was raped and blackmailed to protect me and her brother. I just didn't fucking believe her.

Between the murders at the frat house, and the boys from the swim team coming up dead, I'm not sure what to believe. Every time I questioned her, it pushed her away and fueled her anger towards me. Hating me more day by day. I was so self-absorbed in finding the person who massacred several men, leaving them mutilated and barely recognizable. Keeping secrets about my past and trying to protect my children all spilled over at once.

There were no leads on the killers at large, so I had to go by the book. Interrogate everyone involved. It's my job. I stood there, took an oath to serve and protect, and find the killers who walk among us. Where did that leave Dylan? Neglected, alone, and scared.

My heart is in my throat as my hands shake holding my pistol. As I walk up the steps, I see the front door is cracked open just a bit. I click on the flashlight, shining it in the doorway, checking both left and right. *All clear.*

The house lies in ruins. Books litter the hardwood floor, bookshelves knocked to the ground and a knife protrudes from the TV screen. I continue down the hallway, passing childhood pictures of Dylan and Bentley. They never had a want or a need. I gave them everything and anything they asked for. Except my attention. I point the flashlight down and follow the drops of blood leading into the kitchen. Plates and cups are broken on the tile floor, fresh-cut flowers from the garden litter the counter next to their shattered vase.

Drip, drip, drip. Water falls to the ground.

Whatever happened here, she put up a fight. I continue to follow the blood smeared on the ground leading to the basement. Taking out a rag, because this is a crime scene, I wrap it around the handle gently so as to not wipe off any prints.

Turning the knob, I pull open the door. Nothing, I mean nothing, could have prepared me for what was down those basement steps.

CHAPTER 1

DYLAN

The slow seductive rhythm flows through my body as my hips grind against Amy. Ava sandwiches me in and we get lost in the beat. The Fatal Five won a race tonight, so my brother Bentley, who's the leader of his street racing crew, decided to throw a party at one of the abandoned warehouses on the outskirts of town. This place he calls 'The Den', is packed with people from different towns. My brother and his friends have a reputation for throwing amazing parties.

Taking a sip from my red solo cup, I let the alcohol burn as it slides down my throat. I'm usually not allowed to drink at their parties because they don't want to have to watch me all night. It's annoying how protective they are of me. Luckily, my boyfriend Carter is here and they don't have to worry as much.

"Babe, you guys are up." Carter shouts from the beer pong table. Ava grabs my hand and I grab Amy's, the three of us heading for our turn at beer pong. Something out of the corner of my eye catches my attention and it's Easton, my brother's best friend, dancing with some girl while he stares at me with a cruel look on his face. I roll my eyes and continue to the table.

For years, Easton has been a thorn in my side. He's a part of The Fatal Five and the most lethal one of them all. We all grew up together-me, Amy, Ava, and the guys, living only houses away. Except Easton's house is right next door, and if I look out my bedroom window, I get a clear shot inside his. The amount of times I've seen him fuck girls or jerk off is maddening. *Am I jealous? Maybe, but I'll never tell him that.* We will just continue this cat-and-mouse game he loves so much. Ever since he and my brother and their band of merry assholes started a street racing crew, I see less and less of him.

Carter grabs my waist, taking me out of my thoughts. "You and me later?" he whispers in my ear as he trails kisses along my neck. He wraps his arms around my waist, fingers playing with the waistband of my skirt. I spin around in his hold, placing a soft kiss to his lips. "Only if you do that thing I like." I wink. He growls, grabbing a handful of my ass.

"Then you better win this beer pong game quickly." He breathes biting my bottom lip.

"Come on baby, I'm the queen of pong. Watch me work the table." I giggle, downing the rest of my drink.

"That's my girl," he says, smacking my ass and spinning me around. It's me and Amy versus the last game's winners, Ty and Shelly. They take the first shots and miss. Amy hands me a ball and she shoots first, getting it in the cup. I shoot immediately after her and get it in the same cup. *Game over.* Ty and Shelly stand there, mouths wide open, stunned. *It was too easy of a win.* I blow a kiss to Shelly and she gives me the finger.

Ava slides up next to me, God forbid she's too far away from Amy. They are two peas in a pod. One is never too far behind. Carter grabs me and throws me over his shoulder, and I squeal. He smacks my ass as everyone cheers. I give my girls a two-finger salute and let him carry me away.

As he walks through the crowd, my eyes meet Easton's harsh glare as he has his tongue down some girl's throat. I swallow at his lust filled stare and break eye contact the moment we step outside and the night's cold air hits my thighs. He slowly drags me down his body until my feet hit the ground, pushing me up against the tailgate of his truck and stepping between my legs.

"I'm glad you wore a skirt tonight, Dyl," he groans, sliding his hands up my thighs and pulling my thong down. I step out of them and he picks it up from the ground, bringing it to his nose, inhaling deep. "You always smell so good, baby." I visibly swallow as he removes his black tee, tossing it on the bed of his truck. His body is ripped and that Adonis belt always has my panties melting for him. I bite my bottom lip as I take him in, reaching out to trail my fingers over his muscled pecs and down his abs. I slide my hand into his jeans to grip his hard cock. He groans when my thumb circles the tip. "Fuck, baby," he pants as I stroke him slowly.

"Touch me." I whisper and his hand slips under my jean skirt finding my throbbing clit with ease. He rubs it in tight circles causing me to moan as his lips find mine and I open letting his tongue slide against mine. We both moan as we continue to touch one another.

He pulls back and removes his fingers from my soaked pussy and slides a wet finger into his mouth. "Turn around, baby. I need to feel you wrapped around me." He says. Turning around, I bend over the tailgate and arch my back for him. *I know this will be over quickly.* He bends down to trail kisses along the back of my neck and down my spine as he slides into me painfully slow. I push back into him, wanting him to go deeper, but he pulls out and slams back in, causing me to tighten around his cock. I moan for him as he grips my hips, pounding into me. "I love you Dyl, my forever girl." He breathes against my neck and I tighten around him again before saying,

"I love you too, Carter." He slams into me a few more times before he pulls out and paints my ass with his release. *Another night of it being all about him.* He reaches next to me and grabs a shirt to wipe his release off of me. I get up and slide my thong back on, thinking of a way to end the night with him. It's the same shit over and over again. But I keep up with the facade. *I just don't know how much longer I can fake it.* I pull my phone from my bra and see it's almost two in the morning.

"Babe, I gotta go. My mom will kill me if I'm out too late." I say in a panic.

"I can't wait for next year when you can live in the dorms and no more curfews," he laughs, grabbing my waist, kissing me softly.

"It will be everything we ever dreamed of, baby." I breathe, resting my head against his chest. *Lie after lie.*

"Alright, sugar lips. Let's get you home." He says giving me another kiss, leading me around the truck and opening the door for me. Getting in the truck I look up and my eyes connect with Easton's again, but this time he's smirking at me as he smokes, so I flip him the bird. He shakes his head and gets on his bike, revving the engine.

The drive home is quiet. I give Carter a kiss goodnight and pop a piece of gum into my mouth as I open the white picket fence and walk up the path to the stairs. Mom left the outside light on for us which means she's awake. *Great.* I key in the door code and turn the knob, opening it. Mom is sitting on the couch with a bunch of files spread all over the table. Without looking up, she greets me.

"Hey Honey. How was your night?"

"It was good. We went to dinner and a movie, then hung out at the dorms." I lie, taking off my shoes.

"Wonderful. I'm leaving in a few to head into the office to start a new case. Hopefully, I'll be home sometime tomorrow. Any plans yet?" She asks, finally looking up at me.

"I'm not sure yet. I'll text you if I leave tomorrow. I'm going to head up to bed. Love you." I say as I walk up the stairs.

"Love you too, honey. Good night." She replies.

Entering my room, I turn on the light and strip off my clothes. Walking over to the bathroom, I turn the knob for the shower and wait for it to warm up. Stepping in, I grab the shampoo and lather my hair up. After rinsing, I wash my body from the day.

Everything has been going so great. My grades at the university are top-notch. The girls and I are planning a trip to Aruba for spring break. Carter and I have been existing in a one-sided relationship for the past year. Everything is just so fucking perfect. *Another lie.* Turning the water off, I grab a towel and wrap it around my body. Stepping out of the bathroom, I notice Easton's light is on. I grab my phone from the bed and shoot the girls a text after throwing on a tank top and shorts.

Me: Mani/pedi tomorrow?

Amy: What time?

Ava: I'm down after I meet up with Daddy.

Me: Still fucking the old guy I see.

Ava: He's not that old, and he fucks like a god.

Amy: If wrinkled balls are your thing lol.

Ava: Listen, he buys me whatever my heart desires.

Me: What's the catch? Men don't give shit out for free.

Amy: Ain't that the truth, or they suck you dry lol.

Ava: As long as I'm available when he calls and I fulfill his kinks. He never says no to me.

Me: Do I even want to know what this old guys kinks are?

Ava: Probably not but he's fun. So what time tomorrow?

Me: Lol, 2pm? Sound good?

They both reply yes and I shut my light off. Walking over to my bed, I climb in and plug my phone up as I snuggle under the covers. Five minutes goes by before I hear my window sliding up and boots hitting the carpet. I roll over and see a dark silhouette.

"The little show you put on tonight, was that for my sake or yours?" He asks, taking off his boots.

"Did you enjoy watching?" I snark, lifting the covers from my body.

"No, I didn't. I never do!" he replies, taking off his shirt and jeans.

"Why's that Eas?" I ask as he slides into bed next to me, grabbing my thigh and hooking it around his hip. My breathing picks up as his hand lays flat against my ass, pulling me closer so his cock lays against my aching clit. He looks down at me with a smirk on his face.

"Because I don't enjoy watching anyone touching you, let alone making you feel good." He replies and I swallow at his words. He has no idea how many times I fake it with Carter. No idea that the only person who can bring me to heights I've never imagined, is him.

"Or are you just mad because I haven't let you feel how tight my pussy is?" I giggle and he growls, climbing between my legs.

"Stop toying with me, D. You know damn well I'll fucking take it, but you know I can't, so leave it alone." He warns and I roll my eyes. *I love taunting him.*

"So then why are you here?" I ask, and he smirks.

"I ask myself that same question every time I climb through your window. But tonight, you put on that little show and that can't go unpunished." He breathes as he takes a nipple into his mouth. Flicking his tongue around the hardened peak. I moan at his touch. Even over the clothes, this boy can make my pussy purr for him.

"Always so responsive, Hellcat." He says, biting the other nipple as his hand slides down my sides, gripping my hips. *I can feel how fucking hard he is.*

"Why won't you fuck me? Show me how good you can make me feel." I pant, he stops and looks up at me.

"You know I can't. Just fucking drop it," he growls.

"You can't, or you won't, or do I not do it for you? Is that it? Why do we continue to play this game if you won't even fuck me?" I spit.

"I don't have to explain shit to you. Now shut the fuck up before I shove my cock down your tight little throat and leave you gagging for more." He spits back, raising a brow at me. I go to say something but his mouth hits my panty covered clit and any thoughts I had moments ago are gone. He licks my bundle of nerves until my panties are soaked. He sits up, takes his cock out, and rubs it against the cotton as he slowly glides up and down my slit, teasing my clit and soaking my panties even more with his pre-cum. Between the friction of his cock rubbing my clit over and over again, I'm ready to cum.

"Damn, D. I bet this pussy is so fucking tight and soaked for me," he groans as he continues to slide his hard cock between my lips.

"I think you should find out. Just the tip Eas, just to feel how wet I am for you." I whimper. *I need more and he's just edging me along.*

"Fuck, my cock wants to stretch you out so fucking bad, Hellcat. So fucking bad," he moans, biting his bottom lip. *He looks so sexy like this.*

"Please, Eas. I want to cum on your dick. Just slide my panties to the side. You don't even have to stick it in. Just glide between my wet lips and feel my clit pulsate against you." I beg.

"No, if I feel you, I won't be able to stop." He groans as his thrusts become sharper and harder, applying more pressure to my needy clit. I almost see stars as he thrusts faster against me.

"You're going to make me cum, Eas. Fuck. You feel so good." I moan, rocking against him.

"Don't stop, just like that. Fuck." He groans as I rock faster against him. I love seeing him come undone and knowing I caused it gets me even wetter.

"Cum for me, Eas." I pant as he slaps my clit with his cock, causing me to cum so fucking hard that my back arches off the bed. He bites my nipple as I feel him jerk his cock against my soaked pussy. He cums with a deep growl and ropes of hot cum drip onto my stomach. He sits up and runs his still hard cock through the mess he made, rubbing it into my skin.

"Fuck, D." He pants, trying to catch his breath. Suddenly we hear the rumble of Bentley's bike, and he climbs off of me, getting dressed quickly. He gives me a kiss on my forehead and leaves the same way he came in. I roll over, close my eyes in hopes to drift off to sleep and forget about what the fuck just happened, but my phone pings with a text.

Easton: Sorry Hellcat.

I don't respond. I'll just act like that never happened.

CHAPTER 2

DYLAN

Sitting in the nail salon with the girls, I keep replaying last night's events over and over in my head. I know I said I would forget about it and act like it never happened, but I can't, not with Easton. He always leaves a mark on me and I don't mean literally. It's like he leaves me with a little piece of his soul, but never shows me everything I need and want. He's the reason I stay with Carter. If I'm all alone, I will pine for him, and that's not the type of girl I am. I don't chase boys; they chase me.

Being with Carter is passing time. Do I love him the way he loves me? Absolutely not. I have no idea what love is. It seems too messy for me and I don't ever want to be in love. Not if it always ends up with abandonment. I should be used to that feeling by now, but it doesn't mean I have to like it.

"Are you even listening?" Ava questions, snapping her fingers in my face. I fucking hate when she does that. I look over to her with narrowed eyes.

"Sorry, I was thinking about what to wear tonight. You guys coming to the frat party?" I ask, dismissing her bullshit.

"Yes." They both say like a set of Bobbsey Twins. These two are always inseparable. We all were until we started dating, then the guys took our time away from one another, but I love when we do girl stuff. It takes my mind off other shit.

"But did you hear what I said about Carter?" She quips.

"Obviously not Ava." I laugh.

"Apparently, after we left The Fatals party last night, the frat had girls over and some chick was rubbing up all over your man." She says.

"Interesting. I trust Carter though. I'm secure enough in our relationship not to worry about what he does at the frat house. I know girls come and go." I shrug.

"I know Dyl. I just wanted to give you a heads up about the bullshit being said. I don't want my best friend looking like an asshole." She says sincerely.

"Thanks, babe. I appreciate that. How was your time with Daddy?" I ask, changing the subject. I'll deal with Carter later tonight.

"Five orgasms and new jimmy choo's. I think we can all agree it was well worth it." She gloats but continues.

"Maxwell is a silver fox and something out of a book, I swear. He asked if he could take me away for a weekend so we don't have to hide." She says, as a blush crawls up her face.

"Wait, wait, wait." Amy chimes in. "I thought this was just about the money and dick. Are you seeing one another? What about Ace? Stop gatekeeping and spill the tea." I nod in agreement. Ava giggles. Uh oh. I wasted my breath about the whole feelings thing. Shit. She's already done for. This is a good distraction away from my thoughts of Easton.

"That's how it started, but then we couldn't stay away. I promise you it's not me. He's the one pursuing me, not the other way around, and fuck Ace!" She blurts, and we roll our eyes, knowing to leave that subject well alone.

"Okay, that is not enough. Come on, Ava! Give us all the dirt. Does he have a big dick? I bet he does and knows how to use it better than the guys our age." Amy says, wiggling her brows. I laugh because she's probably right.

"Amy, don't be so crass. But yes, yes he does." She giggles again. "He's wonderful, sophisticated and plays my body like a fucking fiddle. He cooks me dinner and eats me for dessert. Every single time." She says with a smile on her face. She seems happy, but it all seems too good to be true.

"Does he have a friend? Hook ya bestie up." Amy says.

I quirk a brow at her and she rolls her eyes.

"Did you forget you're dating my brother? Don't let him hear that shit. You know how he gets." I quip. Her eyes won't meet mine, which means something has happened.

"What happened? You won't look at me. Fucking spill Amy." I say, getting annoyed at all the secrets going on that I'm unaware of. She takes a deep breath and a lone tear falls from her eye. Fuck.

"We broke up last weekend. He told me that we have grown apart and I'm not it for him anymore. Our relationship has run its course, and we are done." She hiccups as tears flow down her cheeks. I reach over, grab her face, and wipe the tears from her eyes.

"I'm going to kill him when I see him, but you," I say, grabbing a hold of her face and looking into her eyes. "No crying over my asshole brother. There will be other guys who will treat you the way you deserve and if you want to get back at him. Fuck his friends!" I say and they laugh.

"So take a ride with The Fatal Five? No thanks Dyl. I like my life too much to lose it over your brother being a dick." She says, wiping more tears from her eyes. I know she loves my brother, but he's too blind to see the amazing girl she is.

"I'm just saying." I sing. They start chattering about tonight's events at the frat, and I take my phone out to text Bentley.

> **Me: When the fuck were you going to tell me about Amy?**

> **Benny: Well, little sister. I don't have to tell you shit. I'm done with her. It's just that simple.**

> **Me: Oh, I see. Okay. Then I got something for your ass.**

> **Benny: And what is that?**

> **Me: Oh nothing, just a frat party on the row tonight. Might as well bring her along for a nightcap.**

> **Benny: You're bluffing.**

I take a pic of us in the salon. He knows before we go out, we always get our nails and hair done.

> **Me: Multimedia Message Sent.**

Suddenly, my phone starts to ring. Answering, I put on a sickly sweet tone.

"Hello dear brother, what can I do for you?" Looking over at Amy, her eyes widen, shaking her head profusely.

"You are not to go to that frat party tonight, let alone taking Amy," he growls down the line.

"Or else what?" I spit.

"I swear to God Dylan, for once in your life, do as you're fucking told. No frat party tonight. Something is going down and you cannot be there!" He yells.

"Now I'm calling your bluff. If the party is so dangerous, then why haven't you warned me not to go in the first place knowing who the fuck my boyfriend is? Lie better next time, douchebag. Gotta go. It's waxing time." I laugh, hanging up on him as he continues to yell down the line. I put my phone on silent and place it in my bag.

"You're a savage, but you know there will be consequences if we don't listen." Amy laughs.

"Oh, you let me deal with the prince of darkness. I can handle my fucking brother." I wink at her and relax into my seat, closing my eyes. Nothing like a challenge to get my adrenaline going. Tonight is going to be so much fucking fun.

Me and Amy took an Uber to the frat house. Maxwell called Ava, so she chose a night of wine and dine rather than hanging with us. I don't blame her. The partying, the drugs, the boys. It gets old. If it wasn't because I needed to prove a point, I would be doing something much more exhilarating. When we arrived, Carter was very shocked to see me and that has my red flags flying high, so I've been ignoring him. This party is not as big as it usually is and something is seriously off. My phone pings with a text. I reach into my jeans pocket and take it out, seeing its Bentley, I roll my eyes.

> **Benny: Where the fuck are you Dylan?**

> **Me: At the party calling your bluff.**

> **Benny: Leave. NOW!**

> **Me: Why should I listen to you?**

> **Benny:** I don't have time for this. Fucking leave now, Dylan.

> **Me:** I don't have my car! We took an Uber.

> **Benny:** Just fucking get out of there. Don't worry about a ride. Just get the fuck out of there. NOW!

Suddenly the lights go out and Amy screams. I grab her, throwing my hand over her mouth to shut her the fuck up.

"Amy, listen to me. Bentley told us to get out. Be quiet and don't let go of my hand. Got it?" I whisper, taking my hand away from her mouth.

"Y-yeah, got it." She stutters. Luckily, we are in the kitchen and can easily slip out of the back door. I pull her along the steps down to the ground level. Grabbing my phone, I shoot out a text.

> **Me:** What the fuck is going on? The lights just went out.

> **Benny:** Get off the property. Go down the road. Make sure no one follows you. I'll explain later.

Rounding the corner of the house, I collide with boobs and a knife at my throat. I gasp as she presses the knife deeper into my neck and pushes me against the house. A masked man grabs Amy, covering her mouth with his hand, and pushes her to her knees. My heart is beating a mile a minute. I've never been in a situation like this. This is what my brother and his crew protect me from.

The girl with bicolored eyes cocks her head at me and releases the knife from my throat, only to drag the dull side over my forehead and down my cheek to my jawline.

"You're beautiful." She whispers under the mask. I don't move an inch. I'm so scared, but her eyes are nothing I've ever seen before. They're hypnotic. She trails the knife down my neck and around my breast. My breathing hitches when she circles the tip around my hardened nipples. I've never been attracted to girls before, but her, she's fucking gorgeous.

"Someone likes my knife." She breathes.

"We aren't here for them, let's move it along sister," the masked man spits.

"You're never any fun, Prince." She says, pulling out her phone and opening it to show me a picture of a hot guy I've never seen before.

"Have you seen him here tonight?" she asks, trailing the knife down my torso and pressing it against my hip bone. I shake my head no profusely.

"I have never seen him before. I'm sorry." I stammer. She nods and removes the knife from my body. I let out a breath I didn't realize I was holding.

"Get out of here before I change my mind and keep you for myself." She whispers. My eyes widen but she lets me go and I grab Amy and run. We don't stop until we get to the university six blocks away. Holy fucking shit, what and who the fuck was that? I'm not sure whether I'm more scared, or turned the fuck on, by that girl. My panties are soaked. My phone pings with a text at the same time as Amy's phone, taking me out of my thoughts. Taking mine out, I see its Easton.

> **Easton: Where are you?**

> **Me: Come find me, Crow.**

> **Easton: Hellcat, this is not the time to play games.**

> **Me: No fun. At the university.**

> **Easton: Drop your pin and stop turning your location off.**

Me: Come find me Eas. Come play with me.

Easton. Get rid of Amy then.

Me: Maybe she can watch?

Easton: Not an option.

Looking over at Amy, she smiles, "You know, sometimes you are a genius. B is coming to get me." She smiles and I laugh.

Me: Benny is coming to get her.

Easton: See you soon, Hellcat.

CHAPTER 3

Easton

Dylan loves to make our job harder at protecting her. She shuts off her fucking location and does as she pleases. Half of it is our fault. We don't share the inner workings of what we do and who we run with. Tonight was one of those nights that she shouldn't have been there. She didn't fucking listen and her life was at stake, even though they weren't there for her. But that smart mouth of hers could very well get her into some shit and those that shut down the frat house are ruthless and the most deadly killers in the criminal world. Something I don't want her a part of.

Bentley sent me to go get her while he went to get Amy. He damn near lost his shit when he found out she was going with his sister to the party. I haven't figured out if he was pissed because of what was going to go down, or because if he can't have her, no one else can. I feel like Bentley is at a point in his life where he doesn't want to be tied down anymore. It's too dangerous for us to have anyone to care for. It's bad enough we have to keep Dylan safe. Her boyfriend is a piece of shit. I can't wait for the day he steps out of line. His days are already fucking numbered.

Hellcat wants to play a game tonight. It's going to have to be quick because I need to meet up with Spade to hand him the cash we made the other night and pick up some new product. Working for the Cartel has been lucrative, but everything comes with a price and tonight was one of them. I'm glad Preston gave us a heads up otherwise it really could have turned deadly and I don't want a war with the Kings of Chaos and Mayhem. I cherish my life a little too much.

Pulling into the university, I check Dylan's location. Of course, she's at the other end of the stadium. Shifting my car into gear, I drive over and park. Getting out, I light up a cigarette, taking a pull, inhaling the minty smoke as I walk over to the football field and don't see anyone. It's completely deserted. Then I hear the footsteps charging at me and I immediately take my knife out and spin, grabbing her by the neck and holding it to her rapidly beating artery.

"This is the second time someone is holding a fucking knife to my neck tonight. What in the actual fuck,

Eas?" She spits. *Oh, she's mad. This should be fun.* Tightening my grip, I say,

"Well, if you had actually done what you were told to do, this wouldn't be happening now, would it?" I quirk a brow and she rolls her eyes.

"Don't fucking roll your eyes at me D, you were specifically told to stay away from the frat house on Fatal's orders but here we are. So why did you have a knife to your neck?" I breathe, stepping into her space. Her eyes fill with lust as she runs her hands up my stomach to my chest, wrapping her little hands in my shirt.

"Some masked chick with the most gorgeous fucking bicolored eyes I have ever seen," *Hazel.*

"Caught me and Amy as we were running out of there and held a knife to my neck and turned me on in the process." She says, pinching my nipple and I growl.

"A chick and her knife turned you on? Is that what you are telling me?" I laugh, lifting a brow.

"Yes, yes I am. If only you would stop being a little bitch and slide your fingers into my soaked panties, you would see I'm telling the truth and the knife you're holding to my neck is only making me wetter, Crow." She groans.

"Stop fucking calling me that. It's the stupidest nickname. Grow up. We aren't kids anymore D." I say, ignoring her taunts. Not saying my dick isn't hard from her words, but I can't cross that line with her. Not now, not ever. *I really need to just stay away from her.* I let her go and take a step back.

"Come on, I have somewhere to be." I say, walking away. She shoves me and I whirl on her.

"Why are you even here, Eas? Benny could have taken me home with Amy." She yells. *Jesus fucking Christ it's like dealing with a toddler.*

"It doesn't fucking matter, stop acting like a child and lets go." I turn again heading out of the field and she shoves me a second time, not expecting it, and almost fall into the fence. I spin so fast and grab her by the throat, picking her up in the air and slamming her on the grass, not letting go of her throat. She coughs on impact, and I crouch down, getting in her face with wild eyes.

"Why do you make me do this to you? Why can't you just listen, or is this a kink you're into Hellcat?" I spit.

"Fuck you, Easton. You're a grade A prick. Get the fuck off me." She thrashes under my hold.

"What is it that you wanted tonight? Did you think playing a game with me would get me into your panties? Think again, bitch. I don't want what's between your legs. It's getting pathetic how much you beg for it." I squeeze tighter to really send my point home. Her eyes widen as she claws at my wrist. Before she can slap me, I open her legs with mine and grab ahold of both her hands with my free one and hold them above her head.

"Cut the fucking shit." I growl.

"You're a fucking liar." She spits in my face. *I'm going to fucking kill her.* I get up and walk away before I really hurt her. Then I have to listen to Bentley's mouth and that's not what I need tonight.

This time, she follows me to the car and gets in without another word. Looking at the clock on my dash, I see I'm fucking late. Fuck. I speed out of the parking lot and get onto the road to head home. One day, I need to let the little princess next to me fall on her face. I won't always be here to save her. I glance to my right and look at her. She's facing away and I see tears glistening against her gorgeous face in the moonlight. *I don't have time for this shit but Jesus fucking Christ.* I hurt her when I slammed her down on the grass; I need to get my head together. Pulling the car to the side of the deserted road a few blocks away from home, I slam on the brakes.

"D, look at me." I say, grabbing her face gently. She pulls away and I growl. Unbuckling her seat belt, I haul her small body into my lap. She tries to look everywhere but at me, but I need her eyes. There's one way to get her to comply, but the last time I did that, it took me months of work to get away from her. *All it takes is one fucking taste and I won't be able to stay away.* I need to apologize, but I don't know how to do it. Words aren't enough. I struggle daily between doing the right thing and saying the hell with it all when it comes to her.

The way she fits perfectly in my lap. Every moan she makes when my hands touch her seductive body. Those lips, though. They are tantalizing and voluptuous, but her taste makes me animalistic. She doesn't know this, but the last guy who got to taste her is currently pushing daisies. She thinks he ghosted her, but he didn't. I cut his lips from his face and stabbed him 17 times because that's how many times he touched her.

"I said look at me Dylan. Please," I plead, cupping her face. She finally whips her face to mine and if looks could kill, I'd be dead. This is when she's the prettiest, when her eyes are filled with malice and rage. I've fantasized about sinking my cock into her and drowning in her contempt, letting it consume me whole. But the pact I made, the oath I spewed, halts my want for her, but I bet she's so fucking tight. *Fuck!*

"What Easton? Haven't you done enough tonight? Just take me the fuck home." She spits, trying to pull away from my embrace, but I yank her closer. My lips, only inches from hers. A slip of the tongue is all it would take to get a taste of insanity. *The war raging in my head is the real insanity.* I look into her ocean blue eyes and wipe the tears that spill.

"I'm sorry I hurt you. It wasn't my intention to slam you so hard." I whisper.

"You think that's why I'm upset?" She smirks, rolling her eyes as she inches closer, but I don't take the bait. I pull back, stunned at her response as she shakes her head.

"I'm upset because all you ever do is take from me, Easton. Everytime we play this game you take, and then you leave your mark with no promises, no nothing, just a bitter taste." She says, poking me in the chest.

"What the fuck does that mean?" I growl, slapping her hand away.

"Exactly, figure it the fuck out and let me know what the fuck this is because one day I'll be gone and there will be nothing more for you to take, no one for you to play this game with." She yells, climbing off me, but I don't let her. I grab her hips and slam her down onto me. Unfortunately for her, she gets to feel how fucking hard I am for her. *If only I could slam her down on my waiting cock. Maybe then I could get her to finally listen to me.*

"So what you're telling me is, because I have some-where to be tonight and couldn't play your game nor give you the answers you seek, you're going to cry about it?" I laugh, full belly fucking laugh, as my hands glide up her torso and my thumbs circle the outer part of her tits. She leans back against the steering wheel, giving me a great view of her body in such a confined space.

"No, you don't listen to what I'm fucking saying. It's fine. One day, you will realize when it's all too fucking late. Now take me the fuck home." She says, rocking her hips against my cock. I grunt, trying to find words that will make fucking sense.

"Can you sit fucking still while we work this out? I don't have time for this. I'm already late." I say through gritted teeth, feeling the warmth between her legs. It's radiating my already hard cock and her rocking is really not helping the situation down there.

"You're the one who has his hands on me, not letting me go." She smirks.

"Maybe I like looking at you." I raise a brow as her hip continues to roll against me. A little moan escapes her lips, and I thrust up into her. She gasps as my thumbs circle her hardened peaks. Squeezing a handful of her heavy breast I lean into them and rub my face into her cleavage, squeezing her tits against me. *God, she smells delicious.* She rocks faster, causing me to moan into her neck where I trail kisses along her throat and jaw.

"Isn't this what you wanted? For me to make you cum?" I whisper into her ear, licking the lobe. Her breathing picks up from my words and I grab her ass, pushing her harder onto my dick. She rocks faster, pulling at my hair and sucking my neck.

"Fuck, Hellcat." I groan the harder she sucks. *What I wouldn't give to have her on her knees for me.*

"I wish I was sucking something else." She whimpers. *Fuck it.* I pull down her tank and the cup to her lacey purple bra and suck her nipple into my mouth hard, flicking it with my tongue while squeezing her ass. Her body shivers and I'm so tempted to take my cock out and have her ride me until the sun rises, but I can't, this is the best it's going to get for now, so I rock with her knowing she's close.

"Easton, shit. Just like that." She whines as I move her hips up and down my length, pulling her jeans up so the seam will hit her clit even harder.

"Faster, Hellcat. Come on. Make me cum with you, baby." I whisper, biting her nipples one at a time.

"Like that, Eas. Can you feel how wet I am for you?" she pants.

"I bet you're drenched for this cock. You feel how hard he is for you? Only you, Hellcat." I groan.

"Fuck, fuck. Don't stop Eas. Don–I'm cumming, ahh." She screams as her whole body convulses in my arms, burying her head into the crook of my neck and sucking that spot I love. That familiar tingle crawls up my spine.

"Fuck, Hellcat." I growl as my dick twitches and cum pools inside my boxers. *Jesus Christ.* We don't move for a moment. All you can hear is our labored breathing as she lifts her head and giggles.

"Damn Eas, I can only imagine what the real thing could feel like. Shit." I laugh with her and slip her tits back into her bra.

"Awe, such a gentleman." She chides.

"Shut up. Let's get you home before your brother finds us and kills us both." I groan because fuck. This girl is my best friend's little sister and here I am making her cum and getting off on it. *Fuck.*

She slides off me and back into her seat, turning on the music. I get back onto the road and head for her house. *I'm so fucking late.* I don't know who's going to try to kill me first, the Hellcat next to me, or Spade for keeping him waiting.

I'd much rather die by pussy than by the hands of the most lethal man running the Cartel.

CHAPTER 4

DETECTIVE ELEANA ST. JAMES

I was called in not too long ago to meet my partner, Detective April McAdams, at Zeta Kappa Mu on University Drive. Arriving on the scene, the police are taking the appropriate measures to keep the campus safe and secluded from outsiders with barricades placed on both ends of the street. Walking into the frat house, some of the officers are questioning the ones who live here, and the coroner is currently bagging up three bodies. I find April easily enough after getting side eyed by some of the male officers.

"What have we got, April?" I ask, taking my pen and pad out.

"Three homicides, two in critical condition and one with no tongue." She states. I shiver at the no tongue part. This job never gets easy. Seeing dead bodies day in and day out is not for the faint of hearts.

"Any leads?" I ask.

"No one is talking. All we were able to get was they were having their usual frat party and 3 masked assailants came in, turned the lights out and brutally murdered three men. The two that are in critical condition have mainly stab wounds and then we have the one without a tongue." She states walking over to the body bags.

"The way the three were killed is almost a copycat of 'The Carver'. The only difference is, it was rushed, it didn't have the same intricate slices as he did but it's pretty fucking close." She says.

"That was over eighteen years ago. I thought he died. No one ever caught him and the killings stopped. Do you think he's back?" I ask, bending down to look at the victim. She's right. This can't be him. It's borderline too sloppy for him, or maybe it's the time and place which still doesn't add up. I stand up and look at her with a raised brow.

"Someone has to know something. We need to shut shit down and question everyone that was here, starting with the top. Where is the head of the house?" I ask, looking around the room. Something isn't adding up. I just can't pinpoint what it is.

"He's the one with no tongue." She points to the ambulance hauling ass down the road.

"Well, do you have any suggestions? All I can think of right now is to question and wait for the autopsy to come back. Maybe the copycat left DNA behind?" I say as we walk around the room. My team is already taking pictures and dusting everything for prints. Hopefully, we can figure this out quickly.

"We can question everyone here and wait for the team to do their analysis and take it from there." She says before taking out her phone to answer it. She steps away and I continue to survey the room. What really stands out for me is the words written in blood on the mirror above the fireplace.

"Little Red Riding Hood is coming for the Big Bad Wolf. You better hide little bitch."

Taking out my phone, I snap a picture of it. The way it was written is by someone who is left-handed and possibly a female. It's written too nicely to be a man.

"Eleana." I hear my name and turn to April.

"We have another issue tonight. There's been a shootout on County road 55, mile marker 10, on the outskirts of Whitestone and Daggerspoint. Two fatalities and several injured."

"Why are they calling us? That's not our jurisdiction." I quip.

"Cartel leader is down. Now it makes it our jurisdiction." She says.

"Shit, let's roll." I blurt, heading out of the frat house and down the steps towards where I parked.

"You want me to drive?" I ask. April looks at me and smirks.

"Only if you promise to stay the night?" she says, stopping to wait for my answer.

"That can be arranged. My kids are out doing their own thing. I'll just send Dylan a text and let her know I'm working late." I wink.

"Ya know, one day I'd like to not be your dirty little secret." She quips as we get to my car. I walk up behind her, pushing her up against the car, sliding my hands between her thighs. She groans and I kiss her lips lightly while applying pressure right where she begs for it. "Be a good girl or I'll be the only one cumming tonight." I whisper against her lips. She moans and I pull away, opening the door for her. She slides in and shuts it as I round the driver's side and get in. Starting her up, I turn the lights and sirens on and head for the last place I thought I'd see for the rest of my life.

CHAPTER 5

DYLAN

The week has flown by and I haven't seen Easton at all. Every night I leave my window unlocked for him but he hasn't come to see me. I text him and no response. I don't think he's even been home. My brother has been MIA as well, but at least he fucking checks in and that's only because he has to know what the fuck I'm doing and where I am going. It's annoying as fuck. I can't ask him about Eas. It will just send him on a whirlwind as to why I want to know where his best friend is. Anytime I ever bring him up in front of Benny, he loses his shit. I don't understand why, we all grew up together. It's not like he's a fucking random friend. The whole situation is frustrating.

Grabbing my backpack from my bed, I shut the light off, close my door and head down the stairs.

Mom is working on a few cases that have been keeping her at the precinct, which is fine for us. Her being away gives us free rein as long as we check in every so often with her, me more than Benny. I leave the house and get into my car, plugging in my phone and turning off my location. Fatal doesn't need to track me tonight. Once I get to the party, I will turn it back on, but for now, I'm incognito.

Pulling out of the driveway, I roll down the windows and turn the music up, taking in the cool night air. I let the wind flow through my hair and roll over my skin as I drive down the nearly deserted roads.

Thirty minutes later I arrive, pulling down the dirt road to the gate. Keying in my code, the gates open and I slowly drive through to the warehouse. Rolling up my windows and shutting off my car, I grab my backpack and get out. Walking to the door, I press the button and look up at the camera, giving it a little wave. After being buzzed in, I open the door and am greeted by Mr. Gio. He's been guarding this place for as long as I can remember.

"Good evening Miss Dylan, how are you tonight?" he smiles.

"I'm good, just here to pick up my bike and I'll be out of your hair in no time. Is the boss in?" I ask as he leads me into the garage where all the bikes, cars, and weapons are stored. This place is like a toy store for criminals.

"He's here. He will be down in a moment." Gio responds, leaving me to get myself situated. I dress in my racing gear and braid my long black hair before climbing onto my teal and silver Yamaha GYTR super sport. The door shuts and the man of the hour walks towards me with a huge smile on his face. I hop off the bike and run towards him. Slamming into him, he grunts at the impact as I give him a tight hug and he reciprocates my embrace. I feel a bandage on his chest and wonder what the fuck happened.

"It's been too long. I thought you forgot about me." He coughs.

"I could never forget you, Uncle Spade. Never." I say, burying my face in his chest. He gives me another squeeze before letting me go.

"Racing tonight against your brother and Fatal?" He asks with a smirk.

"Yep, how've you been? What happened to your chest? Last time I came, you were away on business." I say, walking back over to my bike.

"Sorry I missed ya kid. Don't worry your pretty head about your old uncle. No one can take me down. How is your mother doing?" He asks, concern written all over his face.

"Hmm, I don't like the sound of that but, she's fine, working as usual. Haven't seen her much since she's been working on two new cases." I say.

"Cut her some slack, she's doing her best," he says, cocking his head.

"I suppose, I just wish things were different and we didn't have to keep this a secret. I don't know my own cousins. Not even your wife." I say, and his face drops for just a moment before he looks at me again.

"I know. Hopefully, one day we can be together. It's just not time yet," He responds.

"Fine. I'll keep up my end of the bargain but, only for you, Uncle." I smile.

"That's why you're my favorite niece," he chuckles.

"I'm your only niece, for fuck's sake." I say, shaking my head.

"Alright, go kick Fatal's ass and I'll catch you later." He says giving me a kiss on the cheek and heading out the same way he came in.

The amount of fucking secrets and lies this family holds is fucking ridiculous.

Climbing back on the bike, I turn her on and rev the engine, put her in neutral and roll to the door. The sensors catch my tires and the door lifts. Putting my helmet on, I wait for enough clearance before putting the bike in gear and heading out. The gates automatically open as I approach, never having to slow down. I turn onto the main road and take off into the night, excited as fuck to smoke my brother and Fatal.

I pull the throttle to rev the engine as I wait for the flag to drop. Taking a deep breath, I center myself. I've been hiding this secret for years. No one knows who the 'Midnight Rider' is, and I plan to keep it that way. If my brother and the rest of Fatal only knew that they were constantly losing to a girl, let alone little ole me, they would kill me.

I'm not shocked to see Easton pull up to the line. I knew after not seeing him all week that he'd be here tonight. He never misses a race. He's an adrenaline junkie just like me. I get it from my Uncle Spade who taught me how to race when I was fifteen. I overheard my mother having a heated argument over the phone one night.

She was saying how she needed to stay hidden, and even though she's a detective, she will still protect her brother. I didn't know then that she had any family.

All she ever told us was that our dad left after I was born and that she was an only child.

So, to find out that everything was a fucking lie, was a straight punch to my heart and I'm pretty sure that was the day I stopped trusting her. That night, after she drank herself stupid, I snooped through her phone and found Uncle Spade's number and stored it in my phone. It's also the same night I found out that my mother is a lesbian and was in a secret relationship with her partner.

I don't understand why she keeps it a secret? It's not like I care about who she goes to bed with.

The revving of the bikes next to me takes me out of my thoughts and brings me back to the present. Some chick in a bikini stands in front of us and waves her little flag. I rev my engine, letting her know I'm ready.

The flag drops and off we go. I let the guys get a little head start and then I gun it for them, whipping past them. The only one who can keep up is Easton, but Uncle Spade works on my bike and hooked me up, showing me a little trick or two when racing. The finish line is up ahead and I let go of the throttle for one second to give Eas that little glimmer of hope before I shift and go full throttle, engaging the nos and speeding past him, hitting the finish line first.

As always, they were beaten yet again, by a girl. Instead of stopping and gloating at my win, I keep going and only stop next to the man holding the cash. He hands me my winnings, and I nod in thanks, putting the envelope in my zippered pocket before heading back to the warehouse. I wish I could see their faces every time I smoke their asses.

A few hours later, I arrived at the after party in my car. I told Amy and Ava that I would meet them there and would text them when I pulled in. Heading towards the end of the lot, I pull into the furthest stall away from the crowd so that when I leave, it's not a hassle to get out.

The after parties are always at The Fatal Five's 'Den', as they call it. It's an old warehouse on the opposite side of Lake Whitestone. Apparently, my uncle owns it and lets Bentley use it from time to time. Bentley has no idea that Spade is family. He thinks he works for the Cartel leader and that's as far as it goes. I'm not sure why my uncle didn't tell him, but it's going to be a fucking mess once all these secrets come to the surface.

Getting out of my car, I take my phone out and turn my location back on before opening the thread to send a text to the group chat letting the girls know I'm here. But I don't even get the chance to. Suddenly, someone grabs me from behind, shoving a cloth over my mouth. I go to scream but I inhale the sweet aroma and the last thing I feel is a pinch in my neck before everything goes black.

CHAPTER 6

EASTON

I've spent the week recovering and avoiding Dylan. I don't want her to know what happened after I dropped her off. Being late to the drop was the biggest mistake I ever made. Spade was shot and his other men died. I, on the other hand, got my ass handed to me by the guys trying to intercept their shipment. What made things even fucking worse, is my mother showing up to the scene with her partner, who just so happens to be Detective St. James. As my mom headed over to speak with the officers on site, I watched my best friend's mom turn and run to the cartel leader with tears down her face.

We all thought he was dead, but another tall man with blonde hair showed up, and carted him away after arguing with the detective until she finally gave in. I'm not sure how she fucking got away with it, maybe the other officers on the scene are in The Cartel's pocket, but it was cleaned up quickly and I dipped out of there unnoticed. I didn't say shit to Bentley. It's not my place. But it sure has my curiosity peaked.

Luckily, Spade survived and was taken care of by his own personal doctor. I had to hear a whole speech about why it's important to be on time, and to watch my surroundings, which I fucking did. If I was sooner, maybe these guys wouldn't have gotten the drop on us. Now I owe him. When he calls, I go. No questions asked, I just do as I'm told.

Taking out a cigarette, I light it up, inhaling the minty smoke. I'm sitting in the main room of our warehouse we call 'The Den' watching half-naked girls dance all around us. I really should find a girl to dump a load in tonight, but I'm waiting to see her, waiting to see what fucking bullshit she's going to purposely pull tonight.

I look to my left and see that Bentley has his eyes glued to a dancing Amy who keeps eye fucking him from across the room. Shaking my head, I take another inhale of my cigarette, bracing myself for impact for what's about to come out of my mouth next.

"Yo, lover boy. Where's Dylan at tonight? Her girls are here, but she's nowhere in sight." I ask nonchalantly. Ace answers first.

"Probably with Frat boy, choking on his cock." He laughs but Bentley doesn't find it funny. Kingston smacks Ace in the back of the head.

"Do you ever think before you speak?" He says, shaking his head.

"That's my sister you're talking about. I don't want to think about her sucking cock. So shut the fuck up before I shut you up." Bentley fires back. I just shake my head as Bentley looks in my direction.

"To answer your question, I'm not sure, I'm not her babysitter. I believe I gave that job to you. So now you have me curious as to why you don't know where she is." He says, now it's my turn to laugh and he quirks a brow. I take another inhale, enjoying the mint filling my lungs.

"Says the one who needs to know her every move." I chuckle and ignore his question, putting out my butt. Antonio comes over and hands us all a round of beers. I take a deep gulp and place the bottle down. Just as I do, some blonde chick comes into our circle and climbs onto Bentley's lap, whispering in his ear. I look over at Amy, who has murder written all over her face. Before I can even get the words out, she's moving fast in our direction. Fuck.

"Incoming," is all I'm able to get out before this little firecracker pulls the blonde's head back in a tight grip, forcing the girl to look up at her. *Oh shit.*

"I don't know who the fuck you are, but you have two seconds to get off my man's lap before I fucking hurt you." She spits, pulling the girl's hair harder causing her to scream.

"Okay, okay. Jeez." The blonde says as she gets up from his lap. Amy lets go of her hair just as the chick calls her a bitch. Before Amy could get her, Bentley has her wrapped in his arms, pulling her away and whispering in her ear. *Well, damn. I didn't know Amy could get down like that. Shit.* Ava comes over with a pout.

"Where the fuck is Dylan? I am not being left with the four of you while B fucks her." She whines and I laugh. She's probably right. If that was me, and my girl was gonna throw hands like that, I'd definitely be taking her somewhere to sink my cock into her.

"We haven't seen her. I was hoping you knew where she was." I say, taking another sip of my beer.

"Last I heard, she was going to text us when she got here, but that was hours ago and I still haven't heard from her." Ava says, sitting down in Bentley's seat and downing his beer.

"You could always come sit on my lap sweet thing and we can talk about the first thing that pops up." Ace says, winking at her. I cover my mouth with my hand, trying not to laugh at the lamest pick up line I've ever heard.

"Eww, grow up Ace." She says with a disgusted look on her face.

"Awe, come on, Sweet Thing, I bet you'd like it." He smirks.

"Unless you have a ten inch cock and live in a penthouse overlooking the lake, I don't want to hear it." She spits back. *Oh shit.* Dylan's girls have some fire in them. Ace's eyes widen, but the look of disappointment riddles his face. He schools his features and gets up to walk away.

"Are you always a bitch?" Kingston asks with a slight snark in his tone.

"No, but I don't need his bullshit tonight. He's the one who ended things, not the other way around." She says. Which she's right, yet again. We all do things we don't want to do because of our pact. Sometimes I think late at night, is all this worth it? Is it worth not being able to love, and be loved in return, all because we lead a dangerous life? Taking out my phone, I shoot Dylan a text while everyone is occupied.

> **Me: Where you at, Hellcat?**

A few minutes go by and I get up to circle around the warehouse, sell a few bags and take a step outside into the cool air. The night is clear and the stars shine bright in the sky. I walk over to my car and stop in my tracks when I hear moans coming from behind a truck. *Why does that truck look so familiar?* My phone pings, pulling me away from getting a better look, and I see it's Dylan.

> **Dylan: Come play with me.**

Of course she wants to play. When does this girl not want to play games with me?

> **Me: How can I? I don't know where you are.**

> **Dylan: Come on Eas. You're smart. Find me.**

> **Me: Someone is being a bad little kitten tonight. Are you at the party?**

> **Dylan: I'm giving no hints, big boy.**

Big boy? That's a new one. Clicking her picture, her exact location pops up, and it's nowhere near here. She's about twenty minutes south of here at the old Academy. That place burnt down before I was born. From the stories I was told, someone bombed it with students still living there and now it's abandoned,no one knows what truly happened. It's like an urban legend, much like the lake itself.

I get in the car and head south towards the academy. That place gives me the creeps. Legend has it, if you listen closely, you can hear old souls scream at night when the first winter hits. Some say you can hear the last girl who drowned there, scream for her loved ones, just like the native princess who killed herself in the middle of the lake. I will never swim there, no matter how hot our summers get. Ain't no mother fucking way.

Driving through the torn down gates, I get this eerie feeling as chills climb up my spine. Why the fuck she chose here out of all places is beyond me. Slowly, I drive past the lake and right to the front steps. Seeing a glowing light four stories up is the only clue of her whereabouts in this fucking place. Taking out my phone, I shoot her a text.

Me: Ready or not, here I come.

I get out of the car and climb the million fucking stairs, wretching the broken front door open. It grinds as it slowly closes behind me. My phone pings and I look down, opening the message.

Dylan: Incoming Multimedia Message. Click to open.

What the fuck could she be sending me? I turn my flashlight on to find the stairwell to climb up to the fourth floor when another message comes through.

Dylan: Incoming Multimedia Message, Click to open.

I click to open the first video. Pressing play, I notice it's us in my car last week. *What. The. Fuck.* It keeps replaying us climaxing, and I can't stop staring at the look on her face. *Pure ecstasy.* I click over to the next video, press play and nearly lose it. I watch, squeezing my phone so fucking hard, as Dylan is tied up by chains in the bathroom getting beat up by five men. All body shots, they're real strategic with their strikes, keeping her face clean from marks. I immediately run up the stairs as fast as my feet will carry me. Why must she be on the fourth floor? For fuck's sake. Another message comes through and I open it while I continue to run.

Dylan: It's five on one Easton. Do as we say and you and this slut will live to see another day.

I ignore it. I don't give a fuck how many there are. I will fucking gut every last one of them for touching her. For hurting her. Getting to the fourth floor I stop. I need a plan. *Think Easton. Think. Be smart.*

Don't let your anger overrun your thoughts. A clear mind gets the job done. Don't be stupid. I don't know what I'm walking into. I don't have any information other than she's hurt and hanging. I took a vow to protect her. Fuck! I can't exactly call anyone for help because the questions asked won't have the answers they want to hear.

I open the door slowly and step into the hall. Big fucking mistake. A gun cocks and I feel the cold metal against my head before I can even take another step.

"Walk, bitch." The voice says. I try to spin around and punch him in the gut, but all that does is get me pistol whipped in the temple. My vision blurs as they surround me. Punch after punch lands on my still recovering body, until the butt of the gun hits the back of my head- lights out. *Fuck.*

CHAPTER 7

DYLAN

*** Content Warning: Chapter 7 & 8 contain ON PAGE RAPE***

"Time to play with us, you little cunt." A sinister voice echoes in my mind. I try to open my eyes, but I can't. *What the fuck is happening? Where am I? The last thing I remember is... Fuck. I can't remember shit.* Tuning everything out around me, I try to center myself. I left the warehouse, drove back to The Den, went to text the girls to meet me, and then boom. I remember someone grabbed me from behind. Memories of a sweet aroma sends white dots to the fore-front. *Flashes of blurred bodies surrounding me as I hang from chains in an old bathroom. I can barely open my eyes as the familiar voices taunt me.*

"You're such a fucking slut. Walking around acting like you're better than everyone." I blink as knuckles slam into my chest as I swing back from the impact, almost knocking the wind out of me. Is that? No. It can't be.

"Benny?" I rasp, my throat tight. Another fist sends me careening backwards again and I cough from the punch to the stomach.

"No, it's not Bentley, you dumb bitch. But he is the reason you are here." That familiar voice laughs and I blink again seeing Carter, Easton, Ace, and a few others, but they are still blurry. I try to clear my vision, but I can't focus. No! They wouldn't do this to me. The drugs are messing with my mind, it wants to take me under, but I keep fighting it. I'm too afraid to let my mind drift. I'm afraid of what they will do to me. Another crack at my body. Then another, and another, and another. I can't fucking breathe. Tears stream down my face. I want to go home. Please let me go home.

"Man, I thought you said this would knock her out?" someone whines beside me.

"It's supposed to, maybe she needs another dose," someone deeper in the room suggests. His tone is so fucking familiar but it's also muffled, like hes trying hard to disguise it, or wearing something over his face. I try to scream but something soft is gagging me. I don't want anymore drugs.

"This isn't what I signed up for. This is how we get caught, you idiots." A high pitched voice says as I hear footsteps walk away from me.

"I have a plan for that. He should be here soon. Let's move her onto the bed in the other room." Someone says. Is that? No. It can't be. A prick in my neck is the last thing I feel before they release my chains. Someone lifts me from the ground and wraps my arms around their neck, leaning my head on their shoulder as I'm carried. I take in a sharp breath and freeze. That smell of musk and cedar is so fucking familiar but I can't put a face to the smell, this drug is clouding my mind. The person carrying me kisses my forehead and places me down on the bed, covering my face with something. My body relaxes for a moment too long as the darkness seeps into my mind taking me under.

Sounds of grunts and scuffling close by bring me back to my present nightmare. I try to move my arms but can't. I'm awake and can hear everything but I can't fucking move. My mind is screaming at me to move, to fight back, but I can't. I'm trapped within myself and there's no way out. Tears stream down my face and a laugh echoes in my ear. *It was so much better when I tuned everything out but I don't want to go back to that. I just want to go home.*

"What a dumb slut. You can feel everything we do to you and there isn't shit you can do about it." His fake, raspy voice, laughs as he runs his hand up my bare thigh. Wait, why the fuck am I naked? I try to kick him away but my legs are in tight metal cuffs that pinch my skin. *I don't like this. I'm scared and I don't know how to save myself.*

"Go on, give us a little show." The voice commands as the bed dips to my right and I stiffen, bracing myself for what's going to happen. A buzzing sound starts and the feeling of an object begins sliding up my knee to my inner thighs. I attempt to close my legs, forgetting I can't fucking move. The object slides further up my thigh, causing my body to riddle with goosebumps, my nipples hardening in the cool air.

"Look at those pretty pink nipples perking up with a simple breeze. She's so responsive. What else can she do? Keep going, bitch." The voice taunts. His voice is so fucking familiar.

"No!" Someone growls and then the sound of a slap echoes the room causing the bed to shake.

"Do it, or the video goes viral." The sinister voice threatens. The person on the bed takes a deep breath and suddenly I feel a warm wetness as they lick my right nipple, sucking hard. *Being touched by a stranger shouldn't feel good. But it's enthralling, the feeling of the unknown.* Feeling his long wet licks all over my large breast, biting my nipple and pulling it in his mouth. The pain mixed with pleasure has me wanting to arch my back off the bed, but I can't. I just lay here completely unmoving, letting this person do as he pleases, taking whatever the fuck he wants. The buzzing object hovers over my clit, pausing and teasing me.

"Cunt face, how does it feel to be helpless and at someone else's mercy while we watch?" The deep voice taunts, "Isn't this what you like? An audience? It's what you've been begging for every time you fuck your boyfriends out in public." The person on the bed growls as the hairs on the back of my neck stand. I know that growl, I just can't think straight. *This is fucking maddening.* The bed rustles and I hear the cock of a gun close by. If I could move, I would have gasped and cowered away, but since I can't do a damn thing, I'm terrified in my mind. My mind is the only thing I can control at this point. But I'm seriously waging a war with myself. Fuck.

"Make her pretty little pink pussy gush for us." A more high pitched voice orders. *The more they talk, the more familiar they all sound. What in the actual fuck is going on?*

"Well fuck. Look at those plump pussy lips. I bet your little boyfriend couldn't make you feel this good anytime he rutted into you." Another voice growls, but this one sounds older, more sinister. I hear a slap but it's not close enough to be the person on the bed.

"Ouch! What the fuck dude?" Nothing is said after that. No response. No noise. This is truly a mind fuck. *I just want this to be over. Do what you need to do and let me go home. I just want my bed. I want out of here.*

"Fuck this. Since you don't want to comply, we are going to speed this little party up. Take your dick out and fuck her. Once you make her cum, you are free to go. She stays though." A whiney voice says. *That's six, including the person on the bed with me. It's the same men from the bathroom plus a new guest. My mind is playing tricks on me. I don't know what to believe anymore.*

"When is it my turn? I can't wait to wreck her and tear that pussy apart with my cock." The high pitched asshole says. *Never. Stay the fuck away from me.*

"Don't worry, we will all get our turn, then we will leave her to fend for herself. No one will ever want her again. Especially after tonight." The older guy says. *Please, just let me go.*

I feel a hard object enter my pussy, but it doesn't feel like it's attached to a person. It's not warm. One can only assume it's a sex toy. I hear someone spit and the warm liquid lands on my clit and something slowly circles my bundle of nerves. I don't want this to feel good, but fuck, he knows just how to touch me and have my pussy purring like a kitten.

The ominous voice laughs, "Fuck, I want to cum just watching her enjoy this." *Thank god I can't see. I don't want to watch that.*

"That's because she's a slut and wants to be ran in on." One of the voices taunts. I can't pay attention any longer. More tears spill from my eyes as I try to center myself again and think of something happy. Maybe if I think of Easton it will help me get through this.

My mind continues to be at war with my body, but when I think of Easton being the one touching me, my heart rate picks up as he presses the toy back against my clit, this time adding a finger to my drenched pussy. All I hear are their laughs taunting me. He presses down harder, holding it there while he finger fucks me slowly, causing my pussy to spasm and gush all over the bed. Tears continue to flow down my face from the embarrassment of what they all just witnessed, but I'm glad they can't see me crying. One thing I'm actually thankful for is the sac covering my head. The laughs don't stop as he continues his abuse to my body.

Orgasm after orgasm is forced from me. Pleasure and pain mix together and it's all too much, but my body craves it where my mind is screaming for help. He finally pulls his fingers from me and I take a breath, hoping that they're done. That relief is short-lived as someone slides between my legs and I'm suddenly hit in the head with something so hard my vision blurs and everything spins to darkness.

CHAPTER 8

EASTON

Knocking her out was the best plan I had. I didn't want her to remember this as our first time together. Not that she knows it's me, but some day, I will have to tell her. There's no way I could keep this a secret. How the fuck am I going to come back from this? This is all she ever wanted from me and I said no every single fucking time. But now? Now I have a gun to my head and threats are being made about her and Fatal.

This was the only choice left. I line my cock up to her already swollen pussy and slam into her as fast as I can to get this over with. I don't want her to wake up while I'm still on top of her. *God, she feels so fucking good. She's so fucking tight and the way her pussy fluttered when she gushed all over my hand, it was perfect. She's fucking incredible, but then I remember that we are in the old academy in front of these pieces of shit, and I need to get my head in the game. Get in, get off and get out.* I can't leave her here with them, but they would be stupid to let me go.

How easy it would be to call the guys and this shit would get shut down. And these five fucks; we would paint the walls with their insides. We are lethal as it is, but when it comes to our property, it's a whole new ball game.

Her beautiful body is riddled with red blotches that will turn into bruises by tomorrow. Once I get us out of this, I'm going to kill them, one by fucking one, for forcing me to do this. I told them to send the fucking video. I would deal with Bentley later if it kept her safe and unharmed. This situation reminds me of last year with Ava. Some guy roofied her and didn't know she was Fatal's property, but he fucked around and found out quickly.

Another prick who's either pushing daisies or cut up in the river. I'm not sure. Ace took care of that one. Because of that night, he and Ava aren't together and I know it kills him to know she's seeing someone else.

Suddenly, I'm grabbed from behind and pulled off of her, slammed into a chair and immediately zip tied, with my dick still hanging out. Garrett looks at me and winks as he climbs on the bed and sinks inside her, grabbing her hips so tight I know there will be fingerprints left in his wake. I pull at my restraint, trying to get free.

"She feels so good. Fucking tight and soaking for my cock. Thanks man, for revving her up for me. I owe you one." He chuckles and I want to fucking go off, but I can't, I don't want her to know I was here. My voice alone will give it all away and I can't lose her like that. Not until we talk and she's safe. Home in her bed. I'll fucking hold her while she cries. I don't care; I just want her out of here.

I continue to strain against the zip ties, the plastic cutting into my skin as the next scumbag I've never seen before, gives Garrett a high five while holding his phone out and recording everything that's going on. A few of these dirtbags I know from university; the Captain of the swim team and his little bitch boys. He lifts the sac just enough to produce her mouth and pinches her cheeks roughly so her mouth opens, then he's slamming his cock down her throat.

I don't wince at his brutality as he looks my way. This just fuels the rage inside me. But what really makes me irate, is the guy standing the furthest away, watching, waiting. I fucking called this shit. *Oh, just wait mother fucker! I'll save you for last, little bitch.* Each guy that touches her will die at my hands and it will be a mutilation. I will leave them unrecognizable.

That old serial killer, 'The Carver' will look like child's play after I'm done with them. Detective St. James better buckle up for the shit storm I'm going to throw her way. I want this shit to make front page news for every mother fucker to see and take it as a fucking warning as their friends start dying around them. What's even sweeter, is that they will know it's me, they will see me coming a mile away.

Garrett cums with a roar on her stomach as the camera man drops his phone cumming down her throat. He pulls out, picks up his phone and continues to record as the next dead fucker steps up and slides into her. Fuck boy number three turns her to the side and pounds into her ass. *Jesus fucking Christ.* She doesn't deserve this. I'm glad I knocked her out, hopefully she stays that way until they're finished.

The guy standing furthest away just watches. He never touches her but he allows this to happen! That's what makes it that much worse. Trust no one in this life. His eyes slowly connect with mine, I snarl at him and he smirks, licking his fucking lips.

They continue to take turns and brag about what they've done. I stopped pulling at my restraints long ago because there is no point. Even if I set myself free, it would be another ass beating and they would most likely just kill us both at that point. I feel my phone buzzing over and over again in my pocket. How the fuck do I explain my absence if that's one of the guys? What story am I going to cook up this time? Tonight is a fucking nightmare. I should have watched her closer. Should have done a lot this week. One of the many things Bentley always told me is when he's not around, I must keep his sister safe, and to keep my dick away from her. I failed at both. Clearly.

The sudden shrill of a scream takes me out of my thoughts. The drugs have run their course and Dylan is now screaming and thrashing around the bed, trying her best to fight them off. But it's no use. They lay blow after blow onto her torso, legs, and arms. Her screams echo the room so loudly and it hurts my heart that I can't help her. I can't save her from this. The last blow is to her face, then the cameraman takes out a fluorescent green syringe and stabs it into her neck, quieting her screams immediately. He waltzes over to me, pointing the phone at my face with a wicked smile on his as he produces another syringe and jabs it into my neck. Then it's lights out for me too. *Shit.*

CHAPTER 9

DYLAN

"Say anything to anyone and their death will be on your hands." He whispers, biting my earlobe. I jolt awake, breathing heavily in my car at The Den. The first thing I notice is that my head is fucking pounding, I'm thirsty as fuck and my entire body aches-especially between my legs. Shit. I look to the left and see all of Fatal's cars are here except for Easton's. It looks like the party goers are still milling around.

I need to get the fuck home and shower this nightmare away before I am spotted. I wince, trying to sit up to start my car. Jesus, my ribs hurt so fucking bad and I feel utterly gross. *What the hell is happening?*

Searching for my phone, I finally find it laying upside down on the floorboard on the passenger side. There is no way I'm attempting to reach it with the pain shooting up my spine and the throbbing in my arms. Thank god I don't have a stick shift because that would be a fucking bitch.

With shaky hands, I put the car in drive and speed out of the lot, heading home with hopes that my mother isn't there. I don't need to be caught and questioned by her. I'd much rather deal with my brother and his questions than hers. It would be a fucking shit storm.

Getting home doesn't take long and as I park in the driveway, noticing her car is missing, the tiniest bit of relief washes over me. *Thank fucking god.* I climb out to the best of my ability and round the passenger side, holding my ribs. Opening the door, I bend down and nearly scream from the pain, pick up my phone and slam the car door shut.

I open the back gate and climb the stairs to the backdoor. Keying in the code, the lock disengages and I turn the knob, pushing the door open into the kitchen. I walk over to the cabinet by the fridge and grab the pain meds, pouring two into my hand and placing them in my mouth. Pulling the fridge open, I take out a bottle of water, open it, and chug its contents, letting the ice cold liquid flow down my throat and into my stomach. My body shivers at the temperature and I throw the empty bottle in the recycle bin as I head up the stairs.

Tears fill my eyes from the pain that riddles me. I can only imagine what I fucking look like. Getting to my room I slam my door shut and throw my phone on the bed. Heading into the bathroom, I open the shower door and turn the water on.

Stripping from my clothes, I stand under the lukewarm water waiting for it to get hot as I let the tears flow down my face. How did this fucking happen? I was drugged, beaten, and raped by multiple men. I should be calling my mom, and going to the hospital to get a rape kit done, but I can't. They threatened to do this again. They also said they would kill my mother while my brother watches.

So, I'll keep my mouth shut for now and get my own revenge on them. A couple things I know so far, one guys voice was so fucking familiar, and they were at The Den. So it could only mean I know them and so does Fatal.

I refuse to stand in this shower and break down. I'm stronger than this. I won't let it define me. I'm not some fucking statistic. I'm not a random girl at a party who was drugged and raped. This was premeditated. There's a reason why they did this to me. I think about all the what-if's as I move slowly to wash my hair and body, every movement hurts.

Getting out of the shower, I dry off and gently run a brush through my hair, afraid to touch my head because of the big lump from one of the guys knocking me out. *Hello headache from hell.*

Walking in my room, like a freaking robot, I keep telling myself that I'm stronger than this. I won't cower. I won't hide. Tears fill my eyes but I don't let them spill. Looking outside my window and across the yard, I notice Easton pulling into his driveway.

I shut my light off and lock my window. I can't deal with him tonight. I slide into my bed, trying not to scream from the pain. At least now I'm safe. No one is going to come for me here.

Feeling around for my phone, I find it easily and plug it into the charger. It lights up instantly with tons of missed calls and texts. I scroll down the list to my brother and mother. Replying back to both of them, I let them know I stayed in for the night, had fallen asleep, and I was sorry for not answering.

Another text comes through. I scroll to the top and see it's Easton. Fuck.

> **Easton: You were home the whole night?**

> **Me: Yes. I fell asleep earlier and my phone was on silent.**

> **Easton: Then why is your window locked?**

I roll my eyes. Of course he tried getting in.

> **Me: I want to be alone tonight.**

> **Easton: Interesting.**

> **Me: What does that fucking mean?**

> **Easton: It means nothing. Are you sure you don't want company?**

Oh I do, what I would give for him to just lay with me in his warmth. Holding me, keeping me safe, but it's never that easy with him. He always takes and I can't handle that tonight. Not after what just happened.

> **Me: I have my period. So unless you have a heating pad, chocolate and want to watch a sappy movie with me, I suggest you stay in your lane.**

> **Easton: Interesting, Hellcat.**

His nickname for me sends shivers up my spine and I want to scream at the pain. Fuck. These pills are doing fuck all.

Me: You have any strong pills? Like recreational shit, Eas. My cramps hurt so bad I don't think I'm going to survive.

Easton: You already know the answer to that. The Candy Man has it all. Pick your poison. But for you my dear, I know what you need. Don't move to open your window. I'll come in the back door.

I roll my eyes again. He could have been coming through the back door this whole time but, instead he climbs the house and through my window. *I don't understand boys.* The soft thud of his boots hit the stairs and my heart starts pounding in my chest as my door opens. I go to sit up and turn on the light but he moves closer and stops me.

"No lights. Just sit up and take the pills. Here, I brought up a bottle of water," he says, handing me the bottle and two little pills.

"Thank you, Eas." I rasp. I can't see his facial expression in the dark but I take the pills and swallow them down.

"Don't try to get out of bed on those. They are really strong. Just relax and sleep and I'll come check on you in the morning," he whispers as he runs a finger down my cheek. I lean into his warmth wishing he would stay with me. As if reading my thoughts, he huffs before taking his boots off and unbuckling his loud belt. He slides under the covers next to me and I freeze for a second too long.

"You good, Hellcat?" He whispers.

"Y–yeah, I'm fine. I didn't expect you to be so warm." I laugh. It's fake but hopefully he doesn't notice.

"Okay, just rest. I'll keep an eye on you for a couple of hours or until your mom gets home. Bentley is staying at The Den with Amy." He laughs.

"Really? They back together? I need them to get their shit together, I'm getting whiplash with those two." I say as his hand finds mine.

"Well, Amy went all feral on some chick at the party for climbing on Bentley's lap. It was quite the show." He says as his fingers entwine with mine.

"Yasss, that's my girl. How was Ava?" I ask, pulling his hand closer to my body.

"She was fine until Ace started running his mouth. Ya know, the usual," he sighs, squeezing my hand.

"So tonight was eventful. I hate that I missed all the fun." I say as my eyes start to get droopy. I take in a heavy breath as sleep starts to take over.

"I wish that's where you were. I'm sorry Hellcat, for tonight." He says, his voice above a whisper.

"Hmm?...Oh, it's okay," I say, snuggling up closer to him. Already feeling the effect of the pills he gave me. Just as my mind drifts off to sleep, I hear him whisper from what sounds so far away,

"I'll kill them all, Hellcat. Just sleep, my beautiful girl."

And that's what I do.

CHAPTER 10

EASTON

Relief swam in my chest when I saw Dylan's cutlass parked at her house. I woke up in my car after they knocked me out, still sitting at the academy. When I decided I was coherent enough to drive, I flew by The Den to see if her car was there, which it wasn't. I tried to track her phone but it was dead. I actually fucking prayed as I drove home, that her car would be in the driveway, and for once, luck was on my side.

My mom texted me earlier in the night to let me know she was working late on a case and wouldn't be home, which wasn't unusual for her, but she still likes to check in. It's been her and I since I could remember. My father was murdered right before I was born, which sent my mother on a wild goose chase to find his killer which still to this day, is unknown. So she chose to join the force alongside Eleana. After going through the academy together, they became partners in the homicide unit.

I went up to my room, took a shower and changed my clothes. All I could smell was mold and fire, and I didn't want to tip her off by that. There was no way I wasn't going to go to her. I had to make sure she was okay. The guilt of what I was forced to do is eating me alive, but why hasn't she called her mother, Bentley, or the cops? I thought for sure her mom would have came home guns blazing after finding out her daughter was raped. But nothing happened. I tried her window, but it was locked. It hurt my heart a bit that she didn't want me near her tonight. I get it, but it didn't change the pain filling my chest.

I lay here next to her, holding her hand, my thumb stroking her soft skin as I listen to her heavy breathing. The sun is starting to rise and I should really go home and rest. I'm not sure I'm ready for her to see how fucked my face is. Plus, my head is pounding and I could really use some sleep. I'm afraid if I rest my eyes we will get caught together, and that's the last thing we need right now. But I can't help but stare at her as she sleeps peacefully, safely in her own bed. I look up at the ceiling and thank god that she's here and breathing. I look down at her and run my finger lightly down her nose and over her lips.

She's utterly gorgeous and even more stunning with tears running down her face. I wish I could stay here with her, wake her up with a sweet kiss to her lips and get lost for hours within one another. But it's not in the cards for us. She's my best friend's sister. Untouchable. Fuck.

Shaking my head, I slowly free my hand from her grip, and she groans in her sleep. I kiss her forehead lightly before putting my jeans and boots on and leave her room. Thank god it's the weekend and we both don't have to worry about classes.

After leaving her house, I look up at her window one more time before entering my own. Climbing the stairs, I enter my room, taking my boots and jeans off. I slide into my cold bed and sleep takes over almost immediately.

Hours later, the sun is shining bright through my window and the annoying sound of my phone keeps going off. Reaching for my discarded jeans, I pull out my cell from the pocket and see it's Ace.

"I'm fucking sleeping. What do you want?" I rasp.

"Just making sure you're good. You walked out last night and never returned." He says, a hint of concern in his tone.

"Yeah, I uhh dipped out. I was fucking exhausted man." I say wiping a hand over my face. I fucking hate lying to my friends. I need to figure out a way to tell them but I need to check on Dylan first.

"If you say so. Well, we are heading into the city to watch a race. We should be back tonight." He says.

"Alright, I'll meet you guys at The Den later. Stay safe." I say.

"Same, E, same." He says, and the line goes dead.

Sliding out of bed, I go take a piss and get dressed. Looking out the window, I see just Dylan's car in the driveway. Grabbing my phone from my bed I shoot a text over to her as I stand by the window.

Me: You up Hellcat?

I look over at her room and see her moving around the room. My phone pings and I head down the stairs as I look at the text.

Dylan: Leave me alone Eas.

Nope, we aren't doing this shit today. I walk out of the house and into her yard, opening the gate and walking up the back steps. I key in the code and open the door, slamming it shut behind me.

"Go home, Easton!" she yells down the stairs and I laugh.

"Not a chance in hell, D. Either you come down here or I'm coming up. The choice is yours." I yell from the kitchen and I hear her huff as she stomps down the stairs. She finally comes into view wearing sweatpants and a long sleeve shirt. But I can see the fucking handprints around her throat and she will not meet my eyes. Her entire demeanor has changed rapidly overnight.

"What do you want?" She says, putting her hand on her hip. I laugh because this girl is always filled with so much sass that I'd love to just fuck right out of her. But instead, I quirk a brow at her.

"Have you eaten today?" I ask and she rolls her eyes.

"Did you just roll your eyes at me?" I smirk but she doesn't take the bait.

"Yes, I'm more than capable of caring for myself when no one is home. I'm not a fucking child Eas." She says, getting mad at me for being concerned about her. *Oh, the fucking audacity of me.*

"Why are you throwing such hostility at me? I came over here to make sure you are okay." I say folding my arms over my chest, leaning against the counter.

"I'm not throwing anything at you," she says, wincing as she folds her arms over her chest.

"Why are you wincing? What the fuck is going on?" I step closer to her and she takes a step back. I hold my hands up in surrender but she takes another step.

"I'm fine, Eas. Let it fucking go." She sneers. I take another step towards her and tears start to fill her eyes.

"Tell me what is wrong?" I demand and she shakes her head no profusely. I step into her space again, caging her in against the wall. Her eyes are cast down and I don't fucking like it. My pointer finger grazes her jaw and she whips her face away.

"Please talk to me." I whisper, pulling her face back to me. Her ocean blue eyes finally meet mine and I can see all the hurt deep within them.

"What is going on, D?" I breathe, trying to keep my tone soft, not wanting to scare her away.

"I can't Eas. Just please go. I want to be alone." She begs.

"I can't do that D. I need you to tell me so I can fix this." I protest.

"You can't fix this." She whispers but I don't give up.

"Did Carter hurt you? Is that what this is about? Are you afraid of what I will do to him?" I question, grabbing her face with both of my hands and she pushes me away.

"No, that's not what this is. Stop making it worse than it needs to be. Just fucking go!" she yells and I take a step back.

"One way or another, I'm going to find out what the fuck is going on." I yell back. But she gets in my face this time.

"I said to fucking drop it Easton. I swear to god just let it fucking go or else." She spits. She moves to try pushing me again, but I grab her hands and she screams. I immediately let go and take another step back into the kitchen.

"See, that right there tells me all I need to know. You either fucking tell me what is fucking going on or I'll go gut the prick." I growl.

"Why do you even fucking care? Why are you pushing this so hard?" She questions. *Fuck*. I can't exactly tell her that I know everything, that I was fucking there. *Fuck*.

"Because you're my best friend's sister, and when I see bruises on your neck, that makes me fucking concerned." I yell and she immediately covers her neck with the hood.

"Because I'm Bentley's sister? That's why you care?" She laughs in my face.

"Get out, just get the fuck out!" She laughs again pointing to the door.

"And if I don't?" I challenge. She throws her hands up and stomps off.

"That's what I thought. Get your shit together. You're coming to The Den tonight. You obviously can't be left alone." I yell down the hall. I turn my back for one second and she comes running down the hall and shoves me into the back door.

"Fuck you. I'm not going anywhere. If all I am is Benny's little sister to you, then fuck right the fuck off ,get the fuck out of my house and stay out of my fucking window. You ain't shit." She yells, shoving me again. She spins and runs back down the hallway and up the stairs, slamming her bedroom door shut, nearly shaking the whole house.

Fuck. I open the back door and slam it shut as I walk out, pounding my feet down the wood steps and out of the yard. Looking up at her window, I see her standing there and I blow her a kiss, she returns it with a middle finger and twisting the lock to her window.

Well, fuck. How am I supposed to tell her that I was one of her rapists? How can I explain it to her without losing her completely? It's a battle that I'm terrified to lose. Because not only will I lose her, but I'll lose Fatal and probably my life, for it all. I need a fucking drink. Taking out my phone I text the guys to see where they are at.

Me: Everyone at the Den?

Bentley: I'm not. Had to make a pit stop on the way back from the city.

Me: Tell Amy I said hi. Lol

Ace: I'll be there in a few. Why? What's up? Tell Amy to come tonight.

Bentley: Both of you can fuck off.

Me: lol guess that's a no. You feel like drinking Ace?

Ace: Stupid question.

Antonio: I got J's for days. It's time to get high, my friends.

Me: LMAO, when are you not high?

Antonio: Good question.

Bentley: Never.

Ace: Stone Pony 24-7.

Kingston: I just got here. We having a party?

Me: A small one. I need to let loose a bit.

Kingston: Done

Ace: See you soon.

Me: I'll be there in twenty.

Later that night, I'm drunk, sitting on the couch at The Den, while half-naked girls dance around and my boys shoot some pool. I can't even stand up. I took way too many shots to make myself feel better. *It didn't work.* I can't get her off my mind. I can't get last night out of my head. I take out my phone and check in with her.

Me: Hellcaatttt, you good baby?

Dylan: Didn't I tell you to leave me the fuck alone?

Me: Do I everrr listennnn baby?

Dylan: Jesus Christ . I'm fine Easton.

Me: I don't believe you, Hellcat. And stop calling me Easton. That's not my name to you.

Dylan: What the fuck? Your name is Easton. Is it not?

Me: Not to you, baby. It's Eas or daddy, or maybe...I don't know.

Dylan: Daddy? I think the real question here is, are you okay Easton?

Me: Mmm yes Daddy. I like that Hellcat. I'm better now that I'm talking to you.

Dylan: Are you drunk?

Me: Nooooo. What are you wearing? Send me a pic.

Dylan: Oh, you are sooo drunk.

Me: Am not. Now give me what I want or I will get in the car and come to see for myself.

Dylan: Don't you dare drive here.

Me: Why? Carter with you? Not making you cum as usual.

Dylan: Where are you? I'll come get you.

Me: I'm fine. At Den. Partying without you

Dylan: You don't sound okay.

Me: I want to tell you something but if I tell you, you will hate me forever and I don't want that. I want so much more D.

Dylan: Who did you fuck? Which one of my girls?

Me: I know, D. Just know that I know, and I will take care of it. I'm sorry.

Dylan: I don't know what you are talking about. Where's Benny? I'm worried about you.

Me: Just know I wasn't left with a choice. And I'm sorry.

Dylan: You're scaring me Eas.

Me: Don't be. I'll never fucking hurt you, baby.

Dylan: I know Eas. Never have and never will.

Me: My ride or die girl.

Dylan: I'm coming to get you. I don't like how you sound.

Me: How do I sound? You can't hear me through a text.

Dylan: Jesus. I'm on my way.

Me: No Hellcat. I'm finnne. It's ok. I deserve it.

Dylan: Deserve what?

The room starts to spin and my phone continues to vibrate. I close my eyes to ease the spins but it only makes it worse. Laying my head back, I try to relax my eyes and let sleep take over me. Right now, dreamland is better than reality. In dreamland, the girl I want, but can't have, was never hurt. Never forced to succumb to the pain and trauma of last night. In my dreams, *she's perfectly perfect.*

CHAPTER II

DETECTIVE ELEANA ST. JAMES

Her body shivers as I remove the rose from her aching clit. She takes a deep breath as I slide my finger in and out of her soaked core, her slender body dripping with sweat. I've been edging her for the last hour, bringing her close to orgasm and ripping it away. This is her punishment for not getting the autopsy results back when I asked for it. "Should have been a good girl, Love," I whisper against her thigh, licking up and blowing on her clit.

"I'm sorry. I'll try harder tomorrow." She whimpers, writhing beneath me as her body chases another orgasm. I add another finger and curl them, causing her walls to flutter around me. Leaning down, I take her little clit into my mouth and suck ever so gently. "Mmm, I love the way you eat my pussy." She pants and I suck harder as her clit ripples in my mouth. "Please baby, I want to cum. Let me cum." She begs. *I love it when she begs.*

Reaching over, I take my gun from its holster and click the safety off. Replacing my soaked fingers with the tip of my gun, I rub it in her arousal before sliding it inside her. Her back bows off the bed as I place the rose back on top of her clit, turning it on. I fuck her pussy with my gun as the rose sucks her little clit. I press the button again and add pressure to the rose so it sucks her harder. She screams as she rides the barrel of my gun and gushes all around it. I remove my weapon and lick her sweet juices before putting it to the side, but I leave the rose, pulling orgasm after orgasm from her. "Ele, it's too much, I can't." She whines.

"But you can, and you will. Give me one more, Love." I demand as I reach up and slap her nipple.

"Oh, God, again, please do that again." She whimpers and I slap her other nipple.

"Yes, yes. Just like that baby. Fuck." She screams as I push the button on high and she squirts all over me, making a complete mess of the bed. Her body convulses as her orgasm consumes her, watching as her core contracts. I should have fucked her tight pussy with my strap-on.

Next time she's a bad girl, I'll peg her ass, too. Shutting off the rose, I give her a second to catch her breath as I lay next to her, her legs shaking uncontrollably.

Suddenly we see headlights and I sit up, peeking out the window to see Dylan leaving. *At this time of night?* It's not like I can call her and ask her where the fuck she's going. She doesn't even know that most nights I'm sleeping right next door. I'll just text her tomorrow and see how her night was. No point in trying to figure out where the fuck she is off to tonight. "Who was it, baby?" April asks, her breath finally calm.

"Dylan is leaving. It's after fucking midnight." I snap.

"Well, we would know what our kids were up to if we just told them the truth about us." She quips. *I don't want to have this conversation.* There's so many lies, so many secrets that I'm not ready to divulge. No one knows my true identity and I don't plan on ever telling anyone. Not even my own kids know who our true family is and that's the way it will stay until my dying day. April's phone rings and she reaches over to get it. I watch as she rolls over, admiring her curves and the dimples above her ass cheeks.

"Fuck, it's the captain." She groans, answering it. I climb out of bed and get dressed. He doesn't call to just talk. This is our call in, so I might as well get ready to clock in.

"There's been a double homicide in Whitestone and it looks like the copycat is at it again," she says, getting out of bed to get dressed. Before she can put her panties on, I grab her and bring her lips to mine.

"We will finish this later, Love. I wasn't done with you." I wink, releasing her, but before I can walk away, she grabs me and slides her hand down my pants, rubbing my clit. I close my eyes, taking a deep breath. *I love when she takes over and touches me.* I shiver as she continues to toy with my clit. I lean my head back against the wall, letting her rip an orgasm from my tense body.

I grab her wrist as she continues to flick, moaning as she pinches my clit causing me to cum hard and fast. I open my eyes and look at her. Taking a deep breath, I pull her into me. "Thank you." I breathe, kissing her nose as she removes her fingers from my pants, sucking them into her mouth. "Always so sweet, baby." She winks, turning away to get dressed.

As much as I love my job, I much rather stay here with her and fuck like rabbits until the sun comes up, but duty calls and a there's a serial killer on the loose.

CHAPTER 12

DYLAN

Driving to The Den in a panic is not what I wanted to do tonight. I don't give a fuck what my brother says, maybe if he was paying attention to his friend, Easton wouldn't be drunk, let alone texting me on some bullshit.

I'm so fucking worried as I speed down the highway to get to him. His texts sounded weird and alarming; he never texts me like that. The only time we ever speak to one another in a sexual way is in the middle of the act, so to say I was shocked by his actions and apologies, is an understatement. A little secret about Easton is that he very rarely drinks. So for him to be drunk as a skunk, means something is seriously wrong.

I'm exhausted from the day and the night before. My body still hurts and bruises are starting to litter my skin in random places. I fucking hate that me and Eas fought earlier today, but he just kept pushing and pushing. I wanted to tell him so fucking bad, but he will tell my brother, who will definitely tell my mother, and just no. I have to keep this shit buried. *Act like it never fucking happened.* My phone goes off and I see a text from Carter.

> **Carter: Hey babe. I know it's late but I'm just checking in. I miss you Dyl, you should have come to the Hamptons with me. But I hope you had fun with the girls this weekend. I love you. Date night when I get back?**

I really should have gone with him, then maybe this shit would have never happened. Arriving at The Den, I put the car in park and hop out as I text Carter back.

> **Me: Miss you too, babe. I hope you are having a wonderful time in Boujeeville. Lol. When are you due back? Date night sounds like fun. See you soon. Love you. xo**

Sliding my phone in my back pocket, I see it's not as busy as it usually is here, which makes this shit even more fucking suspicious. I swing open the door and see barely anyone of importance until I notice the slump figure on the couch.

Shaking my head, I go straight for him. Looking down, I see his phone laying on his chest, so I pick it up and slide it in my front pocket. I rock his shoulder to wake him and he jumps up from the couch, his eyes going wide as he wraps a hand around my throat, squeezing as flashes of last night litter my vision. I try to scream, but he squeezes tighter.

"D? What the fuck? Shit. I'm sorry," he slurs, letting go of my throat. I narrow my eyes at him but I should have known better. Since we were kids, you couldn't wake him up by touching him because he automatically starts swinging. Still, to this day, no one knows why that is, but I'm stupid and wasn't thinking.

He releases my throat and falls back down. Taking a deep breath, I grab his hand and try to pull him up. His hands slide up my thighs and over my ass, slowly inching up to my waist.

"Come here, baby." He smiles, trying to pull me down with him. My eyes go wide as I shove his hands off me.

"Eas, not the fucking place. Come on, let's go to your room and get you to bed." I say as he looks around before he gives my ass a squeeze. *He wants to die tonight. Jesus fucking Christ.*

"Easton Daniels, stop. There are too many people around and I have a boyfriend." I whisper yell as he stands on shaky legs.

"Not long for, Hellcat." He slurs. *He fucking reeks of vodka.*

"How much did you drink tonight and hold on to me, you idiot, before you fall!" I whisper, wrapping my arm around his waist as he wraps his arm around my neck. *Fuck, this hurts. He's so fucking heavy.*

"You smell delicious, pretty girl." He whispers, licking my ear.

"Easton, if you don't stop, I'm going to drop your ass and leave. I'm trying to help you. Now fucking help me get you to your room, then you can spew all the bullshit you want at me." I chide.

"It's not bullshit, Hellcat. I mean every say I word." He smiles again and I laugh as we make it down the hall.

"You can't even speak right, let alone walk. Just shut up and help me help you, Crow." I say, pulling him along.

"I hate when you call me that. You know you're pretty, right? Pretty as a button." He hiccups and there is the smell of vodka again.

"Ok Eas, if you say so." I shake my head as we reach his room and lean him up against the door, feeling in his pocket for the keys.

"To the left, Hellcat." He smirks. *For. Fuck's. Sake.*

"Very funny, Eas. I'm looking for your keys, asshole." I seethe, getting annoyed.

"Just touch it. You know you want to." He taunts. If it were any other time, he would be correct, but it feels wrong when he's like this.

"No!" I say, finally finding his fucking keys. Pulling them out, I put the key in the door and swing it open.

"Why? You don't want me anymore?" He pouts. *Lord. Help. Me.*

"Eas, you're drunk. You don't know what you're saying. Just go lay down." I order, shutting his bedroom door. I look around and there isn't much in here. A standard dresser. A king size bed with nightstands, a small couch and a closet. Typical boring man room. He stumbles to his bed, kicking his boots off and shedding his shirt before plopping on top of it.

Jesus, he's ripped and covered in tattoos. I haven't seen him shirtless in a while because he's riddled with new ink I've never seen before. *Why must he be so fucking sexy?* I clear my throat, taking a step towards him as he struggles with his belt. *Jesus Christ it's like taking care of a toddler.* I fall to my knees and remove his hands from his belt. His eyes lock with mine and he smirks as I roll mine and rip his belt off in one swift movement.

"Damn, Hellcat. You look fucking ravishing with my belt in your hands." He says, licking his lips.

"Would you just lay down and go to bed?" I say, rolling my eyes again and chucking the belt onto the couch as he undoes the button on his jeans.

"Only if you lay with me, baby." He says, scooting over and patting the spot next to him.

"If you stop calling me baby, I will." I snide, raising a brow at him.

"Just shut the fuck up and get with me in bed." he slurs as I move slowly, taking off my shoes and sliding in next to him.

"Come closer and take off the damn hoodie. I need to feel your skin." He orders. But I can't, all I have on is a bra and I don't want him to see the bruises.

"No, just lay there and shut up." I retort, silently begging him not to push.

"Please D. I just need to feel you." He begs. Huffing, I reach over and turn his bedside lamp off, shed my hoodie and throw it to the couch as I lay down beside him.

"Don't make me again say it." He slurs some more and I laugh, turning on my side, trying not to wince. I lay my leg over his hip and my head on his rapidly beating chest.

"Happy now, drunky?" I giggle as he lays his hand on my lower back, rubbing circles right above my pant line causing goosebumps to litter my skin.

"Nope, I prefer you naked." He grunts. *Who is this guy?* Easton is not known for being sweet or forthcoming with information, he's always tight lipped and at arms length. *Do I soak this up for what it is? I know he will forget about it in the morning anyway.*

"Could you even undress me in your current state? Let alone get it up?" I can't help but laugh as I move to place a kiss on his chest. I can still feel his rapidly beating heart.

"Don't insult me, Hellcat. Even if I am really fucking drunk, I can do things to that sexy fucking body that you've never experienced before." He states with such certainty. I look up at him with a raised brow.

"You're lucky to be in this state. Otherwise, this conversation wouldn't even be happening and you know it." I sigh, laying back down.

"Perhaps you're right, but it doesn't change the fact that I want you." He whispers and my head pops up, looking right into his chocolate brown eyes.

"Don't look at me like that. The game we play is all I get with you, but underneath all the attitude and taunts, you have to know how I feel about you, Hellcat." He whispers some more, his eyes never leaving mine. I laugh and he growls, squeezing me tighter, causing me to wince.

"I'm sorry D, I'm so fucking sorry," he apologizes as he rolls over. Hooking my leg higher over his hip, he grabs my face and caresses my cheek gently.

"It's fine Eas. Besides, you won't remember all of this in the morning. Which kills me deep inside, but it's fine. We both know we can't have one another. I have a boyfriend who I'm going off to live with in the dorms next year and probably marry in the future. So this," I point between us, "Is just a fucking game we've been playing. It's all good." I lie, looking down. I don't want him to see the hurt in my eyes and how much this breaks my heart. His pointer finger brings my chin up but I refuse to meet his eye. I can't. It's too much and I'm too exhausted for all of this, but he grabs my face.

"Look at me, Dylan." He growls, pulling me closer and squeezing me tighter, like he doesn't want me to run. I shake my head and he does the unthinkable. He pulls me against his lips and I gasp as his tongue enters my mouth and caresses mine slowly. *Holy fucking shit.* He kisses me so fucking slowly as he grinds his hard cock against my pussy and deepens the kiss, sucking my lips into his mouth.

We don't come up for air, lost in the moment for I don't know how long, but I'm left a writhing mess in his arms. His cock is so fucking hard, I just want to grab it and make him feel good. I trail my hand from the back of his neck down his chest, feeling all his muscles tighten as I slowly slide down to his waiting cock. I run my fingers slowly up his length and he shutters against me, pulling away from the kiss.

"D, I need to tell you something." He blurts but I stop him in his tracks, putting my finger against his lips.

"I don't want to ruin this moment. If this is the only moment I get with you, without stipulation, then let us enjoy one another," I whisper against his lips, sucking his bottom lip into my mouth. He groans as his hand squeezes my ass, running his fingers down my crack to the warmth between my thighs. I know I'm a fucking mess for him, but his mouth does things to me. He deepens the kiss again and I don't ever want to stop.

I have never been so worked up in my life from just kissing and light dry humping, but this man doesn't even need to touch me to set my body on fire. We kiss for hours until we are both spent with swollen lips. I lay my head on his chest, trying to catch my breath.

"I'm sorry, Hellcat. Sorry for everything." He says as I feel my eyes get extremely heavy.

"It's ok, Crow. I'm just going to close my eyes for a little bit. Then I'll drive home." I say in a sleepy tone, but he grabs me tighter.

"No, you will stay with me until morning. We will go to class together." He says, sounding a little more coherent than earlier.

"Okay Eas. Whatever you–" That's the last thing I remember before sleep takes over.

CHAPTER 13

EASTON

A throat clears and I feel a warm body laying on my chest. Her scent hits my nostrils and my dick automatically gets hard. A throat clears again and I open my eyes to see Ace standing in the doorway with his arms over his chest. *Fuck, fuck, fuck.*

"Well now, what do we have here?" He smirks as he looks over the bed.

"Nothing. I got really drunk last night and she came here looking for Amy saw I was fucked out of my face and helped me to bed. We were just bullshitting and she passed out when we watched a movie." I say shrugging my shoulders.

"Hmm, and that required to be done half naked?" He quips. *Fuck. Fuck. Fuck.* How the fuck do I get out of this?

"Stop reading into shit, it's not what you think." I growl. He puts his hands up in surrender, shaking his head.

"Just be careful E. Don't forget the pact. I don't feel like burying you anytime soon, bro." He reminds me before turning and leaving the room. I let out a deep breath. *Jesus Christ. What am I doing?*

"Is he gone?" She whispers and I laugh.

"Yea, Hellcat, he's gone. Time to get up for class." I try to sit up and she slides off me, grabbing the blanket I placed over us last night to cover herself. I'm glad Ace could only see my bare chest on display and not that she was in just a bra. She climbs out of bed with the blanket and I want to laugh, but I know her sassy ass mouth will have something to say, so I keep mine shut and go take a piss.

Fuck, my head hurts. How much did I drink last night? I do my thing in the bathroom and by the time I get out, she's long gone. As much as that grates on my nerves, she knew we couldn't walk out together, not this early in the morning. I change my clothes and notice my phone laying on the top of the blanket. I turn it on and open to the last thing I did last night and see it was a thread with her. *Jesus fucking Christ, Easton. Daddy? Really?* Actually, I do like the sound of that, but Jesus. And I tried to tell her? *Fuck!* I only remember bits and pieces of last night. I'll never forget the hours I spent kissing her, though. Making her luscious lips swollen and how she grabbed my cock.

Damn, I need a cigarette. Grabbing my stuff, I leave my room. I used to crash here a lot, but as of lately, I've been yearning to be home to make sure she's safe and so I could climb into her window and torture one another.

Last night was a disaster. I wanted her to tell me what happened and if she did, I would have fessed up and told her the truth, but lie after lie spewed from her mouth and it just made me madder. I should have stayed home instead of coming here and I certainly shouldn't have texted her. *I'm an idiot.*

Leaving The Den, I light up a cigarette and inhale the minty smoke as I walk to my car. It's a gorgeous day to ride, but I'm not in the mood to gear up. Instead, I get in the car, bring her to life and head to the University. I continue to smoke my cigarette as I blast music and drive to class. It feels like it takes forever to arrive, even with getting lost in my head about Dylan. I really hate coming here. I only take three business courses and sitting in class listening to a professor drag on about profits and losses, is not what I want to do. I'd rather be getting my hands dirty for The Cartel.

Speaking of which, we have a job tonight picking up guns from the Irish Army. We've done this for the past few months but tonight is going to be a little different. We aren't meeting with the usual people. Spade set it up so we can ambush them and I can't wait to sink my knife into a motherfucker.

Later that night, I find myself pissed the fuck off, standing in my bedroom window, watching Dylan and Carter in her room. Taking out my phone, I send her a text.

Me: Get rid of him!

I stand here and wait for her to pick up the phone to read the text. In the meantime, I check-in with Bentley. I left The Den hours ago and went for a ride on my bike to clear my head. The orders went perfectly tonight, except I didn't get to kill like I wanted to.

> **Me: Everything good?**

Almost immediately.

> **Bentley: Yea. He was impressed and gave us extra plus some product.**

> **Me: Sweet. I'll meet up with you tomorrow.**

> **Bentley: Bianca came here looking for you. She seemed pretty upset.**

> **Me: Yea well, she can fuck off.**

> **Bentley: I know. She needs to be dealt with. I don't trust her.**

Me: Neither do I. The moment she set us up, she lost all my trust. She can rot for all I care.

Bentley: Well, take care of it.

Me: If she returns, I will.

Bentley: Alright E. Take it easy and I'll link up with you tomorrow. I've got a whiney bitch in my bed.

Me: Ha! Tell Amy I said Hey.

Bentley: Shut the fuck up.

I laugh because he is so fucking predictable. Arriving home and seeing Carter's fucking car in the driveway immediately pissed me off. I wanted to march up into her room, kick in the door and sink my knife into his throat. But here I am. Waiting, watching, seething that he's next to her. Laying in her bed. Breathing the same air as her. I'm a jealous mother fucker, especially when it comes to the girl I can't fucking have. I remember some of the things I told her, and it wasn't a lie. I want her in the worst way possible, even when I want to strangle her to death. She drives me mad, and now that I've kissed her for hours and felt her whine into my mouth while we explored one another, I can't get enough. I want more. I want to consume her every breath. My phone dings, taking me out of my thoughts.

Dylan: Excuse me?

Of course she would give me an attitude as I stand at my window stalking her ass.

Me: Look up!

Her eyes immediately meet mine and widen.

Me: Get rid of him!

Dylan: Why?

> **Me: If you don't do as you're told, I'm coming over there and removing him myself. Now do it!**

> **Dylan: No, he's my boyfriend and he's spending the night.**

> **Me: The fuck he is. Look at me, Hellcat. Make him fucking leave or I swear to god I will gut him and choke you with his intestines. GET. RID. OF. HIM. NOW!**

She looks up at me again and smirks. *This little bitch.* Always playing mind games. I don't know what she tells him, nor do I care, but within twenty minutes he's out the door. My phone pings again, bringing a smile to my face.

> **Dylan: Happy now?**

> **Me: Good girl. Now go to sleep.**

She looks at me with narrowed eyes. I bet if I was there, she'd try to punch me for pulling some shit like that. I smirk at her and I swear, if looks could kill, I'd be dead. She kills the light but leaves her bedside lamp on as she sheds her shirt.

What. The. Fuck.

I step closer to the window as she removes her bra, tweaking her pert nipples. My mouth waters at the sight. She then turns and slowly slides her pants down showing off her nice juicy ass in a teal thong. I can see her wet lips through the cotton and it has my dick hard. I look down at my phone and send her a text.

> **Me: You're playing a very dangerous game, Hellcat.**

She looks over her shoulder and smirks. Okay. I got something for her. I take my clothes off and stand in front of the window leaning against the pane with one arm over my head, completely fucking naked, while my other hand strokes my cock. She turns around and her eyes rake up and down my body as she licks her lips. A text comes through.

Dylan: Are you fucking pierced?

Me: Wouldn't you like to know?

I look up across the window and she's gone. *What the fuck?* Then I see a flash of black sprinting across the yard. *Oh, she's coming to me for once. This should be interesting.* I spin and lean against the window, still holding my hard cock, stroking it painfully slow as my door bursts open and a half naked Dylan stands in front of me.

"Hey Hellcat, what brings you to my neck of the woods?" I smirk with a chuckle as she walks straight for me, grabbing my cock and stroking it. I lean my head back against the glass and close my eyes. *Fuck, her hands feel magnificent.*

"Eas, I never knew you were fucking pierced. Jesus fucking Christ. He's big." She says as I open my eyes looking at her stare at it. She continues to stroke my length as I pull her to me, shedding her hoodie. Her body is riddled with bruises. *FUCK.*

"Hellcat. You want to explain this to me?" I growl, but she says nothing as she sinks to her knees, wrapping her warm mouth around the head of my cock, flicking her tongue against my piercing.

"Fuck, baby." I groan as she gags on my length. I don't deserve to feel pleasure like this. Not when her body is bruised up. I pull her off my cock and she looks up at me with those ocean blues.

"Get up!" I command. She slowly rises while she runs her hands up my thighs to my stomach and over my chest to my face, where she slaps me. My head slightly moves from the impact.

"That's for the stunt you pulled. Who the fuck do you think you are?" She asks, waiting for an answer. I just smile.

"Your worst fucking nightmare," I spit, picking her up by her thighs and spinning us to press her bare ass against the glass.

"I won't apologize if that's what you're looking for. I don't want to see you with him, especially from my fucking window." I growl, sliding her soaked thong to the side and sinking my fucking fingers into her drenched pussy. *Fuck. She's so goddamn tight.*

"Are you soaked for me, or him?" I groan, raising a brow.

"You, always you." She moans as I milk her walls slowly. *Fuck, I just want to sink my cock into her, but I won't. Not tonight, at least.* I continue to slowly finger her as she writhes against me, rolling her hips to get more friction. She tries to reach down to touch me, but I'm just out of reach. *Good. For once, she listened, so this is her reward.*

"Damn Eas. Your fingers feel so good inside me." She whimpers as she rolls tight circles with her hips. *Jesus, I wish she would do that on my aching cock. Fuck.* Every fucking ounce of restraint I have is fading at the thought of sliding her down this window and sinking inside her.

"Tell Daddy how good he makes you feel." I growl as she tightens around my fingers.

"So good, Eas. Faster. I'm so close." She whines as I remove my fingers with a raised brow.

"Say it, the way I told you to." I demand as I smear her arousal on her bottom lip.

"You feel so fucking good, Daddy." She says seductively, licking her lips and something snaps in me. I fuse my mouth to hers, tasting her pussy and I growl into her mouth as she whimpers when I sink two fingers into her, fucking her hard and fast.

"You don't know how bad I want to fuck this tight pussy." I growl against her lips. She tastes phenomenal. This is the problem with us. We challenge one another and bring each other to the brink of insanity without ever wanting to stop.

"Please Eas. Please just let me feel you." She begs, scratching her nails down my chest. *Jesus. I don't know how much more resistance I have left.* I need her to cum and get her away from me because I'm literally seconds away from saying to hell with everything and taking exactly what the fuck I want. I flick her clit as she whimpers, playing with her nipples. *This woman is seriously my wet dream. She's perfect, even with that sassy mouth of hers. God, I just want to consume her. I want to take her on my bed, against this window, in the shower, outside on top of my car. EVERYWHERE.*

"Eas, I'm going to cum. Fuckkkk." She screams while I rub my thumb up and down her clit, feeling her tighten around my fingers as her warm cum puddles in my hand. I slowly pump a few more times, letting her come down with ease. Removing my fingers, I slide them into her mouth, and like the good girl she is, she sucks them clean.

"Good girl." I whisper against her lips. She looks down at my hard cock dripping with precum.

"Can I make you cum?" she asks with pure lust in her voice, but I shake my head.

"Not tonight. You've done enough." I say, placing her down on her feet.

"What the fuck is that supposed to mean?" She says with a hand on her hip. *She's so fucking gorgeous.* I could argue with this girl day and night, and I still want to fuck the attitude right out of her.

"Nothing. Time for you to go." I say, not making eye contact with her.

"Wow, Eas. You're a real fucking asshole." She growls, picking up her hoodie and leaving without a backwards glance.

She's right, I am a fucking asshole. It's not new behavior, but I needed to get her the fuck out of here before I had her in my bed again. We can't keep doing this, but I've kissed her for hours, felt how tight she is and got a little taste of her beautiful pussy. *How the fuck do I come back from this? I don't, I just drown in it. I'm totally fucking fucked.* I need to tell her the truth. I'm going to lose her no matter what. Carter wins for now.

Walking over to my jeans, I pull out a cigarette and light it. Sliding my window up, I watch as she enters her room, walks over to the glass and locks it before getting into bed. At least I know she's alone and safe, even if she is mad at me. Taking a deep inhale, I try to think how to get out of this so I can have the girl, but I don't think happiness with a woman is in the cards for me.

CHAPTER 14

DYLAN

Easton is such a prick. How can he make me cum so fucking hard and say all the things he said to me for the last two days, then kick me to the curb like I'm the next bitch? I wanted to punch him so hard in his beautiful pierced cock. That man has me all sorts of fucked up lately.

I leave class, not remembering anything the professor was teaching for the last ninety minutes and walk to my car, ready for the day to be over. I have a shit ton of fucking homework and a paper to write on the mind of a serial killer. I really want to research 'The Carver', but I was told he was off limits, so I'm choosing 'Jack the Ripper' and spending the remainder of the night in my room with junk food and soda researching this guy.

Arms wrap around my waist and I damn near jump out of my skin.

"Woah, babe. It's just me." Carter laughs, kissing the top of my head. I roll my eyes wishing they were tattooed arms wrapped around me instead. I take a deep breath and put on a show, spinning in his hold and giving him a quick kiss. He grabs my ass trying to deepen the kiss but I pull away.

"I'm in a rush, babe. What's up?" I ask, but he doesn't give me an answer. Instead, he moves closer, entwining his hands into my hair, kissing down my throat and nipping at my jaw. All this PDA is making me extremely uncomfortable and wanting to crawl out of my skin.

"Carter, baby, I have an appointment I'm late for. I gotta run." I lie, pushing away from his embrace.

"I just missed you, babe. I thought we could get dinner tonight and chill." He says.

"I can't, I've got a paper due and haven't started it. Rain check?" I say, leaning up to kiss him on the nose.

"Sure babe. Call me later when you take a break," he says, walking backwards. I blow him a kiss before turning around, continuing the walk to my car, suddenly feeling eyes on me. I fucking can't stand this shit. I always feel like I'm being watched and it's making me fucking paranoid. Finally making it to my car, I stop in my tracks, tears fill my eyes as I see the words 'Gang Bang Whore' written across my car in spray paint. I look around and see people whispering and giggling. I need to get the fuck out of here. Unlocking my door, I get in and slide the key into the ignition, except she won't turn over. *Fuck.* I smash my hand on the steering wheel as people continue to stare at me. Taking out my phone, I text Bentley.

> **Me: You still at Uni?**

Benny: Na, why? What's wrong?

Fuck, I can't tell him. Shit, what do I say?

> **Me: Just want to see if you want to hang out before I have to start my paper.**

I lie. I'm always fucking lying.

Benny: Sorry sister. I'm kind of in the middle of something.

> **Me: Eww. Tell Amy I'll text her later lol.**

> **Benny: What is with you people? But she said okay.**

Fuck. Well, now I can't call Amy and Ava is in a study sesh for the next four hours. I can't call any of Fatal, except maybe Easton. Fuck. I'm going to have to tell him something. *Fuck. I hate this shit. But here goes nothing.*

> **Me: I need your help!**

I wait a few seconds, looking around at people still gawking at me causing my skin to literally crawl. I refuse to get out of this car until someone comes to get me. My phone pings, it's him.

> **Easton: You want more of my fingers, Hellcat?**

Me: Jesus Christ you're such a pig. I actually need fucking help, but I need you to not question shit and then let it fucking go.

Easton: Where are you? No games D. Just tell me where you are.

Me: Crying in my car.

Easton: Gotta be more specific than that since you have your location off. I swear to God one day I'm going to...nevermind. Drop your pin.

Me: Dropped. Please don't yell at me. And please do not ask questions. I'm begging you.

Easton: We'll see. I'll be there in 5.

Me: Thanks.

I wipe my tears because, fuck this. Why am I letting these fucks get to me? I just want to bury this. Act like it never fucking happened. They got what they wanted. Why can't they leave me the fuck alone? I lean my head against the steering wheel and close my eyes.

I must have drifted off because the sudden pounding on my window jolts me awake and I look to see Easton standing there with his hands clenched into fists at his side. *Shit. He's big mad.* I unlock the door and he swings it open as I cower away, but he grabs me roughly, causing me to scream. He puts a hand over my mouth.

"Hellcat, I swear to God, stop. I would never fucking hurt you. But I'm fucking livid right now. I need you to do exactly what you are told with no attitude, or so help me God, I will destroy your car. I'm seconds away from this place becoming a massacre." He growls and I nod my head as he removes his hand from my mouth. Helping me out of the car, I get to my feet and walk over to his passenger seat and stop in my tracks.

I spin on him and the look he gives me is murderous. I'm ready to walk home at this point, but he opens the back door and I get in, seething. Bianca Pierce is sitting in the front seat, with her perfectly manicured fingers and freshly cut hair looking like she walked out of a Sports Illustrated magazine, wearing a short skirt and halter top.

Easton's eyes never leave mine as he rounds the car and climbs in. He looks in the rearview mirror at me and smirks. *This mother fucker.* He puts the car in gear and we leave the university without another word. I watch as this bitch's hands slide into his lap, caressing his thigh. I wish I had some string. I'd love to choke the life out of her. I take my phone out. I need to text Amy with this shit.

> **Me: Bianca and Easton are back together?**

Almost immediately.

> **Amy: Girl. I don't know what is going on, but I heard whis-**

> **pers that she's pregnant and it's his.**

My whole fucking heart drops. I look up at the mirror and his eyes connect with mine as tears fall. His eyes narrow, but I refuse to look away until he does. A second later, those chocolate eyes are gone, looking at the road ahead of him. I wipe my tears and continue to text Amy as the happy couple talk.

> **Me: Holy shit! Easton's a dad? That's wild.**

> **Amy: I don't like her and I hate that she will be a part of our group.**

> **Me: Well, I wish them nothing but the best.**

I lie, needing to get out of this car and away from him. I feel like I'm suffocating in here with his scent all over me and the smell of her cheap perfume. I didn't realize, until this moment, how much I actually care about him. My heart hurts as I look up at him again and he's already looking at me, brow raised, as I continue to let the tears fall. Last night was it for us. *There will never be an us.* Why did I ever think there would be? He won't even fuck me. Even his drunk words mean fuck all now.

The car comes to a stop and I rush out the door, practically running to the front door of my house. Trying to key in the code, my eyes blur from the tears when I feel him grab me. I spin on him.

"Get away from me." I growl. His eyes widen and he takes a step back. I open the door and turn to shut it in his face, but not before spewing,

"Have a nice life with your baby mama," I spit, slamming the door in his face. Locking it, I fall to the ground and sob. My fucking heart is in pieces. Between the shit on my car and now this, my chest is so tight, it's hard to breathe. I find the strength to get up from the floor and make it up to my room. My phone keeps pinging. I know it's him, so I shut it off, climb into my bed and cry myself to sleep.

Hours later, I wake up to tapping on my glass. I ignore it, rolling over to turn my phone back on. So many fucking text messages come through, but I don't have the energy to read them. Getting out of bed, I see Easton's face in my window and I walk over, grab the string and drop the blinds in his face. The growl that leaves his throat makes the window shudder. I'm not sure if my mom is home or not so I go down for something to eat and see her sitting in the living room watching TV.

"Dylan, is that you honey?" She yells. Taking a deep breath, I walk into the livingroom and sit next to her.

"Want to tell me what the hell happened? Your car gets towed here and I see those nasty words written across the driver's side. What is that?" She questions. *Fuck. I thought Easton was smarter than that.*

"It's nothing. Some kids at school got the wrong car. I'll pay to get it fixed." I lie.

"Interesting. So you don't know who did this? Why didn't you call the police and make a report?" She continues to question. Typical mom, always in detective mode instead of being caring.

"It's fine, mom. They had the wrong car. It's just that simple." I answer, trying to end this interrogation before getting up to go back to my room. *Well, my appetite is ruined.*

"If something happened, just tell me, because that is a pretty big accusation written across your car." She says, but I ignore her.

"Dylan St. James! Don't fucking walk away from me while I'm speaking to you." She scolds, sounding ever so motherly.

"I have a paper to write and a mountain of home-work to do, the car is the least of my problems." I mumble back, walking up the stairs. She doesn't say shit else because, if she really did care, she would have asked the correct questions, which she failed to do.

Getting back to my room, I grab my phone and see at least fifty missed text messages and calls from Easton. I just can't with him. I need to act like he doesn't exist. *Just brush everything aside and act like it never fucking happened.* I'm not in the mood to write this paper, either. I lost all motivation to do anything. Another text comes through. Opening up the thread, I see he is losing his ever loving mind.

> **Easton: Please talk to me.**

> **Easton: I don't like to see you cry like that.**

> **Easton: Please Hellcat.**

Easton: You're lucky Eleana is home.

Easton: Lock me out, it's fine.

Easton: Stop playing games, talk to me.

Easton: I'm seconds away from breaking your window and you can explain to your mom why it's broken.

Easton: Dylan, so help me, god.

Needing him to shut the fuck up, I decide to reply before he blows up my phone again.

Me: There's nothing to talk about. You're having a baby and that's it. Have a wonderful life.

Easton: You don't get to decide this is done. Just because she says she's pregnant doesn't mean I'm with her.

Me: Don't care. I'm no home-wrecker.

Easton: Just stop.

Me: No, you stop. I'm your best friend's little sister that you won't even fuck. This is nothing. Just let it fucking go.

Easton: What if I told you that I don't care about any of that?

Me: I'd call you a fucking liar.

Easton: Why won't you talk to me in person? I can't stand not being able to see your eyes.

Me: Go look in her eyes. Just leave me alone.

Easton: No! I won't. I'm not finished with you!

Me: Well, I am with you. Oh, and thanks for bringing my car home. I thought you would have been smarter than that.

Easton: You will never be done with me because if it was that easy, your eyes would have never shown me how hurt you were in the car. Who told you anyway?

Me: Doesn't matter.

Easton: It does. It matters a lot. Speaking of your car, I will get it fixed. I didn't think about your mom being home. That's my fuck up. But you need to talk about what happened.

> **Me: I don't need to do shit. Are we done? I have things to do. Don't you have a crib to buy?**

> **Easton: So help me, God!**

> **Me: Goodbye Easton.**

> **Easton: No, this is not good-bye.**

Oh, but it is. I open his contact and click block as tears stream down my face. Taking a deep breath, I shut off my light, put my phone on charge and cry myself to sleep for the second time today.

CHAPTER 15

EASTON

One month later...

It's been a whole month since I've spoken to Dylan. She's made it her mission in life to avoid and ignore me, which has only pissed me off further. She fucking blocked me, so I smashed my phone to pieces and I've been slowly spiraling ever since. My hellcat is as stubborn as it comes, but I've been texting her daily, hoping she would just speak to me. I see her at the university looking more miserable than ever, her gorgeous smile long gone, and it's my fault.

Seeing her still with Carter, makes me irate, but I can't say shit. I'm having a fucking baby with the devil. Bianca is a Pierce. Why I ever fucked her in the first place is beyond me. That whole family is a bunch of snakes. But if that baby is mine, I will do the right thing and take care of them both, and she'll make sure she never lets me forget it.

She's like a succubus, draining the fucking life out of me. She wants me to buy everything constantly, and lets not forget, trying to stay with me at The Den. *I'm not into her. She doesn't do it for me.* There's only one girl for me and she's currently out of my reach.

I did fix Dylan's car and left a red rose on the windshield, but still, not a damn word. Nothing. I guess I didn't realize how this would affect her or how much she actually cared for me.

My heart dropped when I found Bianca waiting by my car with a sonogram in her hand. What was I supposed to do, send her away? That's not the type of man I am. But I could have sworn I wore a rubber with her. I don't usually raw dog it. I barely even remember fucking her.

Sitting in my car, I impatiently wait for Mr. Cyprus to deliver some product for Spade. I've become his little bitch boy, still paying my debt for the whole being late and almost dying charade. Money's been steady working for The Cartel, which I'm grateful for, but something has been missing in my life and I know it's her. Even the guys have made comments that I'm on edge and ready to snap at any moment. Obviously

I can't tell them why, so I try to stay to myself as much as I can. A tap at my window takes me out of my thoughts, rolling it down, I see a girl. *The fuck?*

"Can I help you?" I ask with a raised brow. She rolls her eyes, sticking her hand out. I look at her hand, then up at her. She huffs.

"My dad sent me here to make the drop. I don't got all night." She snaps her gum, waiting for the cash, which I place in her hands and pop the trunk. She places the duffel inside and slams it shut, tapping it twice, giving me a wink and dipping like a ghost. I sit here stunned. I wasn't expecting to do business with a female tonight. Why can't communication ever be easy around here?

Putting my car into drive, I get out of here and head to the warehouse to drop the load. I continue to obsess over Dylan, and I'm hoping she will be at the party tonight. *I fucking miss her.* I miss the games we played. Her laugh, smile, her scent. This shit is killing me. I also need to tell her the truth about that night, but if I tell her now, she would kill me on the spot. She already hates me, and I don't blame her, but that doesn't mean I'm letting this go.

I'm hearing rumors that someone has been taunting her; leaving her notes on her car, there was even a flier that went around Uni showcasing a masked girl getting railed on a bed. I specifically went around throwing them all out. It took me hours, but I took care of it. No one should ever see her like that. *Vulnerable and assaulted.*

I need to get the names of all of them. I planned to start with Garrett first. He will squeal like a pig and spill his guts. He's a pussy, he knows he can't take me one on one, hence why they jumped me. I'm not sure what they have on Fatal, but something one of us did, set him off to orchestrate Dylan's gang rape. This week, after swim practice, I'm grabbing him. I just have a few things to tweak before I can move forward.

Arriving at the warehouse, I key in my code, drive up the long dirt road and see Gio waiting for me. He rounds the car as I pop the trunk. *Transaction completed.* Gio stops by my window and hands me an envelope. "From the boss." He says and I nod.

"Tell him I said thank you. See you soon, Gio." I bid my farewell, get back on the road, and head for The Den.

A few hours later, I'm standing next to the pool table readying myself to take a shot. I rear the pool stick back ever so slightly and bang, I send the eight ball flying into the corner pocket, winning the third game of the night. Shooting pool is a great distraction tonight, plus Bianca is here after I specifically told her to stay her ass home, but she doesn't listen. A pregnant woman doesn't need to be hanging around here. But apparently she didn't want to be alone and is trying way too hard to present herself as my girl. My boys know it will never happen. We've discussed it. I don't trust her, and I could kick my own dick in for getting her knocked up. I still have to tell my mother, but I refuse to open my mouth until a DNA test proves anything. Again, I don't trust her, not for what she did the last time. Bentley nudges me to get my attention.

"Yo, where is your head at right now? I've been talking to you for the last couple of minutes." He says with a raised brow.

"My bad. I was in my head about the baby." I respond and he shakes his head.

"It will be okay. I don't like her and we both don't trust her, but you are doing the right thing. You could have just walked away, but you're trying to do what's best." He says, placing a hand on my shoulder, giving it a squeeze.

"I know, but how can I do this when I can't trust her? If I don't do what she wants, she holds the kid over my head. I'm not her bitch. That's not how this works, but I don't want to be absent either. My feelings aren't all the way involved yet. I need to know if it's even mine. Then we can go from there. But right now, something is off and I don't like it." I grunt, and he looks at me with a smile.

"I've had the same feeling as well. Guess we will find out when the time arrives." He shrugs.

"Yeah, but what if it gets us all killed? I need to know now, before it's too late. My gut is telling me this is a set-up. You know the beef between The Pierces and The Rivers? We are their most lucrative business besides the other shit. What if she was sent here to take us out one by one and kill the distro so they can take over our territory?" I whisper as he calls the others over. We really need to get in the office and discuss this shit now. We have a big job in a couple of hours and this party is a decoy. Everyone will think we are here partying, when we are actually taking out some high-end players in the game.

"I'm aware of the history. It's old beef that has been lingering for way too long. There's more to the story than what Preston has told us, though. He's always so tight lipped, it's like pulling teeth to get all the information. He only gives us what we need to know, nothing more, nothing less. He trusts no one. I'm not sure he even trusts his siblings. He keeps to himself from what I can see. But that's not the point here. If she's a spy and setting us up, we need to know now, like you said. Where will she be while we leave to go to this job? She can't stay here. There's too much intel here, and her sneaky self could get her hands on things she shouldn't. All the girls need to be secured." Bentley orders.

"Ava isn't here tonight. She's with her new boyfriend." Ace sneers. I take a deep breath knowing how he feels.

"Where's Amy and Dylan?" I ask. Seeing that we are on this subject, I can ask and it wouldn't be alarming.

"Let's take this to the office." Kingston says as he scans the crowd around us. The five of us take off down the hall and into our office with a big oval table, high back chairs, and about ten screens of cameras covering the grounds both inside and out. Antonio shuts and locks the door behind us. We can speak as loud as we want since we converted this to a sound-proof room. Kingston walks over to the desk, removes a small device from the drawer, and starts scanning the room for listening devices and cameras. The rest of us sit around the table, laying out the plans for our next job. Suddenly, the device lights up like the fourth of July, and we freeze. He moves to the light fixture above the table and removes a little chip from underneath dropping it in Antonio's beer bottle. *I fucking knew it.* He continues to scan the room and finds three more listening devices. *What. The. Fuck.*

"How the fuck is she getting in here? That door is always locked. We need to check the cameras." I blurt, but Kingston looks at me with a dumb look.

"Shut up, I'm not done." He growls in a hushed tone. *Oh, he's mad.* Kingston is a man of few words, and it takes a lot for him to get mad. He's normally a happy guy, but this type of snake-shit pisses him right the fuck off. Once he's finished, he nods, giving us the okay to speak. Everyone immediately starts yelling, but Bentley says nothing, just slams his fist down on the table.

"Shut up, all of you. Me and Eas already had our suspicions. We need to know why, though. We also need to keep this office more secure, especially with us leaving tonight." He growls.

"He's right. This is going to be tricky because she's here with our other girls that need protection, who actually have rank over that sneaky bitch." Antonio adds.

"But we also need to keep the party going. We need people to think we are here the whole time. Especially because of who is here, and I don't mean Bianca. Lee and Ziya Wang are attending tonight, just like we planned." Ace says.

"Okay, so everything is in place, we just need to play our parts. Yes, this new revelation throws a wrench in slightly, but we need someone that we trust to watch this place while we are gone. That's the only thing we haven't decided." I raise a brow and we all sit back to take a moment to think. We don't trust anyone that won't fucking snitch.

"What about Carter?" Kingston blurts. Before anyone can say shit, I'm all over it.

"Absolutely the fuck not. Just because he's with the ice queen doesn't make him trustworthy." I growl and they laugh. Looking over to Ace, he has a smug look on his face. *Fuck.* I see he hasn't let that morning he walked in on us go. Something catches my attention in my peripherals on the screens to my right and I see commotion going on. What the fuck is that? I stand abruptly and walk closer to the screen. What I see has me moving so fast out of the room, swinging the door open and hauling ass out to the main room. My eyes widen as I see my fucking hellcat beating a girl's ass, but not just any girl, my baby mama. I'm frozen on the spot as I watch her slam Bianca's head to the ground and punch her in the jaw. *Fuck. I need to stop this.* I walk up and grab my girl by her waist, haul her ass over my shoulder, and walk away from the scene, taking her outside to cool her the fuck off.

"Put me the fuck down, asshole." She yells. I slap her ass as she pounds on my back.

"Nope, not until you calm your little ass down." I growl as I continue to walk us to my car.

"Let me go, fucker!" She yells. Again, I ignore her pleas as I reach the passenger side door, opening it and tossing her ass in the seat as I slam the door in her gorgeous face., *I missed her so much.* She's screaming her head off trying to open her door as I round the car. *Child locks bitch.* I laugh because she's really big fucking mad. I get in the car, start it up and swing out of the parking lot.

"Where the fuck are you taking me?" She heaves as I glance over at her quickly. *God, she's beautiful. I have to figure out how to make this right.* But first I need to know why the fuck she did that to Bianca knowing she's pregnant.

"You wanna explain to me what the fuck that was back there, Hellcat?" I ask, a small smirk tugging at my lips as I feel her ocean blues drilling into the side of my face.

"Oh, just me calling the bitch out. Seeing it with my own eyes. That the cunt is playing you like a mother fucking fiddle." She yells, throwing her hands up.

"What the fuck is that supposed to mean?" I yell back, stepping on the gas a little harder to get to where I want to take her faster. I need her alone, without prying eyes. I'm a man on a fucking mission and it needs to happen tonight or I may never get the chance.

"It means, dickface, that she's not fucking pregnant. She was throwing back shots while the five of you were in the office." She smirks and I slam on the brakes.

"What?" I yell, turning to look at her.

"Eas, at least pull over to the side, Jesus. Just park somewhere other than the middle of the damn highway." She laughs. *Ah, I missed that laugh. But fuck. She played me? Shit. I need to warn the guys.* Taking out my phone, I shoot a text to Bentley.

Me: Do not let her leave.

Bentley: What the fuck bro? Also, you storming out of here with my sister? Make it make sense my guy!

Me: Dylan has always come first. I'm just fulfilling the orders set for me, Boss.

Bentley: Cut the shit. What is going on?

Me: Apparently Dylan caught Bianca doing shots. She ain't pregnant. I've been played. DO NOT LET HER LEAVE. Tie her ass up for all I care.

Bentley: Fuck. Well at least we won't have to worry about her snooping around anymore.

Me: Roger that. I'll be back before we need to leave. I'm just making sure Dylan is alright. What are we doing with our girls?

Shit. I said our. I hope he doesn't read into it.

> **Bentley: They are to stay here until we get back. This is the safest place for them. Spade is sending guards over to walk the perimeter while we are gone. Everything is in place.**

> **Me: Ok. I'll be back soon.**

I finally find a place to park. Getting out of the car, I round the front and open her door. I sit on the warm hood with my head in my hands. *She fucking played me. But why? What is it we have that she wants? Something doesn't add up.* I look over at Dylan who is standing in front of me staring.

"Thanks for having my back when I least deserve it." I say softly and she rolls her eyes at me.

"It wasn't for you. I've been watching her for the last month playing you left and right. You know she frequents the Frat house a lot?" She asks, and that's news to me. *Damn, this little bitch has been doing recon.* My cock twitches at the memory of her smashing Bianca's head to the floor. *I won't deny it, that was hot.* I hop off the hood and go right for her. She steps back, but she doesn't know that I will chase her to the ends of the earth. She's mine. And there's nothing in the way of making it happen. *Except the Pact. Fuck.*

CHAPTER 16

DYLAN

He stalks towards me and I take a step back but he doesn't stop.

PUT THE WORDS HERE, WOMAN!!!!!!!! bahahahahaha

There are still no words, so we're winging it and handling it like adults.

"Bruh, Dylan.... I was there that night. They forced me to rape you, or they were going to kill us both.

"Oh my God, I can't believe this. I love you so much. Let's live happily ever after and have tiny babies!"

"YAY! You're mine bitch. Let's go tell your brother."

"We can't, he'll kill you."

"Not if I shove you in front of me. Get in the car, hooker!"

"Only If I can give you a little hauk tua. Lemme spit on that thang baby.

....Just kidding. Turn the page.

CHAPTER 17

DYLAN

He stalks towards me and I take a step back, but he doesn't stop.

He grabs my arms roughly and I scream, causing him to immediately let go.

"What the fuck? I'm not going to hurt you, D." He yells as I start to shake. God, I missed him, but he doesn't understand my reaction at being grabbed. I need to tell him, but I'm too scared. I closed off my heart over the last thirty days trying to forget about him and act like he never existed, but the minute he manhandled me and his fucking scent hit my nostrils, everything I worked so hard to accomplish flew right out the window.

"I know, I know, I'm sorry. I just," I stammer as he walks closer, holding his hands up in surrender. I look away as tears form in my eyes. God, I need to tell him, but does this revelation with Bianca change anything for us? I need an answer now. I can't continue this game.

"Don't cry baby. Talk to me." He pleads, walking closer, but I keep taking steps back. I can't. I just need a fucking second to think. I'm so scared to tell him, so afraid of his reaction; his rejection. Tears continue to fall down my face as I try to give him what he wants.

"I–I can't. If I say anything, they will come back and do it again. But I can't take it anymore!" I yell in frustration. He steps closer, grabbing me, trying to pull me closer, but I brush him off.

"Please don't touch me, Eas. I just need to get this out and I can't have you touching me when I say it." I beg as his face drops and hurt forms on his hardened features.

"Please Eas, just listen, and then you can say what you need to say." I growl and he nods, walking over to his car and leaning on the hood. Taking a deep breath, I follow, standing in front of him, feeling really fucking vulnerable at the moment. I'm not sure what to do with my hands that are shaking uncontrollably. I shake them out, but it does nothing.

"It's okay, Hellcat. You can tell me anything, baby." He says and the tears flow harder because I know, I know he's right. Out of all the people in this world, Easton is the only person who never judges, and listens with open ears. I take a deep breath and stand closer to him, grabbing his hand as an anchor. His eyes meet mine and I release a shaky breath.

"Last month, when I told you I had my period and wanted to be alone, I lied." I say as his hold on my hand tightens. He hates being lied to. He finally relaxes his hold, but his eyes never leave mine.

"I was drugged, raped and beaten. Something about Fatal being responsible, and if I said anything, they would do it again." I sob as tears pour down my face. I take another deep breath, already on the brink of crumbling. This is the first time acknowledging what happened to me, of having it buried deep in that suitcase, not wanting to deal with the mess the situation left behind.

Centering myself, I continue, "Not only will they come back, but they will force Benny to watch as they kill our mother," my voice cracks and I feel it in my chest. I can't hold it together any longer. He grabs me, pulling me into his embrace, and I break. My knees buckle, but strong arms tighten around me, never letting me hit the ground.

"I'm sorry, baby. I'm so fucking sorry that happened! You didn't deserve any of it." He whispers as I sob into his chest. I inhale his scent of cigarettes and cedarwood. This man can turn me feral just by the smell of him alone. He lifts my chin to look up at him as he licks his lips.

"I need a name, Hellcat. Do you know who did that to you? Are these the same people who left bruises all over your perfect body? The same ones who fucked with your car?" He snarls as anger flashes across his face.

"Yes, I'm pretty sure it was Garrett, Bryce and George from the swim team, but I can't be positive. I heard their voices, but I never got to see anyone. I know there were five or six men there. The drugs disoriented my vision, amongst other things." I hiccup, putting my face in my hands. I feel his lips kiss my head as he inhales deeply.

"Look at me D, I need your eyes, Hellcat." He whispers, placing his pointer finger under my chin and lifting so my eyes meet his.

"Kiss me, or I'm going to leave and hunt these mother fuckers down and end up in jail for the rest of my life," he breathes, only inches away from my lips. Taking a deep breath, I inch closer and kiss him tenderly. The moment our lips meet, the stars in the sky burst and my heart seizes.

He brings my body closer between his legs, wrapping his arms around my waist tightly as he deepens the kiss, slowly pushing his tongue into my waiting mouth, twirling it with mine. He takes every last morsel of air as he kisses me like he needs to consume me. Tears stream down my face because it's too much. There's so much emotion and so many feelings in this one soul-binding kiss.

I don't ever want to stop. I want to stay here like this forever and give him everything he needs. We share each other's oxygen until there's nothing left. He pulls away first, breathing heavily as he cups my face. I lean into his touch. *I fucking missed him.*

"Tell me what happened, from the beginning." He breathes, but I shake my head. I don't want to ruin this bubble we are in. That shit can wait. I need answers from him first. It's fucking now or never.

"No Eas. We can talk about that shit at any time. I need answers from you." I say sternly as he narrows his eyes at me. Taking a step back he growls and pulls me closer.

"Tonight is not the night for games babe. I'm seconds away from snapping. I've been on edge all month because of you." He growls, and I raise a brow, tilting my head at him.

"Don't give me a fucking attitude. Not tonight. Tomorrow maybe, but tonight, we need to say everything that was left unsaid because I cannot leave here not knowing what the fuck this is." He spits. He's right, we need to lay this out on the table. Taking a deep breath, I run my hands through his curly black hair and look into his chocolate brown eyes. This could be it, he could reject me and then I'm stuck in a loveless relationship with a prick I'm starting to hate.

"Spit it out Hellcat, my patience is wearing thin." He chides.

"Are you with Bianca?" I ask and he laughs, shaking his head.

"No! Are you still with Carter?" He asks through gritted teeth, and this time I laugh while running my hand down his clenched jaw.

"That depends." I smile and he smirks.

"On what, Hellcat?" His hands run down my back and over my ass, giving it a squeeze.

"On your answer to my next question." I laugh, and he smacks my ass, making me yelp.

"I can't play these games anymore. I care about you too fucking much to continue without knowing I have you. So either you take what you want or we walk away from one another." I say with as much confidence as I can muster, bracing myself for the rejection.

"It's not that easy, Dylan. There's a lot more to it!" He says, shaking his head. I take a step back, and he lets me, which gives me all the answers I need.

"I'll call someone for a ride." I say, turning my back to him as I walk towards the road. My heart shatters yet again, leaving pieces to my soul with the same person who cracked it the first time. I can't help the tears that trickle down my cheeks. I shouldn't have said anything. *How can I be so stupid?* I'm so far gone in my head I don't notice when he spins me around, wraps his hands around my throat, and fuzes his lips to mine. He squeezes so tightly, like he's waging a war within himself. Relaxing into the kiss, he releases his grip on my throat and picks me up by the backs of my thighs causing me to wrap my legs around his waist and walks us back to the car.

"I can't let you walk away again. I won't fucking survive. You're on my mind day and night. I need to see your eyes daily. But most of all, I just need you. Every fucking day. Can that be enough?" He pleads, his eyes filled with hurt and hope as he holds my face with both of his hands. He holds my stare, but I shake my head. *I wish it was enough.*

"No. I don't want to be your dirty little secret. I want more, Eas, so much more." I whisper, looking into his sad eyes. I know that look. It's the look of defeat, I've just never seen it on *his* face. Tears pour down my face, dripping from his hands, but I don't care. This hurts to the core.

"B–but it's all I can offer right now. Please D, don't walk away from this." He stammers as tears continue to fall. I remove his hands from my face. *I don't want to let him go.*

"I have to, it hurts too much to stay like this. I'm sorry, but this is goodbye, Easton." I confess as I swallow the lump in my throat. The words feel like acid as they leave my mouth. Why can't this just be simple?

Lightning cracks through the sky as thunder starts to rumble in the distance. We stand there, unmoving, for a few minutes as rain drizzles down onto us. I wipe my tears and he takes a step back, spinning and looking up at the sky. I go to hop off the hood to start my long walk home but he spins back to me, his eyes wide and wild..

"Eas, don't. We tried. We are just not meant to be, not in this lifetime." I hiccup, my breath caught in my throat.

"Fuck that. You're fucking mine. You always have been, and you always will be. Fuck it. Fuck it all!" He snaps, wrapping me up in his arms.

"Wait, what are you saying?" I ask. His mouth is on mine before I can react, as he sucks my bottom lip into his mouth, pulling it with a pop. He cups my face, looking deep into my eyes. Lightning cracks again above us, and the rain gets heavier as it crashes down.

"What I'm saying, Hellcat, is that I fucking love you. You consume me just as much as I yearn daily to consume you, Dylan." He confesses, placing a tender kiss on my lips as the rain pelts over us. I'm unsure if it's the tears that soak my face, or the rain, but I don't care. Easton loves me?

"You-yy-you love me?" I ask hesitantly and he smiles so fucking bright.

"I do, Hellcat, more than you will ever fucking know. Now gimme those lips." He doesn't give me a second to reply before he's sucking my face into his and ripping my tank top right down the middle.

"Jesus, Eas." I pant as he shoves his face into my cleavage.

"I wish I had more time tonight to ravish you, properly." He growls as he licks the drops of rain up my neck, causing me to shiver.

"You're right, I do wish we had more time. Speaking of which. What time is it? Don't you have somewhere to be tonight?" I ask and he freezes for a split second, his head snapping up at me.

"How do you know about that?" he asks with curiosity written on his face as he kisses my jaw. *Jesus, he's so fucking distracting.*

"I overheard Benny on the phone with you the other night. You idiots talk so loud." I laugh and he nips my ear.

"Well, when I get back from the job, I want you in my bed, waiting for me. In nothing but that teal thong." He growls, grabbing my ass.

"I think that can be arranged, Daddy." I purr against his lips as he pulls me tighter against him.

"Don't start, Hellcat. I need to get you back to The Den before I'm late. But after, you're mine, baby." He says through gritted teeth as I caress his taut jawline. I nod, giving him a quick peck before sliding from his grasp and hopping off the car.

"Let's go babe." I wink. He smirks as he adjusts himself, walking over to the driver's side and getting in the car.

"Before we leave here, I need you to come back to me. I'm not stupid, I know the shit you guys are involved in. So please come back in one piece." I plead and he looks at me with that million dollar smile.

"Nothing would stop me from finding my way back to you." He leans over and presses a kiss to my forehead, starts the car, and takes off into the night.

I hope we know what we are doing.

CHAPTER 18

EASTON

Tonight has been the best night of my fucking life, but something is wiggling in the back of my brain that all of this is too good to be true. I smile as I sink my poignard into one of the guards' neck at the Wang Triads compound. We are all spread out around the property. Kingston is rerouting the cameras, Bentley is our Alpha- he calls the orders, Ace is in charge of weapons and ammo, while Antonio is our medic in case any of us go down and Me? I'm the sneak attack they don't see coming. A silent killer in the night. My kill shot is the neck, it's one part of the body that is the quietest and easiest to access. One swift stab in the neck, through the spinal cord, and that's it. Lights out. We work together, like a well-oiled machine; we may have separate jobs, but make no mistake, we are as lethal as they come.

Spade sent us here because the fall of a Queen has dire consequences, and with that, people are rushing to take over certain territories that were never meant for them. The Triads are slowly inching their way into our territory, wanting to be the new arms distro, which cannot happen. There's history there that we aren't privy to, which is really getting on my last nerve. I'm pretty sure we have proven ourselves to be valuable, time and time again, yet here we are. This place is like a fucking maze. Thank God for these night vision glasses, it makes our job so much easier.

There's a guard standing on the other side of this partition. I can tell he is waiting for me to round the corner, but I've got a surprise for his ass. I take my poignard and twirl it in my hand. I love the weight of it in my hold, the feeling of slicing through skin, tissue and muscle makes me feel alive and exhilarated. Lifting the dagger in my hand, I take two slow steps, keeping my breath even, as I stab right through the paper-thin wall, hitting my mark in the throat. Luckily for the partition, the spray back is seamless. Removing my dagger as the body drops, I continue to the next room.

I'm wearing an earpiece so we can communicate as we move around this place. We are only here for one person but have orders to take down whoever gets in our way. I was really hoping for some fighting action tonight because my favorite weapon to use is the sais. It makes me feel like Raph from the Ninja Turtles. The silence on the walkie-talkie crackles over the airwaves; somethings not right. Time to check-in.

"Everyone clear?" I whisper as I turn the corner and see two guards coming right for me. *Fuck yes.* Taking out my sais, I spin them in my hands as the guards charge me. Their walkie goes off, which causes one to be distracted as I spin and send a fast jab of the sai up on a slight angle through both their chins hitting the brain. Lights out, mother fuckers. I remove my weapons and wipe the blood on my pants, then place them back into their holder. Another guy rounds the corner and retrieves his gun. Right before the dickhead in front of me drops, I grab a hold of his body and use him as a shield as the idiot alerts everyone where I am.

Reaching into my back pocket, I grab a throwing star and send it sailing through the air, hitting the moron in the eyeball. He screams, as I chuck the dead body at him, causing him to stumble back. Taking his own gun, I grab him by his collar and twist his wrist, forcing the gun under his chin.

"Where is Kai?" I growl. He says nothing.

"You're dead either way, so spill it." I grit, pressing the gun harder underneath his chin. He replies in his native language that I do not understand.

"Anyone get what he said to me, because I don't fucking understand this language? Kingston?" I grit, hopefully someone is listening. I hear nothing. I usually hear some type of static letting me know we're all here, but it's fucking silent.

"Fatal, answer me before I start leaving the bombs everywhere." I growl. Still radio fucking silent. That can only mean one thing. He has my team. BET. Instead of blowing this guy's head off and giving away my location, I slide my dagger slowly through the bottom of his chin, reveling in the sound of his blood choking him. He falls to his knees slowly and for dramatic effect, I remove my dagger, spin, and kick him in the face, causing him to hit his head hard on the ground leaving a cracking sound in its wake.

Walking silently through this maze, I come across dead guards littering the halls, which is a good sign I'm getting closer to where I need to be. Placing a block next to each room and guard I pass, I press a button on each one, waiting until it lights red. I continue forward until I start hearing voices. I've spent weeks studying the plans for this place, and know where Kai's office is, banking that they are all in there. There's a secret passageway that I want to come out from when I enter that room.

Using my night vision glasses, I click it over for the thermal feature. Looking into the room to my right, there's four standing with three guards behind them, another guard in front of what I assume to be a desk, and Kai standing behind it. Now that I know where everyone is, I leave the room and count to five. Walking into the fifth room, I go to the back and push the shelf to the side and enter, sliding it back to close myself in.

Walking down the narrow hallway, I count again; this time to six. I take out a remote and flick the switch to one, two and three, setting off three bombs and causing the place to shake as I slide the secret door back open. I needed to make some noise so this fucker didn't get the drop on me. The guards leave the guys to see what was happening. As I enter the room slowly, I silently retrieve a small dagger and walk up behind Kai and pierce his neck. I hold the weapon to his artery, applying just enough pressure that any sudden movement will end his life.

I look over at my team and see a smile on Bentley's face. The others look a little roughed up, but no injuries as far as I can tell. Ace quirks a brow at me and smirks.

"Now that we are all here, we can get this little show on the road." Kai says.

"It's funny how you think you're still in control here. Those guards that just left, they're dead." I chuckle as my brothers put on their face masks.

"Did you know your father worked for the most ruthless players in the game? I'm impressed to see you're much smarter and more lethal than him. It's a pity you and your friends chose the wrong syndicate to work for! You could've been an asset to me, but you and your little friends, your time ends here. Be careful who you trust. Not everyone wears the same face as you." He spits, trying to distract me, but it won't work.

He could tell me my father is alive and it still wouldn't make an ounce of difference. My father was a piece of shit, I've heard the stories over the years, so that tactic does fuck all in my eyes. I flick the switches for four, five, and six. The walls and windows rumble again. Bentley shoots the guard standing in front of Kai, and I apply the perfect amount of force to slice his artery wide open.

"The Kings send their regards," I whisper, throwing his body to the ground. Placing my mask over my face, I rummage through his desk for a flash drive, finding four different ones and putting them in my pocket. We move quickly to get the fuck out of here as I continue to flip switches.

Standing outside, I flip another switch and pass it down the line where they do the same. The compound blows up like the Fourth of July, sending shards of wood, glass, and furniture into the night sky. We stand there watching the fire and smoke billow out and cloud above us for a moment before we hear the sirens. The wailing sounds getting closer, pulling us from the scene as we all pile in the van and high tail it out of here, heading for the warehouse. Looking around at the team, we all take our masks off, and Kingston has the biggest grin on his face.

"Check your accounts." He orders. As Bentley hands me his phone while he drives, I log into both of our accounts and holy fucking shit.

"A mil each?" Ace shouts. I'm stunned at all the zeros. I look over at Kingston who still has a grin on his face.

"I was able to hack into Kai's account, drain them into an offshore one and then split it six ways. I sent Spade his cut and we each got ours." He whoops and we all laugh as Antonio takes out a joint and sparks it.

"Celebratory J." He laughs, taking a hit and passing it around.

This night turned from shit to one of the best nights we've had in a long time. Now to get back to my woman so I can show her how much I fucking love her.

CHAPTER 19

DYLAN

It's been hours since all of Fatal left for their job and I'm beginning to get worried. Eas told me he loved me, but I never got the chance to say it back to him. During the drive back, he held my hand the entire way to my house so I could grab a new shirt. Once we got there, he pressed me against the front door and kissed me like he couldn't get enough of me. I made him wait outside though, if he would have come upstairs, we wouldn't have made it back to The Den.

Eas gave me the rundown of what was expected of us girls tonight. We had to keep the party going, act like it was any other night, and make sure our newest guests have a good time; which was simple enough. Lee is piss drunk and his sister is grinding on some guy from Uni. No one suspects a thing. Amy keeps looking at her phone and I can see it in her eyes, she's worried too. I grab her, bringing her to the dance floor and start moving against her. I'm hoping the guys start trickling in soon so we can ease our minds. I haven't told her about me and Eas. I'm not sure why I'm keeping secrets, but I don't think now is the right time.

Thankfully, we haven't seen Bianca at all tonight. Hopefully she's tied up somewhere. That bitch is a straight snake and I'm almost positive she's fucking Carter, I just can't fucking prove it. But it doesn't matter because I'm kicking him to the curb. I can finally be free. My phone vibrates in my bra. I take it out and take a deep breath.

> **Eas: Hellcat, we will be there in a few minutes. Have Amy go into Bentley's room and take your sexy ass into mine.**

> **Me: Are you sure that's a good idea? We could just go back to my house.**

> **Eas: No, Bentley is taking Amy there, so I told him you will stay in his room and I'll keep an eye on you.**

Me: Eww, I am not sleeping in his bed. You both can get fucked.

Eas: Hellcat....just shut the fuck up and do as you're told. Tell me when you are both in the rooms.

Me: You're making me nervous.

Eas: Don't be. I want you in nothing but a thong when I get there.

Me:

I nudge Amy and whisper in her ear what the plan is. We slowly move off the dance floor and grab a drink from the bar before walking down the dark hallway to the guys' bedrooms. Amy enters Bentley's first and I continue down the hall making a left, his bedroom is right next to the office that no one is allowed in. Opening his door, I'm immediately hit with his scent. Taking out my phone, I shoot him a text.

Me: We are in the rooms.

Eas: Good girl. If you hear any commotion, do not leave my room. We have to handle something first and you two don't need to witness it.

Me: Fine, but hurry up. I don't need anyone walking in here seeing me naked in your bed.

Eas: I'll fucking kill them.

Why does his threat make me so hot for him? I put my phone on the nightstand, slide my shoes off and remove my tank, bra, and leggings. Walking over to his closet, I see his racing jacket hanging. I remove it from the hanger and put it on. His fucking scent is everywhere. I take a deep breath as butterflies swim in my chest. I can't wait to be alone with him tonight. He better not pull some fucking shit because I swear to god, I will lose it. My phone pings and I walk over to the nightstand to pick it up.

Eas: Put my stereo on, baby. It's about to get real loud in here.

Me: Okay, move it along, I'm waiting.

I snap a picture and send it to him.

Eas: Jesus Hellcat. I'll be right there, give me ten.

Leaving him on read, I walk over to his stereo just as I hear glass shatter and people screaming. Turning it on, DMX blasts through the speakers, drowning out the chaos. I love that he listens to the same music as me. I sit down on his bed and wait for him to arrive, thinking about the entire night as a whole. I can't believe I told him what happened. I know we aren't done with the conversation seeing as I left questions unanswered, but I just didn't want to ruin the bubble we were in.

When we are alone in our own little world, I don't want to worry about anything in life. I just want to feel, and be in the present with him, completely consumed by one another. What started as an innocent cat and mouse game, turned into something entirely different.

The door suddenly bursts open, causing me to jump out of my skin, and there he is, dressed in all black with his weapons still strapped to his body. His chest is heaving as he stares at me with lust in his eyes. He slams the door, locks it and takes off his holsters, laying them on his dresser. He moves to the small couch in the corner, sitting with his legs wide, leaning back as he stretches his arms behind him. "You look gorgeous in my race gear, Hellcat. I need more pictures of you." He says, lust in his voice as he raises a brow.

"Is that right?" I sass as he moves to loosen his tactical belt. I sit up and straddle the bed so he can get a better look at me in his gear. *If he only knew I've beaten him in multiple races.*

"Don't move a fucking muscle," he orders as he takes his phone out, snapping a picture of me, then continues to take off his belt. Once he's finished, he sits up and removes his shirt with one hand as he unbuttons his jeans. My mouth waters at the sight of him. He sits back against the couch, looking at me with a smirk on his face.

"Crawl to me, baby. Nice and slow." He commands, and I slide off of the bed, slowly getting on my hands and knees as I crawl to him, never taking my eyes off his sexy body. I make my way between his legs and look up at him, his eyes meeting mine as he bends down some to capture my lips in a quick kiss. His finger trails down my jaw to my neck and over my breasts, shivering at his touch when his thumb runs over my hardened nipples.

He uses both hands to slowly push his jacket down my shoulders, letting it drop to the floor.

"You're so fucking beautiful, Dylan." He whispers, causing a blush to creep up my cheeks. He pulls me from the floor, closer to him. I move to breathe in his addictive scent but all I can smell is blood. I pull back, and grab his hand as I climb off the floor.

"You stink of blood, Eas. Time to get you cleaned up. Put your clothes in a bag to burn, then meet me in the shower." I say, letting go of his hand, walking through the bathroom door and turning on the shower. I step in and lean back against the wall, watching him watch me as I let the water cascade down my chest. His chest heaves as he watches me slide my hand into my thong, giving my clit a flick.

"Fuck this," he growls, walking into the shower still with his jeans and boots still on, not giving a fuck. Getting on his knees, he shoves his face between my legs, biting the soaked cotton and sucking it hard into his mouth.

"I've fantasized about your sweet pussy in my mouth for so long. Fuck, you taste so good, Hellcat," he groans, shredding the thong from my hips as I moan in pleasure. I run my hand through his dark curly hair as the caked up blood coats my fingers. He licks each thigh before sucking my swollen clit into his mouth. I buck at how sensitive I am. His hands squeeze my ass as his tongue swirls my clit, sucking it in and out of his mouth, giving it a little bite.

I moan as I pull his hair with one hand, pinching my nipple with the other. He slides a finger into my drenched pussy and I tighten around him, laying my head back against the tile wall as I throw a leg over his shoulder, shoving his face deeper into me. He growls, sucking harder, lapping up my arousal.

"Your mouth is amazing, Eas. Fuck my life." I pant, biting my bottom lip as he picks up the pace, causing my body to shiver even though I'm under the hot spray.

"Your taste drives me wild, baby." He growls as he continues to slowly bring me to the brink of orgasm.

"Fuck, Eas. I'm going to cum." I yell, and he pulls away.

"Not yet, Hellcat. I want you to drench my cock." He says, looking up at me as the water falls onto his beautiful face. He stands, lifting me by the backs of my thighs and presses me into the cold tile while he pulls his soaked jeans and boxers down.

"Are you sure about this? Because once my cock sinks into this tight fucking pussy, there is no going back." He breathes, looking deep into my eyes and I nod.

"Say it, Hellcat. I need to hear your words." He growls, rubbing his cock up and down my slit as his piercing hits my clit with enough pressure that I'm ready to gush all over him.

"Yes, Eas. Take it!" I growl. Before I take a breath, he thrusts up into me in one swift movement and we both groan.

"Fuck baby, your pussy grips my cock so fucking well," he moans, taking a nipple into his mouth, pressing me harder into the shower wall. He pulls all the way out and slams back in, causing me to tighten around him.

"This isn't enough, I need to worship you." He says, taking us out of the shower and placing me on the counter, still slowly thrusting in and out of me. My legs shake because I'm so fucking close, but I also don't want this to end. I take a deep breath as he rubs the towel over my shoulders, kissing along my jaw. He slowly pulls out only to slam back in.

"Jesus, Eas." I pant, holding onto the counter for dear life.

"I know, Hellcat. Look at how your pussy sucks my cock in, it's like it doesn't want me to leave." He growls, looking down at our bodies bound together. *It's such a beautiful fucking sight.* I love how he bites his lip with every thrust and how his forehead divots like he's in deep thought and then the way his abs tighten, Jesus Christ. Lord forgive me for I have sinned, this man before me is the Devil himself, waiting to possess my soul and I'm ready to be possessed by him.

He pulls out, placing his hands on my thighs and sliding them down my legs as he lowers himself in front of me, perfectly eye level with my drenched pussy. He moves his hands to untie his boots, never taking his eyes off of me. He leans in, groaning as he inhales my scent, dragging his tongue painfully slow up and down my slit as he continues to take his boots off. *Fuck, I need more.*

Once they're off, he kicks them to the side and places his hands back on my thighs. As he moves to stand, his tongue continues to drag up my center, over my hips and up to my breasts, sucking my nipple into his mouth. I moan as he stands between my shaky legs, pushing his jeans and boxers all the way off before he throws me over his shoulder, slapping my ass. I yelp at the sting it leaves behind but I don't care. I want him. All of him, now, before I seriously combust. He throws me onto the bed and takes a step back, grabbing his cock, slowly stroking it. I bite my lip as he squeezes the tip of his dick.

"You ready to let Daddy worship you?" He asks.

I'm more than ready. Let the games begin.

CHAPTER 20

EASTON

Climbing on the bed, I slide between her sexy fucking legs as she looks up at me with those ocean blues. *She's so fucking stunning. I'll never get bored looking at her.* I run my hands up her thick thighs, squeezing them. I trail my hands up her torso and cup her full breasts, toying with her hard nipples. She moans at my touch as her body riddles with goosebumps.

Bending down, I lift her hips, line my cock up and slam into her as I take a nipple into my mouth. She laces her hands through my curly hair, pulling at the strands that meet my neck. Her back arches as I pull out and slowly push back in, rolling my hips so my piercing hits that spot deep inside her. Her eyes roll as I continue to give her short, hard thrusts, over and over again. Her nails claw down my chest leaving welts and I revel in the pain. *I wish she would make me bleed.*

"Eas, you feel so good." She pants and I pull out again, kissing her lips, jaw and down to her neck, sucking the tender spot below her ear as I slide my hard cock between her wet lips, hitting her clit. She whimpers with every thrust as I kiss down her chest, biting each nipple, swirling the tender peak with my tongue. Her nails trail down my back and grab a handful of my ass as I continue to slowly thrust into her perfect pussy, pulling out only to rub my cock down her slit, my precum coating her swollen clit. I pull away and walk over to my stereo to turn up the volume. I want my girl to scream my name as I fuck her all over this goddamn room.

Walking back to the bed, I slap her clit with my cock and she jolts, sitting up and grabbing my face, sucking my lips into her mouth. I wrap her long wet hair around my fist and tug as I lick down her neck, leaving little bite marks, but she pushes me away and I raise a brow. She looks at me with a grin as she climbs off the bed and slides to her knees, wrapping her hot mouth around my cock, taking me to the back of her throat. My Hellcat swallows around my length and I moan, biting my lip. I wrap my hand around her hair again and push her further down my cock, causing her to gag.

"Holy shit Hellcat, just like that baby. Gag on Daddy's cock." I groan as she takes me all the way down, her nose touching my pelvis. She stays there for a moment breathing through her nose and swallowing again.

"Fuck, your throat is so fucking tight. Fuck, baby." I moan again as my legs start to shake. *This little bitch can suck my cock for the rest of my life.* She comes up for air, stroking my length and giving me a little hauk tua, sending me almost over the edge as she looks up at me, taking my entire length again, gagging as spit begins to drip down her chin.

"You look fucking breathtaking on your knees for me. This is where you belong, baby. Sucking my cock, taking all of it. Fuck, I love this mouth, Hellcat. Dont fucking stop. Gag harder," I order and she listens like the good girl she is. She gags so fucking hard, her throat tightening so much that I almost dump my load down her throat as she looks up at me with mascara running down her gorgeous face.

"Don't be afraid to run your teeth along my shaft baby. I like the pain. Fuck, baby, I wish I could take a picture of how sexy you look." I moan, flexing my abs as she continues to gag on my cock. *This girl is fucking perfection.* I grip her hair, pulling her off my cock with a pop and she smiles up at me. I use my free hand to smack her in the face with my dick, smearing her spit and my precum along her plump lips. Her tongue darts out but I grab her face and force her to look at me.

"Don't you dare lick them." I command, bending down to lick her lips, feeling as she groans into the kiss.

"You taste so fucking good Eas, I want your cum down my throat." She purrs.

"Mmm, don't worry, we have plenty of time for that." I growl and she rolls her eyes.

"Did you just roll your eyes at me?" I ask, my brow raised at her little sass.

"Sure fucking did." She quips. *Oh, this little bitch.*

"Get up, walk over to the dresser and bend the fuck over." I command, and she does one better, she drops to the ground and crawls past me, swaying her hips as her round ass jiggles and her pussy lips glisten in the dull light. I grab my cock and slowly stroke it, groaning as she stands, legs spread, bent over and stretching her arms out in front of her as she holds onto the dresser.

I walk up behind her and smack each cheek, watching as her porcelain skin reddens with each hit. She looks over her shoulder, smirking at me. I grab a fist full of her long black hair and pull it all the way back,sucking her lips into my mouth. She moans as I take my cock and line it up with her entrance.

"Hold on tight baby." I growl before slamming into her. I pull out and slam into her again, pulling her hair harder as she moans loudly. I roll my hips, pushing in deeper as she meets my thrust, shaking her ass on my cock. *The sensation is fucking wild.* I let go of her hair and grab her hips tightly, leaning over her, kissing down her spine, leaving bite marks anywhere I can.

"Fuck, Hellcat. You're so fucking tight. This pussy is fucking mine." I growl, pounding harder and harder as her tits bounce.

"Eas, I'm going to cum so fucking hard." She whimpers and I reach around rubbing tight circles on her clit.

"Cum on my cock, baby. Tighten that fucking pussy, let me feel it." I groan.

"Fuck, Daddy, just like that. Don't fucking stop!" She screams, rolling her hips, grinding on my fucking cock as I flick her clit.

"You're on the pill right?" I ask, no intention of stopping, and she laughs.

"Yes, Crow. Fucking fill me." She commands as her pussy starts to flutter around my length while I slam into her harder and harder.

"I'm cumming! Fuck, I'm cumming so fucking hard. Don't you fucking stop!" She screams as her pussy gets so fucking tight. I pinch her clit, causing her pussy to ripple and explode around me. I slap her clit rapidly and she gushes all over my cock.

Fuck yes. My girl's a squirter. I slow down because I'm nowhere near done with her sexy ass. I pull out as she heaves for breath, but I don't care. I spin her around and fuse my mouth to hers, cupping her face with both my hands as her chest continues to rise and fall. I pull away, looking into her ocean blues.

"I hope you're ready for more." I pant and she smiles wide.

"Go sit on the couch," she commands and I back up not taking my eyes off her until my calves hit the couch. I sit and wait for her. She reaches into my holster and grabs one of my daggers. I tilt my head in curiosity as I raise a brow at her as she stalks over to me and straddles my lap, grabbing my cock and lining it up with her entrance, slamming down onto me. My head falls back against the headrest as my Hellcat rides my cock. I grab the dagger from her hands and hold it to her neck.

"Ride me like it's the last breath you're going to take" I growl and she grinds on me, clawing down my chest, causing blood to seep from the cuts. I press the dagger harder into her neck and she moans, rolling her hips, bouncing on my cock.

"Fuck, baby. You feel so good, Hellcat." I groan, lightly dragging the dagger down her neck, to her chest, circling around her nipple, flicking the tip on her sensitive peak. I thrust up into her and she throws her head back, moaning my name, as I continue to glide my dagger down her stomach and twirl it across her hip bone, slicing into her so delicately. Her body convulses at the pain, causing her hips to roll.

She leans down to kiss me, biting my bottom lip and flicking her tongue against mine. I push her hair to the side, pulling away from the kiss and biting her shoulder as she slows her movements, panting my name. I place the dagger aside, grab her hips with both of my hands tightly and bounce her on my cock as I thrust up into her, hitting that spot deep inside her, causing her to grind harder against me.

Fuck. I start to feel that familiar tingle up my spine but I'm not ready to cum yet. I grab a hold of her ass and lift us off the couch. She wraps her legs and arms around me as she continues to slowly bounce on my length. I bend down slightly to grab the dagger and slice down her shoulder blades as I walk us over to the wall next to the door, slamming her into it.

"Fuck Eas, I'm going to cum again." She whimpers. I pull all the way out and slam into her over and over again. Dropping the dagger to the ground, I shove my face into her tits, leaving bite marks all over them. She tightens around my cock, meeting me thrust for thrust.

"Just like that Hellcat. I'm going to fill this fucking pussy." I growl as she flutters around me, her whole body shivering at the intensity of her impending orgasm. I reach down between us and pull her clit flicking it and she screams, soaking my cock as my name leaves her lips. I slam deep into her a few more times before I cum so fucking hard inside her. I don't slow down until every last drop spills from my cock. She smacks her head against the wall, laughing and I take a deep breath before I look up at her.

"I love you, Hellcat, there's no coming back from this. Even if it means my life." I whisper as tears glisten in her eyes.

"I love you more, Eas. Ride or die, baby." She whispers back, kissing me slowly, swirling her tongue with mine as I remove us from the wall without pulling out of her. I walk us over to the bed and lay us down. We continue to kiss until we're a panting mess again, ready for round two. I pull away taking a deep breath and move her hair from her face, cupping her cheek as I rub my nose against hers causing a smile to bloom across her perfect face.

"You want to kill them with me?" I ask and she laughs, knowing exactly what I'm asking.

"I thought you would never ask." She whispers, cupping my face.

"I'm not as skilled as you, but this can't go unpunished and if I'm going to become a killer, I wouldn't want to do it with anyone else." She says and it's like music to my ears.

This girl really was made for me and I can't wait to spend the rest of my fucking life with her. I'm a shithead for not coming clean, but hopefully, I can make up for it. Then I'll have to deal with Fatal. *Fuck. One day at a time.* She grabs my face kissing me deeply as she straddles my lap sinking my cock back into her wet pussy.

This is home.

CHAPTER 21
DETECTIVE ELEANA ST. JAMES

It's been over a month since the frat house killings and we still aren't any closer to finding out who this new serial killer is. What's even worse? The Carver is back and bloodier than ever. He's not even being clean about it. It's almost like he wants to finally be caught. Me and April stand in the pool house at the university looking at the corpse of a teenager who we can not identify. We will need to send his teeth in to get a match. There was no wallet or anything at the scene. It's gruesome. His face looks like someone repeatedly kicked it in leaving nothing but shattered bones, his skin was removed and thrown in the pool. Whoever did this, cut every limb off and threw it in the pool leaving nothing but a naked torso sliced to shit. The only way we know he's a male is because his genitals are hanging out of his broken jaw.

I'm at a point where I can't profile the killer. This kill doesn't scream 'The Carver' to me. His kills are more poetic, where his copycat loves to leave riddles. This one is just so much worse. We have nothing to lead on. The cameras were wiped and the IT guys tried to follow the IP address but it kept bouncing back here. It won't go any further than this university.

Taking a deep breath, I walk out of the exit doors to get some fresh air. This paperwork is going to be atrocious. Between the serial killers and the Triad compound being blown up, I don't even know where to begin. There's a fucking war brewing, and as much as I need to stay far away from it, I'm also neck deep in it. Staying hidden is starting to get harder and harder with each passing day.

When you have been running from The Cartel most of your life, and now your own flesh and blood-the one who saved you from it all-is the leader and in over his head, it will cause you to not sleep at night. I don't need the FBI zeroing in on my brother, or his business, so I try to cover up as much as I can. I'm exhausted.

We have been working for over a hundred hours straight and it doesn't look like we will be getting to go home anytime soon. Suddenly the door swings open and April comes out, stalking over to me.

"We might have a lead, but you're not going to like it." She says and I sigh.

"What is it?" I ask, suddenly feeling like I'm not going to like what she has.

"Last students seen leaving the poolhouse were Easton and Dylan, apparently looking to be in a rush." She says.

"Does anyone else know about this?" I ask.

"No, just the blonde girl named Bianca who came over to give me a tip when I went out the front looking for you."

"Okay, we need to keep this airtight until we speak to our kids." I say, giving her a stern look.

"I know, Ele." She says.

"It's time to call a meeting at home. Are we doing this together or separately?" I ask and she looks at me and laughs.

"I'll call Easton, but I can't make any promises that he will show. Why don't you talk to Dylan by yourself. Maybe it's a misunderstanding." she says with a shrug and I nod.

Only one can hope.

CHAPTER 22

DYLAN

After Easton fucked me six ways to Sunday, we laid in each other's arms until the sun came up. He fell asleep as he rubbed circles on my hip, the sound of deep snores letting me know he was knocked out. I, on the other hand, was too in awe of what transpired earlier, so that there would be no sleep in sight for me.

I promised him I would end things with Carter when we go back to school. I'm not the type of girl to break up with someone through text message. *That's for pussies.* I feel like a weight has been lifted off my shoulders, knowing I'm not stuck in a loveless relationship and I can finally be fucking happy.

Well, we have to tell my brother, which is another mess in itself. Honestly, I could care less what Bentley thinks, but Eas does. He told me that the pact they made was after Ava was date-raped at a party last year and that they didn't want to involve women in their lives. It's too dangerous with the life they lead and the enemies they create. That incident is what created the rift between Ace and Ava. My girl was so hurt and scared. It was a fucking mess, but I understand why the guys wanted to pull away. The oath they took was to protect me and none of them were allowed to fuck me. I was off limits, especially if feelings were involved, but it looks like Bentley broke the pact, and then when he realized he couldn't have Amy, he pushed her away, but we all know he loves her, even if he won't admit it to himself.

So our argument is; 'Fuck you, we're together.' Fuck the oath and their fucking pact. It means shit. I can put my life on it that Eas will always keep me safe and honestly, I signed up for this. I know what it means to be with a man like him, especially one who works for my uncle. *I kept that part to myself. There's no need to divulge all of the truths in one night.* There are too many secrets and I don't want to argue.

Pounding on the door causes me to jump out of my skin and scream. Easton's eyes fly open and his hand wraps around my throat, squeezing so fucking hard. His eyes are wild and clouded making it obvious he's not really seeing what the fuck is happening, or what he is doing, so I slap the fucking shit out of him, his head shaking as he blinks rapidly and lets go of my throat. I scamper away to the bathroom, slamming the door and locking it as he roars in anger.

That shit has got to stop. I'm not going to sleep next to him if that's how he's going to wake up. A crash causes me to jump as I hear yelling and stuff being thrown around the room. I shake as I stand in front of the mirror, looking at all the bite marks littering my skin. *Jesus, he marked the shit out of me.* The knob rattles and a hand slams on the door. "I'm sorry, babe. Open the door and let me explain." He pleads.

"Not until you calm the fuck down, Eas." I yell.

"I am calm, but the more you stand in there, with this fucking piece of wood between us, the more I want to kick it the fuck down. So please open the door or I'll fucking do it." He heaves as I walk over and flip the switch to unlock the door. It flies open and I jump back.

He comes barreling in and I take a few steps back, my ass hitting the counter. He doesn't stop until he cages me in, lifting me on top of the cold porcelain. He cups my face, placing a tender kiss to my lips. "I'm sorry for scaring you, and most of all, hurting you. Are you okay?" he asks, looking for marks around my neck. I grab onto his wrist, leaning into his touch.

"I'm fine." I whisper, but he shakes his head.

"You're not fine. I scared you and I don't fucking like it." He growls.

"First tell me who the fuck was pounding at the door, then explain why in the hell you grabbed me like that." I quip. He takes a deep breath and rubs his hand over his face.

"Either we suck at our job or we have a rat in the ranks, because at some point, Bianca got out of here and no one saw her. Kingston went over the security footage and there was a glitch, then boom, she's out of the gates and hopping into a blacked out G-wagon," He grits.

"That fucking bitch. You should have let me fucking finish the job when I was bashing her fucking head into the floor." I growl. *I fucking hate that girl.* I've only been around her a handful of times, but I know a snake when I see one and she's the worst of them all.

"Ya know, it's fucking hot hearing you say that shit." He groans, kissing my neck.

"Down, boy. You have more explaining to do. Now carry me back to bed and tell me a story." I command as he lifts me off the counter and does just that.

"Good boy." I laugh, patting his head. He tosses me down on the sheets and crawls next to me bringing the comforter with him. He wraps his body around me, pulling my ass against his hard cock. *Always such a horn dog.*

"Did I ever tell you the story of when I was thirteen years old and a man kidnapped me?" he asks as I try to turn around to look at him but he doesn't let me.

"No. Just listen," he says, kissing my shoulder. "I don't remember where my mom was when I was woken abruptly out of my sleep. It was so dark and I couldn't see anything; my first reaction was to scream and fight, but the man stuck a needle in my neck and the next thing I know, I'm waking up in a basement with meathooks attached to the ceiling. The white tiles were stained from old blood and there were metal tables lined in the middle of the room with carts full of knives and saws. I was fucking terrified. I couldn't remember how I got there or if it was even real. He told me this is what my father would have wanted; for me to become a man trained through different situations. This shit went on for years. I was afraid to sleep. I tried to tell my mom, but she didn't believe me. She said my father was dead, and so was the man he was associated with, but I'll never forget his face, the face of a monster. I made my first kill that year." He takes a breath before continuing.

"A woman, to be exact. Which is also the same woman who I was forced to lose my virginity to, after I killed her. He was a sick fuck. He said my father was excellent at pleasing him. One day, he wanted me to do sexual things to him and I refused. He called me a pussy and beat me, electrocuted me and drowned me in a tub of ice water. I thought he was going to kill me. I've never been so scared in my life." He whispers as I wipe the tears from my eyes. I don't want him to think I pity him, but that's a lot for a child to hold onto. And to have your mom not believe you? He must have felt so alone and that breaks my fucking heart.

He takes another deep breath and continues, "This shit lasted until I was damn near eighteen. He made me into the ruthless killer I am today and it fucking sucks that after all this time, I still wake up like this. I'm glad I don't have nightmares about it, but when startled awake, I go right for the neck. I can't help it. That's one of the many reasons why I don't allow women to stay overnight. I'm too afraid I'll accidentally kill them." He says, holding me tighter.

"We will have to figure out a way to make it work because I like being in your bed with you." I whisper.

"Yeah? Feeling is mutual Hellcat." He laughs, kissing my shoulder.

"So who was this guy and what happened to him? He obviously stopped taking you. Finish the story." I say.

"I'm really not sure what happened to him. It stopped so abruptly that I actually went looking for him, but he was a ghost; there was no trace of him, like I made it all up." He says.

"Why would you go looking for him?" I ask.

"Because I wanted to kill him. I wanted to do to him what he'd done to me." He growls and I lean into his chest, hoping to calm his racing heart, but he continues. "Last night you said you know what me and the guys do. Do you know who we work for?" He asks.

"I do. The Rodriguez Cartel." I answer.

"That's correct. What do you know about them?" he presses, kissing down my neck.

"I know that they are the most powerful, ruthless players on the East coast." I lie. Thankfully, he can't see my face, otherwise he would read that lie so quickly.

"Correct again Hellcat. My boss saved me one night from one of the mans 'trainings' and I'll forever be grateful. The man, along with their fathers, had done the same thing to him and his brothers when they were thirteen. It's a really fucking messed up story." He yawns. My heart warms hearing that my uncle saved him.

"Alright, enough story-time. Let's get some sleep and then you can take me to breakfast and we can plot out our kill." I yawn because that shit is fucking contagious. He squeezes me tighter and envelopes me into his body.

"If we don't go to sleep soon, I'm going to take you right here. Hearing you want to plot out a kill over breakfast makes my dick unbelievably hard for you baby." He growls, pressing his cock against my ass.

"And I wouldn't stop you," I laugh.

"I love you, Hellcat." He breathes against the back of my neck, yawning again.

"I love you too, Crow. Now shut your eyes or you're not getting pussy for a week." I laugh.

"Yes, ma'am." He grunts. I close my eyes and drift off to sleep thinking about a little boy who was all alone with a monster.

CHAPTER 23

DYLAN

A few days later, I'm sitting in my room, trying to finish writing the paper that is due. If I don't get it turned in, I'm going to fail the semester. The atmosphere at Uni has been sullen. We killed Garrett the other night and it was the most riveting thing I have ever done. It was totally fucking gross, but it made me feel better inside. He wouldn't give us the name of the person who orchestrated my rape, but he sang like a fucking canary giving us Bryce's name. Right after that, Eas cut his tongue out and taught me how to stab someone in the back of the neck with a dagger, without having so much spray back.

He said the artery on the side of the neck and the throat make the biggest mess. He also showed me how to use a bone saw which is much sharper than your standard wood saw. Next week he wants me to learn self-defense, so that if I'm ever put in a situation like that again, I will be more alert and ready. *I'm excited as fuck to do that.* Plus, it will keep my body in shape and my stamina up, because Jesus fucking Christ, the way this man fucks and the amount of stamina he has, is outrageous. I can hardly keep up or I'm a pillow princess that loves to be worshiped. It can go both ways.

I'm almost done with this fucking paper as I wait for Eas to get here. His mom wanted to talk to him about something and then we're going to dinner to plan out our next kill. My phone pings and I see it's a text from my mother.

Mom: Are you home?

Not a *'Hey, how are you?'*, just straight to the bullshit.

Me: Yep, writing a paper for class in my room.

I hear footsteps climbing the stairs and then my door opens. She peeks her head in and I look up, giving her a fake smile as I place my laptop aside. She walks in, still dressed in work attire which consists of black pleated pants, a dress shirt and a blazer over it with her badge hanging from the belt and gun still in its holster. She comes in and moves to sit on my bed. *Now she's making me nervous.*

"Where were you the other night?" she questions. *Here we go.*

"Can you be more specific?" I ask as her eyes narrow. Uncle Spade told me to cut her some slack, but I fucking can't. She never treats us like her children. It's always detective mode. My phone pings and I pick it up, seeing it's Easton.

> **Eas: Mom just questioned me. We were at the school together. You locked your keys in the car and waited in the pool house for me to come get you, as instructed. Got it?**

> **Me: Yea, mom just came into my room questioning me too. I'll let you know what happens. I might need a ride out of here, so be ready to save the day, baby.**

Eas: Just say the word and I'm there.

"Can you put your phone down while I'm speaking to you? When did you become so disrespectful?" She probes and I roll my eyes.

"Carry on Detective." I quip.

"I'm really getting sick and tired of your attitude. Now, where were you the night before last?" She asks.

"What time?" I say, getting up and placing the laptop in my bag, along with a change of clothes because I know this isn't going to end well.

"Nightfall." She says.

"At school, researching a serial killer for the paper I have to write, that you interrupted me finishing." I answer, continuing to gather my shit for the night and sending Eas a text to be here in five.

"What time did you leave?" She presses.

"I don't know...ten. I left and noticed I locked my keys in the car, called Easton, and he told me to wait in the pool house until he got there." I shrug.

"Then what?" She asks, and I roll my eyes.

"Then nothing. He came, saved the day and we left." I yell, throwing my hands up in the air.

"Watch your tone, young lady. You and Easton were spotted at a crime scene by a blonde eyewitness." She quips and I laugh, placing my hand on my hips.

"Oh, let me guess. Bianca was her name?" I assume.

"How do you know that?" She questions some more.

"Because the bitch has it out for Easton and me." I answer, grabbing my stuff, ready to head out the door.

"Where do you think you're going?" She probes.

"Out, mom. Anything else you want to know?" I snap.

"With who?" She asks.

"Why do you care all of a sudden? You never cared before and now I'm getting the Riot Act because some dumb bitch ran her mouth." I snap again.

"Don't speak to me like that. I'm your mother. You show me some goddamn respect." She yells and I can't help but laugh in her face as I walk out of my bedroom door. She continues to yell as I walk down the stairs.

"Dylan, I am not done talking to you." She follows after me.

"Well I'm done talking to you. No matter what I say, you don't believe me. So why even bother wasting my breath?" I yell back.

"So is it true? You were raped, or were you just passed around like a gang bang whore?" She spits and I spin on her, getting in her face.

"You would think that, wouldn't you? It's real rich coming from a fucking liar like yourself. No wonder Benny never wants to be around you. Why don't you go lie to your little girlfriend next door? Does she even know who you truly are?" I spit and she gasps, putting her hand over her mouth as I look her up and down. "Bet she doesn't know the real cunt beneath the uniform." She slaps me across the face causing my lip to bleed. She's lucky I don't spit it in her face.

"Get the fuck out of my house, you ungrateful little slut, and don't come back!" She orders. I leave with a smirk on my face as I slam the front door, walk down the steps to the white picket fence, swing it open, and climb into Easton's car. *Fuck her. I fucking hate her lying ass.* I look over at Eas and he gives me a smile as he leans over to wipe the blood off my mouth.

"You good baby?" he asks with a raised brow.

"Just get me out of here. I'm not welcome here anymore." I growl as I look up at my childhood house. She's always going to be a miserable human being that's all alone. I don't think I'll ever fucking understand her.

"Alright baby, 'House De La Crow', coming right up," he says in a terrible French accent which makes me laugh.

"There's that smile. The plan of the night: food, school work, plotting and fucking, in no particular order," he chuckles, lighting a cigarette which I steal because her calling me a whore and slut grates on my last nerve, but he rips it from my mouth before I can take a hit.

"I need to take the edge off, Eas. She said some fucked up shit to me in there." I growl and he shakes his head.

"Well, you're sure as shit not fucking smoking cigarettes. You can drink once we get to The Den, or I'll even ask Antonio for a J. Those are your options," he quips, and I huff.

"I'll give you road head." I smirk and he looks over at me with a smile.

"As much as I would love to have those luscious lips wrapped around my cock, I'm going to have to decline," he laughs.

"You're no fun. Dickhead." I pout, and he laughs harder.

"I don't want to kiss an ashtray, so shut the fuck up and chill out," he orders.

"But I'm stuck kissing an ashtray. Make it math, asshole." I shoot back.

"You love how I taste. You fucking moan every fucking time I swirl my tongue with yours." He smirks and I huff again because he's right. I fucking love every inch of him.

Sitting back, I seethe as I watch the sun disappear into the clouds, closing my eyes for a moment. I fucking hate fighting with my mom but what she said really cuts deep. I didn't ask to be fucking raped, but I also should have told her, but fuck her. It still wouldn't have made a difference. It would have been the same old song and dance. Question after question, instead of her holding me, telling me everything would be okay. Nope, not my mom. There's not a caring bone in her fucking body. Easton clears his throat, taking me out of my thoughts as the wind whips my hair from him throwing his finished cigarette out the window.

"I hear the wheels turning in that beautiful head of yours. Talk to me, baby." He says.

"She knows I was raped and accused me of wanting it. She even called me a 'gang bang whore'." I confess, noticing as he tightens his grip around the steering wheel.

"Fuck, how did she find out?" He asks, and I shake my head.

"I'm not sure, but what I do know, is that fucking bitch Bianca is gunning for us. So the first chance I get, I'm taking her ass off the board." I promise, and the rest of the car ride is silent.

One way or another, they will all fucking pay.

CHAPTER 24

EASTON

Arriving at The Den, I pull in and shut off the car. Turning to her, I see a red hand print across her face as tears stream down her swollen cheek. I don't care if that bitch is her mother, she needs to keep her fucking hands to herself or I'll cut them the fuck off. She turns to me and I cup her face, wiping the tears away. Her ocean blues shimmer in the fading sunlight. *This fucking girl is so goddamn gorgeous and I'm one lucky son of a bitch to have her as mine.* I place a gentle kiss on her cheek and lips.

"You're not any of the things she called you. If anything, you're my little slut that I love to gag with my cock. And if she ever hits you again, it will be the last thing she does." I warn, and she grabs my shirt pulling me closer to her as she kisses me slowly, flicking her tongue against my bottom lip. I moan, but pull away.

"If we continue this here, we will never make it inside. I would much rather lay you out on my bed than fuck you in my back seat." I smirk and she smiles. *I love that smile.*

Climbing out, I round the car as she gathers her things. I open the door and offer her my hand, which she takes. I pull her up and take the bag of stuff from her and walk through the front door. The guys are littered around and have already started drinking. Bentley is out of his seat first, coming right for me.

"What the fuck did you do to her?" he accuses, grabbing her chin and turning her face to get a better look at the mark on her cheek.

"First of all, back the fuck up, brother," she seethes as she pulls her face out of his hold. "Second, why don't you call mommy dearest and find out. She's the one who hit me, not Easton. So sit down and shut the fuck up." She spits. *Goddamn, my girl is a little firecracker today.*

"Wait, what?" He says, rubbing his hand over his face and this time I chime in.

"The fact that you really thought I would ever hurt her is fucking wild to me." I growl as his steel-gray eyes meet mine.

"Listen man, I'm sorry. I jumped to conclusions, I know you wouldn't hurt her." He confirms and I shake my head.

"Also, while we are here, the pact and the oath are fucking bullshit. The rest of us have to suffer while you play house with Amy? Fuck that. And don't fucking say she doesn't mean shit to you, because I'll make a call and have a dude come scoop her little ass up real quick and see how you fucking feel about it." I spit and he grabs my collar.

"Do it and see what the fuck happens." He growls as my little Hellcat tries to push him off me. My eyes connect with hers and she shakes her head at me, letting me know this isn't the time.

"Get off me." I spit, pushing him off.

"What is this about anyway? Since when do you care about the pact and the oath?" He presses, but I shake my head, walking away.

"Doesn't matter." I growl, continuing to walk away leaving Dylan to deal with her brother. I need a moment to get my head right. I dig into my pocket as I walk down the hallway to my room.

Taking out a cigarette, I light it and inhale the minty smoke. Getting to my room, I unlock my door and swing it open, then slam it shut, walk over to my stereo, turn it on and the volume up. I sit down on my couch, leaning back as I smoke. That mother fucker has some nerve thinking I would ever hit his sister let alone a female. I may be violent and aggressive, but I've never been that way with a girl before.

Finishing my cigarette, I put it out and strip from my clothes, throwing them in the hamper. I walk into the bathroom and step into the shower, turning the knob on the hottest it will go, I stand under the spray trying to calm down. We have a race tonight and I want to take Dylan for a ride. Thinking about her calms me. I hate that we can't be together in the open, yet. I was ready to lay it all out on the table, but she knows his temper and it wasn't the time. *I just want to be able to kiss her whenever the fuck I want.* Warm arms wrap around my waist and I take a deep breath.

"Did you lock the door?" I ask as she runs her claws up my chest.

"Yes, he stormed out feeling like an asshole for accusing you of hitting me. Ace followed him out but Kingston and Antonio are sitting around drinking." She whispers, kissing my back.

"It really fucking bothers me that he assumed so quickly. I'm a killer, not a fucking woman beater. He knows better." I spit and she sighs.

"I know Eas. Just let it go. He just needs to cool off and everything will be fine." She reassures me, running her hands down my stomach, gripping my cock with both hands. I hiss and lean my forehead against the tile wall as she strokes my length, rubbing her thumb over my piercing.

"Fuck, Hellcat." I growl, and her grip tightens as she strokes me faster.

"Turn around, Eas." She whispers and I spin, looking at her naked body. She drops to her knees, wrapping her warm mouth around my cock, sucking the tip slowly as she runs her nails down my shaft causing me to hiss again. *Fuck, this girl.* She takes all of me down her tight throat, swallowing me as her nails pinch my balls.

"Gag baby. Let me see those eyes water." I command and she does just that.

"Such a good fucking girl." I praise as she continues to gag harder, saliva dripping down her chin. I groan as she looks up at me with mascara running down her face. I pull her off with a pop as strings of saliva leave her mouth.

"You're so perfect," I praise. "How did I get so lucky?" I ask as she stands.

"You're not so bad yourself, Crow." She giggles and I shake my head.

"What is with you and that fucking nickname?" I laugh, curious for the answer.

"I've known you all my life and you have always been a clever little fuck, but also a problem solver. Anyone can throw anything at you, and you always come out on top, just like a crow." She says and I smirk.

"So you have been watching me all this time?" I press, scooping her up into my arms, walking out of the shower and placing her on top of the sink. Her cheeks blush as I call her out.

"Don't be shy baby, I'll let you know a little secret. You remember that boy who ghosted you?" I ask, raising a brow.

"Yeah, Mark Finkle. What about him?" she asks with a curious tone.

"He didn't ghost you. I fucking killed him for touching what's been mine all along. Wanna know how I did it?" Her eyes widen at my confession.

"You did what?" She yells and I laugh, bringing her lips to mine.

"I stabbed the prick seventeen times because that's how many times he laid a hand on you. I don't think you understand how hard it is not to kill Carter for touching you. But his time is fucking coming, best believe that," I promise. She cups my face bringing her lips to mine, kissing me slowly. She pulls away before I can deepen the kiss causing me to growl.

"You really do love me, huh?" She smirks, and I lift her ass up as she wraps her arms and legs around me like a monkey.

"Fuck yeah I do, Hellcat. You are all I need, baby." I confess, wanting to show her how much I need her, but there's a knock on my door.

"Eas, open up. We need to talk." Bentley yells from the other side of the door.

"Oh, shit." She curses. Wiggling out of my arms, she grabs her clothes and hides in my closet. I laugh because Jesus fucking Christ, I don't know how much longer I can keep this shit hidden.

I slide boxers and black ripped jeans on before sinking my feet into my combat boots. Walking over to the door, I pull it open and step aside for Bentley to come in.

"Before you say anything, I need to ask you something." He blurts and I nod.

"Did you know Dylan was raped?" He asks, anger written on his face. *Fuck*. This isn't my story to tell. *What the fuck do I say? Yeah man, I was there. I'm the first one that got inside of her. Fuck.*

"Yeah, she told me not too long ago," I say ashamedly, and he punches me in my face. My head whips on impact and I growl as he grabs onto my shirt. *I deserve that.*

"Why didn't you fucking tell me? That's my fucking sister, you prick." He roars as spittle leaves his mouth.

"Because I'm handling it and it's not my fucking story to tell. If she didn't tell you, it's for a reason, asshole. Now get the fuck off me," I yell, pushing him, but he doesn't budge.

"Handling it? I want fucking names, Easton. Now!" He commands, taking a step back.

"I said I'm fucking handling it. I've already killed one." I say through gritted teeth, spitting blood onto his shoes, he swings at me again, but I lean back and send a quick jab to his nose. His head snaps back as blood leaks down his face.

"I'm going to kill you!" He roars, charging at me as we collide with my dresser, sending my stereo crashing to the ground. Suddenly, my closet door bursts open and Dylan screams.

"Fucking stop. Stop fucking fighting you idiots." She hops on Bentley's back, trying to pull him off me but he tosses her to the ground. *I fucking see red.* I push him off me and grab my dagger, gripping him by the throat. Dylan screams my name again, making me lose focus and he headbutts me, blurring my vision for a second. I take a step back and shake my head, trying to get my vision back, but he punches me in the gut.

"Fucking stop. Please stop! It's not his fault." She screams as I get my bearings and he rounds on her.

"What the fuck were you doing in his closet?" He screams, picking up my lamp and tossing it over her head.

"Bentley, if you don't back the fuck up off her, I will fucking kill you," I threaten.

"Huh? Answer me, Dylan!" He screams in her face and she cowers. *Fuck this.* I grab my sais, not thinking of anything but her, but when my eyes connect with hers, they widen in fear.

"Easton, NO!" She screams at the top of her lungs as my door bursts open and Kingston and Ace take in the scene. Kingston grabs Bentley first.

"Get him the fuck away from her before I kill him." I order, looking straight at Kingston as Ace comes into view.

"Don't fucking touch me. Get the fuck out of my room." I growl.

"You're both fucking liars. This isn't fucking over! Do you hear me? Far from over." Bentley says through gritted teeth as Kingston drags him out. Once he's gone, I place the sais down and Ace steps in front of me.

"Dylan, get out," Ace commands and I growl.

"Who the fuck are you to make her leave? I'm not going to hurt her. Get the fuck out of my face." His eyes never leave mine.

"Dylan, I said leave." He commands again and I get right in his face.

"Enough, I'm not fucking leaving without him. So you can all go fuck yourselves." She snaps, walking over to my bed picking up my keys, raising a brow at me.

"You coming?" She asks, and I nod, grabbing her hand and a white tee from my dresser, leading her out of the room, down the hall, into the main room and out the front doors. No one says a fucking word as we leave. *Fuck this and fuck them.* I'm done with the bullshit.

CHAPTER 25

DYLAN

Jesus fucking Christ, this is a mother fucking shit show. I walk over to Easton's car as he wipes blood from his face. He looks up at me with sadness in his eyes.

"Take my car and meet me at my house. I'm going to grab my bike. I want to take you somewhere later." He winks, and I nod, climbing into the driver's seat and starting it up.

"Do you want me to wait?" I yell from the window, but he shakes his head 'no' as he walks around to the garage where all their bikes are kept. I put his car in reverse, back up and throw it in drive, spinning the tires as I leave the gates like a bat out of hell.

Getting on the highway, I turn the music up and roll the windows down, letting the air whip against my skin. I just keep shaking my head. *My mother and her big fat mouth.* I can't blame Easton though. He was backed into a corner and I would have done the same thing if it was me. I wasn't going to remain in that closet while they beat the shit out of each other. I know guys will be guys, but I saw the look in both of their eyes, they were going to kill one another, and my heart can't take losing them both.

I hear the rumble of Easton's bike as he pulls up beside me, flashing his phone at me. I grab my phone from my back pocket and look at his message.

Eas: Follow me. I don't want to go home.

I look over and nod at him as he gets in front of me. I follow him as I jam out to Halsey. It doesn't take long to get to his destination. He makes a left turn slowly driving down a long dirt road. He comes to a stop and I park next to him.

Holy shit. The view on top of this mountain overlooks a huge river with nothing but more mountains in the distance. The sun has fully set, with purple and blue hues, and a hint of pink as the stars shine brightly. I shut off the car and get out as he removes his helmet, climbing off the bike.

He looks so fucking sexy in a white tee that hugs his muscles, black ripped jeans and combat boots with his curly hair a fucking disaster. *My pussy purrs for this man.*

"You eye fucking me Hellcat?" He smirks and I blush.

"Me? Eye fuck you? Never." I say with a smile as he walks over, pressing me against his car.

"Liar." He breathes against my lips and I laugh looking away from him toward the view.

"This place is beautiful, Eas. Do you come here often?" I ask.

"It sure is," he whispers, not taking his eyes off me, causing the blush to deepen in my cheeks. He cups my face, looking for injury, but I shake him off.

"I'm fine. He didn't hit me. I just fell on my ass, no biggie. Are you okay?" I say with a shrug, trying not to make a big deal over it. He pulls away kicking the dirt and I walk over to the front of his car, leaning against the hood with my arms folded over my chest.

"I'm fine, don't worry about me. I'm sorry you had to witness that, but I will never stop protecting you, no matter who it is. Even if you send me away, I will always make sure you are safe. I told you just hours ago, no one gets to hurt you and I fucking meant it, Dylan." He seethes.

"It's fine, Eas." I say, wanting to change the fucking subject. *I've had enough for one day.*

"It's not. We should have told him, but it's your story to tell, not mine. Am I glad you trusted me enough to tell me something so traumatic? Yes, of course, but it was your choice to trust me and not him. I can't help that, yet I'm to blame. Your fucking mother has a big fucking mouth though." He growls.

"Indeed she does. Where do we go from here? I can't go home and I certainly do not want to be around my brother. He can get fucked for right now. I think we all need a minute to cool off." I state as he looks out into the distance.

"We will worry about that later," he answers.

"Fine, but will you come hug me please? I need to feel you." I demand, and the smile that crosses his face makes me melt into a puddle. He walks over to the hood of his car and wraps his arms around my shoulders as I hug his waist, inhaling his scent.

"I love you Eas, no matter what." I confess and he bends down to capture my lips with his. He slowly kisses me, swirling his tongue with mine as his fingers entwine in my long black hair. He groans as I suck his tongue flicking the tip. He pulls away, looking into my eyes.

"I love you more, Hellcat. Always." He breathes against my mouth, nipping at my bottom lip. I grip the bottom of his shirt, pulling him closer to me. I grin as an idea pops into my head.

"Hey babe, do people come here a lot?" I ask and he shakes his head no.

"I come here often to clear my head and I've never seen anyone else here before." He states, trailing kisses down my neck. I push him away and shed my tank. His eyes widen as lust bursts in them. I slide off my shorts and walk over to his bike, raising a brow.

"Ever fuck a girl on your bike?" I smirk as he stands there dumbfounded.

"Good, now bring that sexy ass over here and make me cum." I demand and he smirks, stalking over while removing his tee with one hand as his abs flex at the movement. He unbuttons his jeans, pulling them down slightly, taking his cock out, and stroking his length while biting his bottom lip.

"It's really a fucking sin how gorgeous you are Crow." I moan, sliding my fingers into my thong, flicking my clit. He growls as he continues to stroke himself, squeezing the tip of his dick as precum pools around his piercing. He gathers it up with his thumb and runs it over my bottom lip. I immediately lick it, loving the taste of him as I continue to play with my clit.

"Why the bike, Hellcat? If you were on the hood of my car I'd have you cumming all over my face."

He groans as I circle my clit faster at his dirty fucking mouth, causing me to moan as I sink a finger inside my pussy and my eyes roll into the back of my head, feeling how wet I am as he watches my every movement.

"I thought the bike would be a little more challenging." I pant as I add another finger. Looking up at him, he strokes faster as he listens to the wet sounds my fingers make with every thrust.

"Fuck Eas, I want to cum." I beg and he lifts me onto the seat, opening my legs and sliding my thong aside to look at my fingers sliding in and out of my soaked pussy.

"Let me taste your fingers." He commands. I remove them from my core and slide them into his waiting mouth. He moans at my taste, sucking my fingers clean as he steps closer, lining his cock up with my entrance and slowly sinking in. I throw my head back, moaning his name.

"Eas, you feel so fucking good, baby." I whimper and he moans as he holds onto my hips tightly, slowly milking my walls.

"I'm so close, baby." I whine as his thrusts become short and sharp, making me want him to go deeper and harder. I grab onto his shoulders and claw down his back as he growls, biting my shoulders.

"So fucking tight Hellcat. Cum on my cock, baby, soak me." He orders and I reach down, flicking my clit.

"Fuck, fuck, fuck." I scream as my orgasm hits hard and fast. He lifts me off the bike, slamming me onto his cock as he lays me on the hood of the stang. I tighten around him causing his movements to become erratic. "Fuck, Dylan. So. Fucking. Tight." He growls as I feel spurts of cum paint my walls. He slows down his movements, milking my walls, and I moan.

"You feel so fucking good, Eas. If you don't stop now, I'm going to cum again." I whimper and he takes that as a challenge, pulling out of me, lifting my hips and sucking my clit into his mouth. "Fuck, Eas, faster baby." I pant as he laps up our cum, spitting it onto my clit and licking me furiously. "Just like that. Shit. Fuck. Baby. I'm cumming!" I scream and he bites my clit, slamming a finger inside me and I ripple around him, cumming all over his face.

He slows his movements, licking and flicking slowly as my clit pulsates against his tongue. He lowers me down on the hood and looks down at me as his chim glistens in the moonlight.

"Fucking perfect." He smiles, kissing up my body to my lips. I kiss him back and swirl my tongue around his, reveling in our taste. He pulls away too soon and leaves a kiss on my nose causing me to giggle. He sits up and tucks himself away as I sit here panting like a bitch in heat. Climbing off the hood, I fix my thong and slide my shorts and tank back on.

"Damn, is sex with you always that good?" I grin and he smirks.

"Oh just wait, Hellcat. You ain't seen nothing yet." He winks and I fucking melt all over again. Now what do we do?

It's been a few days and we haven't returned home or to The Den. We've been staying at a little Airbnb, but today we have classes, and I need to go break up with Carter. Between my mother, brother and Carter, my phone's been blowing up nonstop. I will only answer Ava and Amy at the moment. *Fuck everyone else.* Until they all fucking calm down, I'll stay away for the time being. Easton dropped me off at Uni so he could go do a job for my uncle with the promise that he would be back in a few hours to pick me up.

I had texted Carter before class to meet me by the football field when my session was finished.

I've been standing here for twenty minutes waiting and I'm starting to get impatient. Looking at my phone, I scroll social media as I continue to wait. He's got another ten minutes before I leave and he can eat a dick.

Five minutes goes by and he finally arrives. "Hey baby," he says, trying to hug me but I take a step back, holding my hand up.

"Listen, this has been fun and all, but I'm done. I don't want to see you anymore." I say, looking up at him and he just smirks.

"Really? Well, Dollface, it doesn't work like that. You don't get to decide when you're done with me," he growls, grabbing my arm roughly.

"Let me go, Carter. You're fucking hurting me." I spit, pulling away as pain laces up my arm. His grip is so tight, it's going to leave fingerprints.

"No, you fucking cunt. I should make you get on your knees and suck my cock for thinking you're in charge here." He growls in my face and I spit at him. His hand rears back and he punches me in the face, causing me to fall in the grass.

"Know your place, whore, and do what the fuck you're told. When I call, you come running, understood?" He says, spitting in my face.

"Fuck you, bitch." I yell and he back hands me, causing me to bite the inside of my mouth.

"Get in line or else." He says, kicking me in the stomach.

"Fuck you!" I rasp and he kicks me again laughing.

"Just another dumb bitch!" He spits on me again then jogs off the field, leaving me on the grass, in a ball. Tears stream down my face as I whimper for Easton. I can't fucking breathe. *I just want Eas.*

"Please. Someone help me." I rasp but no one will hear me. I can't take a deep breath, so I hold onto my stomach as I cry from the pain. I try reaching for my phone, but I can't find it. The sky starts to spin and the last thing I remember is Easton's name trailing from my lips.

CHAPTER 26

EASTON

Something is seriously wrong. I've texted Dylan a million fucking times since leaving Spade's warehouse. He didn't have a job for me when I arrived. Instead, he wanted to warn me about someone from our past who was spotted lurking around, and needed to remind me how dangerous he is. *That shit could have been said over the fucking phone.*

Class ended hours ago. I've called and texted repeatedly and nothing. I swear to god if this is some kind of game she's cooked up, I'm going to shove her gorgeous face into a fucking pillow and make her scream my name until her throats' raw as I fuck her little pink pussy so fucking hard, she won't forget why she's so damn sore.

Slamming my hands against the steering wheel, I drive to The Den. Maybe her class got out and she called for a ride even though I promised her I'd be back for her. *Think Easton. Think.* Where the fuck could she be?

Picking up my phone, I dial her again. *Come on baby, pick up. Please pick up.* Nothing. I pull up her location and it circles like it's trying to load but can't. *I swear to god she never fucking listens.* I don't do these things to piss her off, it's for her fucking safety. She's not a stupid woman. She knows more about us than I thought, so you would think her location would be on.

"FUCKKKKK!" I yell out, pounding my fist into the steering wheel again.

I pull into The Den like a maniac, slamming on the brakes and throwing the door open. I run inside. No one is fucking here. It's quiet as fuck. Jogging to my room, praying she's sleeping in my bed, I swing open the door but everything is exactly how we left it.

Fuck. I pull at my hair in frustration because I shouldn't have fucking left, but yet again, I had no choice. When the boss calls, I go running. I need to realize that I can't always be with her, even if that's the only place I truly want to be day and night. "Fuck!" I roar, picking up my stereo from the floor and hauling it across the room as it smashes against the wall. Anything I get my hands on goes flying; TV, lamps, night tables and clothes.

Taking the sais from the holster, I spin them in my hands, climbing onto the bed and slice into the mattress like a hellhound shredding flesh. I don't stop until my arms get heavy and I can no longer fucking breathe.

Taking a step back as I try to control my breathing, I take in the damage I have caused. My heart continues to race just as fast as my mind does. *Think. Easton. Fucking think. Could she have gone home? Wouldn't she at least text me if she had?* I grab my holster and strap it to my jeans, adding a few more knives.

Walking over the mess to my closet, I grab my racing jacket and slide it on. Her fucking scent hits me like a ton of bricks. *I need to find her already.* I slam my door shut and jog back out to my car. Hopping in, I throw her in reverse and head home, praying that's where she is, because if she's not, I don't know where else to look and then I'll have to alert everyone that she's missing.

My fucking heart is beating so fast. What if he took her? What if this is his way of getting to me through the one I love? Fuck, Spade is right. Even if I didn't want to see it, I can never underestimate an Ace, especially when the Ace is gunning for the Queen. The sun is starting to set which is going to make this hunt so much fucking harder.

Racing to the house, I weave in and out of traffic, not giving a single fuck about lights and stop signs, she means too much to me to slow down. I will not fucking stop until she's in my arms again. I really hope I'm fucking overreacting but my gut is telling me otherwise.

Pulling along the curb in the middle of both of our houses, no one is parked in the driveway. *Where the fuck is everyone?* Climbing out of the car, I hop the picket fence and run up the steps, jabbing in the key code and swinging the door open. "Dylan!" I yell, running up the stairs to her room and finding nothing; no sign of anyone being here. Glancing out her window into mine, I see no movement, but fuck it. I leave her room and run down the stairs and out the front door, hopping the fence again into my yard. I jog up my three steps, enter the code, and swing the door open.

"Dylan, you here?" I yell. Again, nothing. Running up the steps to my room and again for the umpteenth time tonight, NOTHING! I'm ready to fucking destroy this room too, but my mom will throw a bitch fit and I do not have the time to deal with her and all the questions that come with it.

Taking a ragged, deep breath, I leave the house and get back into my car. The only other place left to check is the University. *Someone had to have seen her there.*

Luckily, Uni is only minutes away as I try to calm the fuck down. When I get like this, I can't fucking think straight. Spade always taught me to think first, then react, and I'm doing the complete opposite. I'm losing my shit, but I can't hold in all this rage. It's fucking Dylan. I'll never be able to calm down when it comes to her. She means fucking everything to me.

Picking up my phone, I dial her again. It rings and rings and rings, and then it picks up and I hear a whisper.

"Dylan, where the fuck are you?" I scream into the phone, but the voice sounds so far away and the connection keeps breaking up.

"Dylan, if you can hear me, baby, press a button if you are still at school." I say calmly as the line beeps.

"Okay, baby. That's good. Can you tell me where you are?" I ask, and again it's like she's so far away, whispering. What the fuck is going on?

"I can't hear you, Hellcat. You can hear me, right? Press a button for yes." I instruct, waiting for the beep and I get nothing.

"Dylan, I can't fucking find you. I need you to help me get to you. I'm heading to the school but I don't know where to look." I say, praying to God she can hear me. The line beeps and I hear a faint,

"Help me, Eas," and the line goes dead. I drop the phone and pound both hands against the steering wheel as I scream. Entering the college, I find an empty area and park. Picking up my phone again, I call her and she picks up.

"I'm coming baby, you hear me, Hellcat? Tell me where you are. Press a button once for the same spot I dropped you off at. Press it twice for no."

Beep beep. *Okay process of elimination.*

"Okay, are you inside the school stuck somewhere?" Beep beep.

"Are you inside at all?" Beep beep.

"You're doing so good, baby. I'm so proud of you. Are you outside?" Beep.

"Alone?" Beep.

"North side press once, south side press twice, east side press three times. I'm parked on the west side and don't see you." I say, and she beeps three times.

"Okay, east side it is. Tennis courts?" Beep beep.

"Soccer field?" Beep beep.

"Football field?" Beeeeeeeeeeeeeppp.

"Ok baby. I'm coming. Don't hang up. I'm right here Hellcat." I assure her as I race through the parking lot to the other end of the school. Pulling up to the fence of the football field, I get out, bringing my phone with me.

"I'm here, baby. I'm right here." I growl, finally spotting her laying in the grass. I run as I hang the phone up and shove it in my back pocket. Skidding to a stop, I fall to my knees as I take her in. Left eye swollen, bruised cheek, blood on her face as she holds her stomach and chest with one hand and the other is almost out of reach from her phone.

My hands shake with anger as I remove my jacket and lay it over her as I grab her phone and put it in my pocket before I lift her into my arms. She tries to move her arms to wrap around my neck but can't. "It's okay, baby. You're safe now. I got you." I whisper, kissing the top of her head.

"Thank you." She whispers as she begins to cry in my arms. I'm trying to stay calm and not question who had done this because I don't want to scare her with the rage that is fucking building all over again. I just need to make sure my girl is okay before I make my next move.

Opening the passenger door, I gently place her in the seat, and she winces. I grind my teeth so fucking hard as I take a step back and shut the door quietly. Rounding the car, I get in and put her in gear, heading out of the lot.

"I'll take you to the hospital to get checked out." I say as I grab her hand to hold.

"No, take me to Spade's." She whispers. Maybe I didn't hear her correctly. I turn out of the parking lot and get on the main road.

"You want to go where?" I ask as I bring her hand to my lips.

"Spade's. Take me to the warehouse." She says, clearing her throat. *The fuck?*

"How do you know about Spade?" I say through gritted teeth and she looks at me with those gorgeous ocean blues.

"He's my uncle." She reveals and I damn near swerve off the road.

"He's your what?" I ask, shock written all over my face. How the fuck is she related to Spade and why haven't I known that my entire fucking life?

"My uncle. He's my mother's brother. Do the math Eas." She rasps with irritation.

"You've been keeping this a secret for how long? Does Bentley know? Am I the only one out of the fucking loop?" I growl, tightening my grip on the steering wheel.

"I've known for years, just about as long as I've known that our mothers are fucking." She confesses.

"Same about our moms, but you still didn't answer the question. Does your brother know?" I press.

"No, he doesn't, neither does my mom. I guess you can say I've been keeping a lot of secrets locked in my head." She whispers and I just nod because she's not the only one. *Fuck.*

"Why are we going to Spade's?" I ask and she sighs.

"Because he can call his Doc and not alert my brother, or mother, on this. I can trust him to keep my secret. He fucking owes me." She grits.

"Hey, don't get annoyed with me. I'm just trying to help and understand what the fuck is going on. I couldn't find you for hours, Hellcat. I searched everywhere for you and I need a new mattress." I add as she weakly squeezes my hand.

"I'm safe now, but don't ask me who did it until later. And when I do tell you, I need you to promise that you won't up and leave me. We will do it together because I'm sick of the games these fuckers are playing, and it's time to get my hands bloody. Killing Garrett wasn't enough. They all need to die. Every single one of them that hurt and touched me without my consent." She growls and I swallow thickly because I'm one of them and I deserve to pay for what I did.

Sooner or later, I'm going to have to tell her. I'm just so fucking terrified of losing her and I know Fatal will kill me. I guess my impending death is inevitable.

The rest of the car ride is quiet as I internally beat myself up for not coming clean after it happened. If I would have told her the truth, maybe what's coming wouldn't happen or maybe she would have never spoken to me again and lived her life without me.

The cards will fall where they may. But what is Raph without his April O'Neil?

CHAPTER 27

DYLAN

We pull up to the gates and Eas goes to punch in his code, but I grab his arm to stop him. He looks at me with his brows furrowed.

"What is it, baby?" he breathes.

"Nothing, just punch in my code 1431. It will alert him differently than your code would. He will be waiting," I say softly as he nods his head, doing as I asked. The gates open and he drives through slowly down the dirt road. I didn't want to go home, and I certainly did not want to go to the hospital. I knew coming here was the best bet for now. Taking a deep breath, I try to center myself for what's to come.

"Eas, thank you for finding me. I'm not even sure how long I was lying there calling your name." I whisper as he squeezes my hand that he still hasn't let go of.

"I would scour the earth to bring you back to me, Hellcat. I fucking promise you that." He growls, pulling in front of the doors that swing open to my very worried-looking uncle. He hesitates for a second before coming to my side of the car, opening the door as his eyes widen, then narrow as he takes in my face. He automatically pulls a gun, cocking it and presses it against Easton's temple. *Jesus Christmas.*

"I don't care how long we have known each other, Easton, what the fuck happened to my niece?" My uncle spits and I roll my eyes.

"Jesus, Uncle. He didn't do this. Put the fucking gun away. God, you men and your overbearingness." I chastise as he removes the gun from my man's head, sliding it into the back of his jeans.

"Between you and your fucking nephew, I don't know who is worse at this point. But I'll tell you, just like I told him, I'll never fucking hurt her. She's mine, and I fucking love her. So if you're going to point a gun at me, at least have your facts straight because I'll slaughter the world for her, Boss." He spits and my uncle grunts, but for a moment his eyes light up with love and longing and then dull with sadness. It was almost like he was in a memory or having deja vu.

"I respect that, but watch your fucking tone, and get your asses inside. I'll call the Doc." He orders, stepping away. Easton climbs from the car and rounds it, ignoring my uncle watching his every move as he comes to my side.

"Do you want me to carry you, or can you walk?" He asks and I shake my head.

"I can walk, just help me up. I think my rib is broken." I admit and he growls, lifting me gently from the seat.

"You know, I should have seen the signs all along. All you Rodriguezes are stubborn as fuck," he states as he walks to the door my uncle is holding open.

"You are not to call my brother or my mother. This shit ends here or the deal is off." I say sternly as we pass the man I'm speaking to.

"I know, but I want answers." He demands as Eas mumbles a 'get in line' at him.

"Yes, I will give you both what you want after I get checked out, and maybe a glass of water or something, would be nice." I say, my tone dripping with sarcasm.

"Not until after you are seen. We need to make sure you don't have any internal bleeding just in case you need emergency surgery. If you eat or drink now, it could affect that outcome. So chill out and let's wait for the Doc." My uncle retorts as he leads us to the entertainment room.

"Be a good girl, Hellcat. Stop with the sass." Easton whispers and I roll my eyes as he places me down gently on the couch, kissing my forehead and handing me my phone from his back pocket as his starts ringing.

"I need to take this, but you need to turn your location on and don't ever shut it off again. So help me God." He seethes.

"Yea, yea. Go answer the phone." I say, shooing him away. He leaves the room as my uncle leans against the bar.

"Does he know about Midnight Rider?" He asks with a smirk and I smile, shaking my head.

"He'd be pissed, more than he already is, but clearly he knows we are related. He also knows Bentley is not privy to this information. I trust him to keep his mouth shut." I say and he nods as his phone chimes.

"Uh. Do you happen to be in the mood to meet another uncle and a cousin?" he asks with a smile and my eyes light up at the thought.

"Really? Now?" I ask, super fucking excited. I've been waiting for this moment to meet more of my real family.

"Yeah, they're almost here and the Doc should be rolling in any second. How's your mother?" he asks and I roll my eyes.

"Dylannnnn." He warns and I huff.

"There's a lot I need to tell you, so once I get examined, I'll have to start from the beginning. As far as my mother goes, we got into a big fight. She said some pretty messed up things to me, spewed some serious accusations and kicked me out. I'm not innocent in all this, but I'm sick of her shit. Sick of her lying to me and being all about the job instead of caring and loving. Bentley doesn't even know how to love or show affection. He just barks orders and yells at me. The only person who shows an ounce of love and affection is you and Eas." I sigh, taking a deep breath as he comes to kneel next to me, grabbing my hand.

"There's a lot you don't know either. I only know love because of my wife. If it wasn't for her, I'd be just like your mom. Cold and probably dead. My Queen taught me how to love and be loved because me, Juan, Nicolas and your mother Isabel were brought up with no love after your grandmother died. We were trained to be killers, except for your mom. I didn't even have a relationship with her. It was never allowed with any woman, but that's a story for another day." He says, tapping my hand.

"I'm sorry your childhood was like that, and now I understand a little bit of why she is the way she is." I say with a frown.

"That was just the tip of the iceberg, kiddo." He laughs, shaking his head.

"What did you fellows do now?" A very short, bald older man says, walking over to my uncle, who laughs.

"Nothing this time, old man. This is my niece, Dylan. Can you please check her over? She will explain to you her injuries. Anything she needs, she gets, just send me the bill. Before you say anything, I will pay the extra for the emergency call. There's drinks at the bar, you may help yourself. I'm going to step out to give her some privacy and keep her hellhound at bay." He laughs, leaving me with the Doc.

"Hello Dylan. I'm Dr. Harold Liebman, but you can call me Doc like the others do." He says, laying out his bag of supplies.

"It's nice to meet you and I apologize for disturbing your evening." I say and he shakes his head.

"Now, now, child. No apologies necessary, your uncle pays me good money. Now tell me, what brings me here tonight?" He asks, giving me a quick look. His tone is so soft spoken that it makes me feel at ease and comfortable to tell him what happened.

"I was attacked by my boyfriend; well now ex boyfriend–" I start to say and he interrupts with a raised brow.

"It wasn't that gentlemen with the tattoos outside yelling on the phone was it? Because I'll go right out there and kick his ass for hurting such a pretty girl like you." He says with a wink that makes me smile.

"I bet you can take him. I put twenty bucks on you, Doc." I reply with a smile which makes him chuckle.

"But to answer your question, no. He found me and I made him bring me here." I answer, truthfully for once.

"Ok, good. Now continue." He says and I tell him everything that happened as he examines me. It turns out, I do have a broken rib, but there's no internal bleeding and the swelling in my face will go down in a few days. He left me with a bunch of pain meds and told me I need to be on bedrest until I can either laugh without wincing or climb a flight of stairs. Which brings me to my next issue. Where the fuck am I supposed to stay without raising suspicions or anyone knowing what the fuck happened? *What the fuck did my life become?* Easton walking in the room and shutting the door, brings me out of my thoughts.

"How's my girl doing? Those meds kick in yet? Ya know, we can go stay at a hotel if you want?" Easton suggests and I shake my head.

"Oh yes, the meds have kicked in and I feel great. But no, staying at a hotel is too fucking expensive, and two weeks is a long time on bedrest. I still need to go to school. The semester is almost over, then we are off for Spring break. I'm supposed to go away to Aruba with the girls." I say with a sigh, and he looks at me with a raised brow.

"You think you're going to Aruba with just the girls and I'm supposed to what? Sit around with my thumb up my ass? Not happening, Hellcat." He spits and I laugh.

"Uh, yeah I do. You might like it up the ass." I giggle and he growls.

"The only thing going up anyone's ass is my cock into yours." He says, licking his lips.

"Settle down, because the only thing your cock is touching is those hands." I warn and he rolls his eyes. *I fucking love this man.* As I go to lean over to kiss the man I love on the cheek, cold metal is pressed into my skin and I gasp. Easton notices and the smile on his face isn't what I expect when someone has a knife to my neck.

"Hazzellll." He warns as she rounds the corner of the couch, still holding the knife to my throat, and straddles my lap. My eyes widen because she's the same girl who held a knife to my neck at the frat house, except this time, I get to see her up close and personal. Those fucking eyes. One is bright blue and the other is turquoise green. Fucking stunning.

"Easy Haze, she has a broken rib." Easton tells her with a smirk. Hazel cocks her head as we take each other in. *Again, why does this girl turn me on?* She's got a banging little body with her long, curly black hair flowing down her back.

"I like her, Easton. Can she be my new pet?" She asks with a sinister smile that has my nipples hardening as she runs her nails over them.

"She's mine and I don't share." He growls, but I don't give a fuck what he says. I don't take my eyes off her as I slowly run my hands up her thighs. She smirks, leaning in and whispering.

"I bet you taste like skittles and danger." I lick my lips as I palm Easton's hard cock. He grunts, watching the scene unfold in front of him. She presses the knife harder against my skin and I moan as she runs her nose along my jaw and down my neck, licking the blood that drips. I moan again, gripping Easton's cock harder as Hazel brings the knife to the crease of my lip, creating a small slice. She looks into my eyes and licks the blood and slowly kisses me, twirling her soft tongue against mine, causing me to shiver as she slides her other hand behind my neck, pulling my head back against the cushion so she can deepen the kiss. Easton clears his throat, but we ignore him as I continue to pump his cock through his jeans. He growls my name, but I'm too lost in a trance with this girl on my lap. She pulls back and runs the tip of her knife around my lips and down my chin, slicing just a little bit, my eyes flutter at the sting.

"You ever been with a girl before, little pet?" She breathes and I shake my head no, but she raises her brow.

"No, I have not." I whisper, and there's that sinister smile again. She looks at Easton.

"Watch out, Candyman. I might just steal your girl." She winks, but he doesn't say shit, his eyes are hooded with lust as he watches us. She takes the knife and cuts the straps to my tank, letting the strings fall. She lifts her green tank over her head and the sexiest tattoo I have ever seen is inked on her torso and wraps around up to her shoulder. I'm pretty sure the other end goes down her hip. It looks fresh, like she just had got it done. The way the bleeding roses drip makes them look dead hanging on the vines. The sharp thorns look like they pierce into her skin, sparkling red diamonds in place of the blood that would otherwise be there. The realism of this design is stunning.

I trace my finger along the vines and she shudders beneath my touch. She moans as I lightly flick my nail against her hard nipple. My shorts are soaked and my clit is aching to be touched as she takes the knife again and cuts the middle of my bra, spilling my tits free with a bounce as my chest heaves in anticipation. I've never reacted so strongly towards a female before, this is an entirely new experience that I don't want to end anytime soon.

She unclips the front of her bra and I reach up to touch her soft flesh, pinching her nipples between my fingers, causing her to rock slowly on my lap. I lay my head back, taking a shuddering breath as soft lips graze my hardened peaks one at a time. I moan at the sensation, needing and wanting more. She licks, sucks and bites so slowly, making me pant as I tighten my grip on Easton's cock and pinch her nipple with my other hand, squeezing her full tits roughly.

She licks up my chest and bites my neck, swirling her tongue around the cut she left earlier. I grip her hip tightly, trying to roll my hips, but with a broken rib, it's making it extra hard to create the friction I need. The pain meds are helping tremendously, but I don't want to cause anymore damage.

Easton growls next to me as I unbutton and pull down his zipper, freeing his dripping cock. I rub my thumb over the tip, gathering his arousal, bringing it to my lips and sucking it clean. He growls, but I grab his cock tighter and stroke his length, squeezing the tip just how he likes it. He throws his head back, groaning and thrusts up into my hand.

Hazel grabs my face, sucking my lips into her mouth. I deepen the kiss, sucking her tongue, and she moans as I pull her nipples, flicking them as she continues to rock in my lap. I suck her tongue harder and she opens her mouth wide enough for Easton to see me sucking the length slowly. His hand wraps around mine, squeezing with a moan.

"Fuck," he hisses as I suck her all the way into my mouth and pull away slowly. He grabs my thigh, pulling my leg towards him to open me wider and slides my soaked cotton shorts to the side, revealing how fucking drenched I am.

"Damn, Hellcat. You're so fucking wet." He groans as he sinks a finger into me slowly and I pull away from the kiss as I watch Hazel lay the dull side of the knife against my throbbing clit, pushing a finger inside me beside Easton's. I groan as they milk my walls, rocking my hips slowly.

"Come on, Hellcat. Cum for us." He commands as they both finger me faster. I slide my hand up Hazel's thigh, pushing her shorts to the side, rubbing my thumb over her clit as I push a finger into her tight, wet pussy.

"Yes, just like that, little pet." She moans, flicking my clit with the knife as I stroke Easton faster with my free hand. I flick Hazel's clit as she continues to ride my fingers. We all pick up the pace as moaning, whimpering and growling echo the space around us. Easton cums with a long growl all over his stomach.

"Fuck, Hellcat. Show her how hard you cum, baby," he orders, trying to catch his breath.

"Cum for me, little pet, soak my hand, skittle pop." She commands and I pinch her clit, feeling her tighten around my fingers as my orgasm hits hard and fast.

"Fuckkkkkk." I whimper as she fuzes her lips to mine, getting lost in the kiss as we continue to fuck one another, not stopping until I feel cum dripping down my tits. Another grunt spews from Eastons lips as warm wet cum gushes between us as we suck, lick and bite each other's lips. *Fuck, she's amazing.* We remove our fingers from one another and slide them into Easton's mouth together.

"Taste us." I pant, and he holds both of our hands while he sucks us clean. Pulling away, I laugh.

"Well, holy fucking shit. That was unexpected and fucking hot." Easton grunts. I look over at Hazel and I see sadness in her gorgeous eyes. But as quick as it was there, it vanishes. She leans in and places a tender kiss against my swollen lips whispering,

"Welcome to the family, cousin," then gets up, snaps her bra into place, throws her shirt at me and walks out the door.

Well shit.

CHAPTER 28

Easton

Hazel makes her grand exit and I full belly laugh as Dylan turns to me with narrowed eyes. "Did I really just make my cousin cum, and you knew the whole time?" She punches me in the arm and I laugh harder.

"You did, you fucking prick!" She yells, hitting me again. I hold my hands up in surrender as she puts Hazel's shirt over her bare tits.

"She's not your blood cousin. She's Spade's daughter, but not by blood." I confirm.

"You're such a dick, you know that right?" she says, shaking her head as I grab her face, kissing the woman senseless.

"And you're fucking amazing and perfect. That was the hottest fucking thing I have ever seen in my life." I confess as a blush crawls up her cheeks. She looks away, changing the subject.

"Well, now that I'm relaxed, can we sneak off to bed?" She asks with a little pout, but I shake my head.

"Hellcat. You haven't told me exactly what happened, nor have you given me any names. So let's hear it and then I'll take you to bed and update Spade while you rest. I was thinking tomorrow we can go back to The Den. I already placed an order for a new mattress to be delivered in the morning. The cleaning ladies are there now, cleaning up my mess." I say, looking down with shame. I lost my shit again and couldn't control my rage. How can anyone expect me to keep it together when Dylan is involved? I can't, and will probably never, be able to.

"Fine, but hey, look at me. Don't beat yourself up over a mattress Eas. At least it's not something you can't come back from. It's a fucking bed. It's okay babe." She reassures me, but there's that little voice in the back of my head calling me out on all the things I won't be able to come back from. *Fuck.* I want to take her away for a weekend. Just get out of here and be alone, well not alone, alone. I want to take her to see one of my friends that I haven't seen in awhile. The Wicklow brothers own five hundred acres of land in Pennsylvania, they have four wheelers and side-by-sides to ride. I think time away, and introducing her to new people, is just what we need. I think I'll shoot Alaric a text in the morning and see when he's available. Hopefully, we can get down like old times, and have a TMNT movie marathon. I'll have to bring my sais to show him. Dylan clears her throat, taking me out of my thoughts.

"What has you smiling over there?" She asks, poking me in the cheek.

"Ouch, them daggers are sharp, Hellcat. Put the claws away. I was thinking about taking you up to visit a friend of mine in Pennsylvania. I think we would have a lot of fun with him and his crazy ass brothers, they even have a girlfriend, and she has friends too, so you won't be the only girl there." I say grinning.

"Any friends of yours are friends of mine. Let's do it." She smiles.

"I'll text Alaric tomorrow and set something up for when you're healed more. They have a lot of land and toys to play with and I don't need you to make progress just to break a rib again." I suggest and she nods.

"Sooo, bed?" She says with a smirk and I shake my head.

"Nope, not until you spill baby." I retort, leaning back against the couch. She huffs then takes a deep breath. I brace myself for impact because I can feel it in my bones that once she spills the name, I'm going to lose my fucking shit.

"It was Carter." She blurts, squeezing her eyes closed as I get up and slam my fist down on the pool table with a roar. *It was Carter who did this?!* My chest heaves as I replay her words, but I don't hear her screaming my name, and I certainly don't feel Spade punch me in the face. All I see is red as my fists collide with someone. I'm hit in the face again, but there's no stopping me until I see the tall blonde guy with a knife digging into Dylan's throat.

"Get the fuck away from her!" I spit as my chest continues to heave. Spade gets in my face, trying to get me centered, but it doesn't help.

"What do we have here? Such a scared Little Creature you are, little girl." He laughs sinisterly into her ear but then his bright blue eyes meet mine and he winks. "I advise you to calm down. All it takes is a flick of my wrist, and her rapidly beating artery will spill beautiful ribbons of crimson that I love so much." I growl, pressing into Spade.

"I know you're trying to help me, but get him the fuck off my girl. Now! I will not calm down until he backs the fuck up." I spit.

"He can't help you. By the time he gets to me, her blood will be all over the carpets, such a pretty little painting." He taunts, and I narrow my eyes at him. He doesn't know me very well because I can take my throwing star and hit him faster in his neck than he can drag the scalpel across her throat. I smirk at the thought.

"Trust me, Blondie, I may be his running boy, but you don't know what the fuck I'm capable of." I grin, but Spade chimes in before anything else is said.

"Jameson, let your niece go! Taunting him with her is not how you calm someone down! You of all people should know this! Put the scalpel down and go find something to do before you make this worse than it already is!" Spade yells and Jameson's face drops, letting her go and taking a step back. I take a deep breath, counting to ten over and over again until my breathing is even.

"Eas. Look at me." She orders, but I can't, not yet. Then small hands cup my face, forcing me to look at her. She smiles and brings her lips to mine. "Please calm down baby. You scare me when you're like this. I'm fine. I'm safe. I'm here, with you. That's all that matters right now." She reminds me and I take another deep breath. I look up at Spade and Jameson as they stare, dumbfounded.

"She reminds you of someone, doesn't she?" Spade says to his brother, and he nods, storming the room with Spade on his tail. I wonder what that was about. Hands pull me back to the forefront and soft lips kiss mine, bringing me right where I always want to be. *With her.*

"Take me to bed, please. I need you to lay with me until I fall asleep." She whispers and I nod. As much as I want to leave here and find that prick, I can't. She comes first and his time will come. Once she falls asleep, I have something else that needs to be handled and hopefully that will help calm me down. She pulls me by my hand and leads me out of the entertainment room to another room three doors down. I hear groaning from the room across the hall. I have no idea who is in there, but she giggles, opening the door to the room we are staying in. It's a simple space with a TV, dresser, king-size bed and a bathroom attached. I shut the door, locking it behind me. Dylan sheds her clothes, then crawls across the bed and gets under the covers. *Jesus, she's so fucking beautiful.*

"What kind of meds did the Doc give you, if you can crawl across the bed with a broken rib?" I ask with a raised brow, and she smiles, shrugging her shoulders.

"No fucking clue, but I feel fantastic. I think you should get naked and show me how much you love me." She smirks. *Jesus, this girl.*

"As much as I would love to sink my cock inside that tight pussy, I can't, not when I'm like this, and especially not while you are injured. I don't give a fuck how spectacular you feel." I say, shedding my shirt and kicking my boots off. "I'm not in a gentle mood, Hellcat and any other time I'd fucking wreck that little cunt, but I can't tonight." I growl, crawling over to her as she sighs, cupping my face.

"Okay, baby. Can you at least hold me?" She pouts and I suck that sexy bottom lip of hers into my mouth.

"Yes, baby, I can do that." I say, kissing her cheek as she rolls on her good side. Once settled, I scoot behind her, pulling her into me as I trail my fingertips over her arm and down her hourglass hip to her thighs and back up, causing her body to riddle with goosebumps. "Baby? Can you tell me what happened? I promise to stay calm." I plead and she takes a deep breath, telling me everything that happened from the moment I dropped her off, until I found her. I kissed all her bruises and told her how sorry I was until she finally fell asleep. I laid there, listening to her light snores, not wanting to leave, but I have to update Spade and apologize on top of going to kill Bryce.

Hours later, I'm walking the trail at the old academy, planting little speakers that will lead to the

Whitestone Lake. I found out through a few sources that Bryce runs these trails every Thursday night before he makes a deal with a new crew that has come to town. Me and Bentley discussed this shit earlier in the night and Kingston is looking into who the fuck these assholes are. Once we have all the intel, we will move in on them. I also let Spade know this information after I was done updating him on Dylan. I didn't tell him everything, just that she's been dating Carter for a while and we have been messing around on the side and decided to make things official-ish.

After class, she broke up with him and that's when, and why, he attacked her. Jameson wanted to go hunting immediately, even Hazel was listening in and had a few choice words to say about it. I think she's really taken a liking to my girl. Spade calmed them both down and I assured them all that I would take care of it. I was given a time frame to handle it, or they would be taking matters into their own hands, but Spade knows how much of a ruthless killer I am. I'll get it done, no matter what. I hear a door close and I get into position, blending in with the forest. I give him a few minutes to feel comfortable and think he's all alone. Taking out my phone, I press play, watching as an ominous voice taunts him.

"Bryceeeee, come out, come out, wherever you areee," sings through the speakers as I watch Bryce nearly piss himself. He's looking all around trying to figure out where the voice is coming from. He backs up down the trail as I crack a twig with my boot and step out in plain-sight. He can't see my face hidden under the hood. I press play and the voice growls, "Run, little hog, run!!" and he takes off down the path nearly tripping over his own feet. I give him a few seconds of a head start before I take off after him. I continue to let the voice taunt him through the speakers.

"Whoever you are, l-l-leave me alone!" He stammers and I laugh.

"Please, if it's money you want, I'll pay. I have rich parents. Let me cut you a check." He yells as I catch up to him, giving him a little push, causing him to trip but not fall just yet.

"No amount of money will get you out of this. You know what you did." I growl as I continue to chase and give him another push.

"You have the wrong guy. I didn't do anything!" He yells with a hiccup. I'm pretty sure he's crying. What a fucking pussy.

"That's a lie." I growl, sending a star to his left achilles tendon. He screams on impact and loses his footing. He still doesn't fall but it shit for sure slowed him down. I slow my pace, letting him hop on one foot further down the trail.

"For every lie you tell, I will make it hurt." I laugh as he gasps.

"Please, I know nothing. Just let me go." He begs, but all the begging in the world isn't going to save him.

"Does Dylan St. James ring a bell?" I growl and he stops for a second, looking back at me, trying to see my face.

"What about her? They made me do it. I didn't want to, but they threatened my scholarship and my family, man. You have to believe me." He pleads and I throw another star, hitting the other achilles tendon and he drops, screaming in pain.

"Bullshit!" I yell, shoving his face in the dirt. I remove both stars from his ankle and wipe the blood off on my pants, putting them in my holster.

"Please, please. I'm sorry. What do you want from me?" He asks as spittle flies from his mouth and tears cover his face. I bend down and remove my hood, getting in his face so he can see exactly who is about to end his pathetic life.

"Who sent the orders?" I growl.

"I-I don't know." He stammers, but that's not good enough.

"Wrong answer," I spit, wrapping my hand around his throat, squeezing until his eyes bulge. He slaps at my hand in a panic and I release some of the pressure.

"It was Carter! He was the one who told Garrett to round everyone up and told him she wanted us to run a train on her. I didn't know they were going to drug her and hurt her like that! They went too far, man." He says, taking a deep breath as I remove my hand from this neck.

"Interesting, being that I was there, I didn't see you once try to stop anything. You went right along like a bitch, and for that, you're dead." I say taking out my sais.

His eyes widen as I lean in and whisper, "The Candyman sends his regards," just before I stab under his chin, through his face, hitting the brain. I drag him by his face the rest of the way through the trail, down to the lake.

Removing the sais from his face, I dip it in the water and wipe it off on my pants, placing it back into the holster. I pull his head into the water and take out my twelve inch hunting knife and slice into his flesh, ripping through the muscle and tissue, removing his head from the spinal cord and letting it float away with the current.

I contemplate on what I want to do next. Do I just roll the body in the lake and call it a day or do I chop him up? A yawn hits me, making the decision for me. I roll the fucker into the river, watching as he floats and sinks a bit. I walk back through the trail, retrieving my speakers on the way, as I get back to my car.

Throwing my holster and speakers into the trunk, I change my jeans and place the old ones in the garbage bag to dispose of later. Getting into the car, I start her up as I light a cigarette, inhaling the minty smoke as I put her in gear and roll out slowly. The new crew won't be here for another twenty minutes, but I trust no one, so I take it easy leaving here with no headlights on until I get back on the highway.

Two down, three more to go. *Now I just need a quick shower and my girl in my arms.*

CHAPTER 29

Dylan

A week later, me and the girls decide we need a night to ourselves. I told Easton I was staying at Amy's for the night and Amy told Bentley she was staying with me at our mom's house. Hopefully, the boys don't ask each other questions because I haven't been home in weeks. My mother apologized when I went home today to drop off some stuff and grab my car. I let her know I'd be home tomorrow. Luckily, Ava doesn't have to answer to anyone, so she doesn't have to worry about getting caught. I take out my phone and shut off my location. He shouldn't need to look where I am if he knows I'm at Amy's. I pull the visor down and reapply my lip gloss.

"You guys ready to shake your asses and get fucked up?" I giggle.

"Oh, yes. I've been waiting for a girls' night away from the guys." Amy laughs as she passes me a joint and I take a deep hit. *Ava's been quiet tonight. I don't know what's going on with her, but I hope tonight will cheer her up.* I take a hit and pass it to her and she takes it, inhaling deep before coughing.

"Girl, when was the last time you smoked?" I laugh as she passes it to Amy.

"It's been a minute. Is that Antonio's shit?" She asks and Amy shakes her head.

"It sure is. I'll only get it from him. At least I know it's not laced with some crazy shit that's out in the streets as of lately." Amy says, passing it to me. I lean back against the headrest and take another hit.

"This shit is fucking good. I'm already high as fuck." I say with a giggle.

"He calls it 'Giggle Grass'." Amy says. She's right, it's very fucking fitting.

"You guys ready to get in there? Let's do a round of shots and go shake our asses." Ava whoops.

"That's my girl. Let's do this!" I yell and we all laugh, piling out of the car.

We decided on a bar in Whitestone called 'The End Of The Rivers' where no one will know us. We enter the barn-like swinging doors and head straight for the bar. The place isn't packed, but it isn't empty, either. There's a lot of biker dudes in here playing pool and cards in the far back. There's people on the dance floor and the music is jumping. The bartender walks over with a big smile on his face.

"Hey ladies, I'm Slash. What can I get for you?" Ava orders us 'sex on the beach' shots and we throw them back the second he sets them in front of us. I order another round of shots and a mixed drink for myself. I'm not a beer girl like these other two. Once my drink is ready, I hand Slash a hundo, telling him to keep a running tab, and Amy hands him fifty for a tip. I grab a pain killer from my pocket and pop it in my mouth, washing it down with my drink. I haven't told anyone that I'm still in pain, they would never allow me to leave the bed, so I take the meds when needed and I know tonight-it's going to be a must.

Ava grabs our hands and leads us to the dancefloor. We grind to the music, letting our hips sway as the beat flows through our bones. We dance for what feels like hours as sweat drips on our skin. Amy pulls us off to get more drinks from Slash and we step outside to cool down. The cold night air feels refreshing on my arms and legs considering I'm wearing a skirt and tank top. I take a deep breath and look to my right where I see a bunch of guys wearing biker vests, smoking a cigarette. I walk over to see if one of them will share with me.

"Hey fellas, anyone have an extra one for me?" I say as my tone drips with honey, pushing my tits out. The tall guy with dark hair, green eyes and tattoos on his neck, licks his lips and hands me a cigarette. I place it between my lips and he lights it for me. Taking a drag, I blow out the smoke. "Thank you." I say with a smirk.

"No problem, pretty girl." He replies, rubbing his fingers down his chin as he looks me up and down. I wink and turn back to the girls who are giggling. We share the cigarette as we check out the four guys. They are really fucking hot for a bunch of bikers. Once the cigarette is finished, we go back inside for another round of shots. The room is already starting to sway as the pain meds kick in full force. I'm drunk, but I'm not done partying yet. After throwing back the shot, we get on the dance floor and the guys from outside come over and start dancing with us. We giggle, thinking nothing of it. *It's just dancing, what harm can it do?* The tall man wraps his arms around my waist and grinds his hip behind me.

"You're fucking sexy. Anyone ever tell you that?" He groans in my ear but I don't respond as he tightens his hold, pushing my long hair to the side and biting along my neck. *This shouldn't feel good coming from a stranger, but it does.* It feels so fucking good as he pushes his hard cock against my ass. *Damn, he's huge.*

I look over at Amy, who's making out with the blonde guy, and Ava is a panting mess with two of the other guys. The redhead is playing with her nipples and kissing down her neck while the dark-haired guy has his hand up her skirt. *God damn, my girls give no fucks tonight, so why should I?* I push back against his hard cock, rolling my hips against him.

He squeezes my hip with one hand, pushing me harder against him as his other hand grabs my tit, running his thumb up and down my hard nipple. His other hand leaves my hip and trails up my stomach and both his hands squeeze my tits, pinching my nipples. *Fuck, this feels so good.* I grind harder, rolling my hips again as one hand travels down my stomach and into my skirt. He pulls at the front of my thong, creating the perfect friction for my aching clit.

"I bet your pussy is tight as fuck, pretty girl. I would bet my life on it that you look like a goddess with no clothes on." He says, groaning as I pant. The room starts to spin and I laugh, pulling away, but he grabs me harshly.

"You're a fucking tease. You know you want it. Look at your friends, begging to be touched by my guys." He growls in my ear, but I can barely see straight as my head starts to lull to the side.

"That's okay, baby. I'll still fuck you while you're unconscious. It makes it even easier for me to do as

I please." He spits, but he stiffens as the barn doors swing open and closed. I continue to sway to the beat as a familiar voice hits my ears.

"Get the fuck away from her." Easton threatens. *Fuck, we are in so much trouble.* I look at the girls who look at me wide eyed as Bentley and Ace circle the other guys. I look back to the doors and see a very fucking mad Easton. Shit. I don't know how much he saw, but I know I'm in so much fucking trouble.

"Who the fuck are you?" Tattooed neck growls. Easton takes a step forward, taking out a dagger from his holster as the guys pull their guns out. I roll my eyes because they have no idea who they are dealing with. I step back and grab onto Amy and Ava's hands whispering, "You know we're fucked right?"

"Yep." They say in unison.

"Are you both aware of what our guys do?" I ask, and Ava's stupid ass chimes in with her bullshit.

"'Our' guys? You and I don't belong to any of them. Amy's the only one whose stuck with the mother fucker."

"Umm, that's not entirely true." I reveal and they both look at me with wide eyes.

"Girl, if we weren't in the middle of this shit, I'd be all over your ass with questions." Amy whispers.

"I know, I know. Just keep it to yourself. I'll explain later." I whisper back.

"It's not Ace, right?" Ava asks with sadness written all over her face and I shake my head,

"No, Aves. I would never do that to you. I know you love him, even when you deny it." I say and she nods with a little smile.

"But you both didn't answer the fucking question." I whisper as everyone around us gets real fucking tense.

"Yes we know. They kill, and work, for The Cartel." Ava whispers and Amy nods in agreement. Taking a deep breath, feeling kind of relieved that I don't have to mask what's about to go down.

"Then brace yourselves. Easton looks like he's seconds away from losing it and the others aren't looking so calm themselves." I warn and they nod. The redhead lunges at Ace but he's too quick for him. Ace retrieves the gun, pistol whipping him in the face and points the gun at his friend.

"Move a muscle and I'll blow your fucking head off." Ace spits.

"You don't know who you're fucking with." The dark haired guy grits. And Bentley laughs.

"You think being a biker bitch makes you lethal? You ain't seen shit yet." The bar seems to clear out and the music is lowered. I look over at Slash and he winks. *What the fuck does that mean?*

"These sluts were begging for it." The blonde yells to Bentley who just continues to smirk. *Uh oh.* It's fucking coming. I look over to Easton who won't fucking look at me. *Fuck.*

"This little thing was grinding all over my stick, begging me to take her to the bathroom to fuck her hard." He laughs. *Oh fuck no.* Amy's eyes widen as I grab her beer bottle and smash the bottom off as I walk over to the lying mother fucker and hold the sharp end to his neck.

"Wanna run that back? This time tell the truth or I'll sink this bottle into your fucking neck and watch you bleed out all over this filthy floor." I spit. Easton growls, but the guy laughs as he grabs me by the throat, tossing me onto the floor as the bottle scrapes his neck and shatters onto the floor beneath me. Fuck, my hands land in the broken glass and my healing rib screams at me. Easton doesn't hesitate and smacks the hand that holds the gun. It goes off and the bullet goes wide, smashing the front window. I cover my head naturally as the girls run over and huddle on the ground with me.

Easton takes his dagger and slams it into the guys' neck as he drops to the ground, choking on his own blood. I look back at Bentley as he stabs the guy in the eye with some type of pick. The guy screams as Benny brings him to his knees and slices his throat wide open. Last but not least, Ace has the one guy on his stomach as he steps on his spine holding an arm in each hand, pulling until you hear bones breaking from the pressure. He lets his arms go but grabs his head, pulling it as far back as it will go and more crunching of bones echo the room along with his screams. Ace pulls back harder as he pours something down the guy's throat, then holds his nose to force him to swallow.

I watch closely as his Adams Apple bobs, and then Ace takes a small torch from his pocket, lights it up, and brings it to the guys mouth, immediately catching fire. *Holy shit. That's savage as fuck.* He holds him like that until his body starts to shake uncontrollably, then he tosses him to the ground, leaving him to burn from the inside out.

Suddenly the barn doors swing open and Uncle Jameson walks in. I need to remember not to call him that in front of Bentley.

"Slash, get me a shot of tequila please." Jameson orders as he takes in the scene.

"Well, well, well. What do we have here? No one could call me for some fun?" He looks around asking, but no one moves.

"Who the fuck are you?" Bentley asks venomously as Jameson cocks his head. *Jesus, just like Hazel.*

"You look just like him. It's the eyes I see." He says, and Easton finally chimes in because this secret we have been all keeping, is about to explode if Jameson doesn't shut the fuck up.

"We will clean it up, don't worry." Easton says.

"It's fine, the clean up crew is already on the way. I just came to see why this happened in my wife's bar." He asks, taking the shot and pouring it on the floor, reciting some shit in a language I've never heard before.

"It seems our girls decided to come have a night out without letting anyone know." Easton says through gritted teeth as we finally pick ourselves up off the floor.

"Come Little Creatures." He commands and Easton growls.

"Don't worry, Candyman, I won't hurt her." He smirks as Bentley's eyes narrow. *Fuck.* We walk over to him and he takes my hand.

"It's nice to see you again, Little One." He smiles and I roll my eyes.

"It's nice to see you not holding a knife to my throat this time." I smirk and he shakes his head. *That's fucking weird.*

"You remind me so much of her. This is the type of shit she would do, so I don't blame these guys for coming in here and protecting what is theirs." He says, shaking his head again as he stares at me for a little too long. I nod my head and pull my hand away.

"You are all free to go, run along now before I change my mind." He orders and me and the girls scamper out, trying to get to my car before the boys can catch up. I may have been drunk earlier, but all of that shit sobered me the fuck up, real quick. I open my car door, but before I can climb in, Bentley yells across the parking lot.

"The Den! Now!" I nod and look over at Easton who finally looks at me. I can't get a read on him so I get in the car and start it up. Taking my phone out, I check it, knowing he blew it up. Turning the screen on, I gasp; one hundred and fifty missed calls and a shit ton of text messages. I'm in soooo much fucking trouble. Pulling out of the parking lot, the boys follow us.

"Was it worth it?" I ask, and they both groan.

I take a deep breath and prepare for the shit show that's about to happen the minute we get to The Den. We fucked up big time.

Hopefully, all the yelling will turn into multiple orgasms, or a red fucking ass that will sting for days.

CHAPTER 30

EASTON

After everything that has happened, this fucking bitch turned off her location, again, and then fucking lied to me. If Bentley hadn't said they weren't home, I would have never known.

"Who was that guy?" Bentley asks, and I sigh, I'm getting really sick and tired of lying to him.

"Spade's brother. I met him the other night," is all I say because, it's not a total lie, I'm just omitting some details.

"I've never seen him before." He responds and I nod.

"Listen man, there's some things you don't know, and I need you to just fucking listen." I say and he nods, clenching his jaw. *Fuck, at least he's driving so he can't hit me.*

"A couple of weeks ago, Dylan was attacked by Carter for breaking up with him." I grit and he snaps his head towards me, but I point at him to watch the road. *I don't feel like dying today.*

"I had dropped her off for class and went to see Spade. Hours had gone by and I hadn't heard from her. Long story short, none of you were anywhere to be found, and neither was she. When I finally got her, she had a swollen eye, a bloody lip and she could barely move. She begged me to take her somewhere other than the ER to get looked at, so I took her to Spade's." I say and he slams his hands on the steering wheel.

"You took her to Spade's, really, what the fuck? Why didn't she call me?" He yells, Ace is silent in the back seat, which is odd for him, but I keep going.

"Spade called in his personal doctor and paid for everything. She had a broken rib, which she's still healing from, but once she was settled, I made her tell me who it was and when she did, I lost my shit. Spade punched me in the face a few times and that's how I met Spade's brother, Jameson. Needless to say, I can't find Carter. He fell off the face of the Earth, but I want his blood on my hands. Dylan does too. I told you all from the beginning I didn't trust him." I remind, glancing over at Bentley, whose eyes are wide. "You really underestimate your sister, man." I say, and he shakes his head. I think in his mind, Dylan is this innocent little girl who's been sheltered from this world, meanwhile she's neck deep in it, but I can't say all of that. At least not yet.

"Is it you killing off the guys on the swim team?" He asks and I nod.

"It is. I told you I was handling it." I raise a brow.

"Does Dylan know?" He looks my way and I nod again.

"She helped with Garrett." I laugh and he slams on the brakes.

"What the fuck Eas? I don't want this life for her. Why would you bring her with you?" He yells.

"Man chill. She's fine. She deserved the kill and again, you underestimate her." I smirk.

"Well, I don't fucking like it, but it does explain her behavior tonight with that guy." He says as we continue down the road, almost to The Den.

"I thought it was kind of hot." Ace chimes in and we both narrow our eyes at him. He gives me a smirk, letting me know he sees through my bullshit.

"At this point, all these girls need leashes." I add, ignoring Ace's wiggling eyes. Taking out a cigarette, I light it and inhale deeply. I'm glad my revelation about Carter went better than I had expected but I can't believe she lied to me and let some guy grind on her. Seeing this fuck, with his hands and mouth on what's mine, took me over the edge.

"How are we playing this once we get back?" I ask. I need to get her ass alone.

"I'm not sure, I'm seething right now, but I really want to tie Amy to my bed and make her beg for mercy." He laughs.

"I'll deal with Ava. We have some talking to do anyway." Ace says.

"I guess I'll deal with the Ice Queen?" I add, hopefully, no questions arise, but Ace catches my eye, and he smirks. *Fucker.*

"Is there something going on with you and my sister?" Bentley asks, *Fuck. Fuck. Fuck.*

"Yeah, is there something going on with you and the Ice Queen, Eas?" He says, tilting his head, mocking Bentley.

"Shut the fuck up, Ace. That is not how I sound." Bentley says, pulling into the parking lot right on Dylan's ass. He shuts off the car and hops out. Ace turns to me with a smile on his face.

"You're welcome," he sings and I punch him in the arm. We get out of the car and it seems both Amy and Ava passed out on the ride home. Bentley is already scooping Amy in his arms, kissing her on the forehead and taking her inside. Ace reaches in and grabs Ava, who is smacking him as she climbs out of the car on wobbly legs. She stares at him for a moment before he presses her against the car, cupping her face and kissing her. I smile, watching to see how this plays out as I internally root for Ace to get his girl back. He pulls away as she touches her lips with a gasp, then he hauls her over his shoulder, taking her inside as she pounds on his back. One loud smack is heard before the door fully shuts, leaving me shaking my head. I look over at Dylan who is staring at me.

"Don't give me that look. You fucked up tonight. Now get in my fucking room and don't say a goddamn word." I order and she huffs, slamming the door and stomping inside. Taking a deep breath, I follow, staying right on her ass as she tries to open my door but can't, so I cage her in against it. She leans her forehead against the wood and I inhale her scent, growling as I take my key from my pocket and put it in the knob, unlocking it. "You smell like another man. Get your ass in the shower and clean the filth off of you." She gasps at my harsh words, opening the door and running straight for the shower. I don't care if my words hurt. She's hurt me enough tonight, and I can't concentrate knowing she smells like that dead biker scumbag. I strip from my clothes and boots, put on gray sweats and sit on the couch waiting for her.

A few minutes later, the door to the bathroom swings open as steam bellows out. She walks into the room and stands in front of me. I look up at her gorgeous face and our eyes connect. I can feel the heat radiating off her and the fire in her glare. She drops the towel, revealing her perfect fucking body. I look from her eyes down to her full breasts as her breathing hitches. I reach up and pinch a nipple before sliding my hands down between her thighs. My thumb grazes her swollen clit, and she gasps as I slide a finger into her already soaked cunt. I look up at her, seeing her eyes full of lust and want. "You wet for me, Hellcat? Or for the biker who had his hands all over you?" I spit venomously as she visibly swallows. I slap her clit, causing her to cry out.

"You fucking lied to me," I slap her again, "After everything that just happened, you fucking lie and turn off your location?" I question her, standing up from the couch.

"This shit isn't a game, Dylan. Your safety is what matters most to me. What if we didn't get there in time or what if they would have hurt all three of you? Then what, Dylan? Then fucking what?" She takes a step back as my chest starts to heave. "Answer me!" I yell and she takes another step back, shaking her head.

"I'm sorry Eas. We just wanted a night of fun away from this place." She stammers, and I get right in her face.

"So you lie and concoct a story like two stupid bitches-" I don't even get the rest of the sentence out before she slaps me across the face and I growl, grabbing her by the throat, giving her a squeeze in warning.

"Call me a bitch again, Eas, and watch what happens. God, you're so overbearing, this is why I lied. Because all you do is smother, smother, smo-" I stop her mouth mid sentence, tossing her onto the bed as she yelps. I flip her over, pull my sweats down and bring her hips up just where I need her. I slap her ass hard, leaving a handprint.

"I smother you? I. Smother. You. Guess what, bitch? Smother this." I slam her face into the bed as I line up my cock with her entrance and with one brutal thrust I'm balls deep in her soaked cunt. She tightens around me as I slam into her at a brutal pace. *Fuck, she's so tight.*

I wrap her hair in my fist and pull her head up. She gasps for air, then moans the deeper I thrust.

"That's right, little bitch. Take this dick!" I growl as she continues to tighten around me. I slap her cheeks on each thrust, not giving a fuck how red her ass is getting. She pissed me right the fuck off with her bullshit.

"You're lucky I don't fucking gag you with my cock until you turn purple for being such a stupid fucking bitch." I spit.

"Fuck you, Easton! He had a bigger dick than you. He probably could have made me cum quicker." She growls. I pull out, walk over to my dresser, open the drawer and pull out one of my many hunting knives. She heaves as she glances over her shoulder with narrowed eyes. I twirl the blade in my hand and smile.

"Lay flat on your back, legs and mouth open." I command, and she turns, laying down as I asked. Climbing on the bed between her legs, I sink my cock into her needy little cunt. I take the blade and nick her clit, rubbing the blood around her lips. Trailing the blade up her stomach and over her tits, I nick each nipple and let the blood drip. She moans as I continue to leave cuts on her body. I bring the blade to her face and press it long ways across her lips, letting the sharp metal cut the creases of her mouth.

"Bite the blade. If you speak, it will cut you. So I advise you to shut the fuck up and take it." Her eyes widen as I add a little pressure to the knife, watching as the blood drips from both sides of her mouth.

"Such a good little bitch." I growl, slamming into her over and over again. I toy with her clit until she's a writhing mess beneath me.

"Let this be a lesson, Hellcat. No one will ever make you feel good enough. No one will ever make you cum as hard as I do." I groan as she tightens, biting the blade harder as more blood drips down her mouth.

"This pussy is mine, Hellcat. Fucking mine. You understand me?" I moan as her pussy ripples around me. Tears drip down her eyes as her orgasm hits her hard and fast, but I don't stop, not until she cums again, gushing all over my cock. I pull out and paint her pussy and tits with my cum. I run my fingers through the mess, remove the blade gently from her mouth, and force them down her throat.

"Swallow, like the good little bitch you are." I command, and she swallows with a moan as she gags. I remove them and scoop up the blood and tears from her face, bringing those same fingers to my mouth, licking them clean. She looks up at me as I cup her face.

"I love you, Hellcat. You and only you." I remind her and more tears pour from her eyes.

"I love you too, Eas, I'm so sorry for tonight. I promise not to do that shit again, but I need you to give me some breathing room." She pleads.

"I don't know if I can give you that right now, but I'll try. Just give me some time. I just want you safe baby because I won't survive if something happens to you again." I say as I pull out and lay on top of her, resting my head against her rapidly beating heart. Placing my hands underneath her back, I wrap them up around her shoulders.

"I know Eas, I also need to work on all this, too. As much as you guys have always protected me this is all new to me since we have been together. I'm not used to it fully." She whispers and I sigh because she's right. This is new to both of us and I think, to me more, because I've never been in a relationship and I'm new at navigating all these feelings and emotions.

"Was what I did just now too much for you? I know I'm not perfect, but this is me. Take it or leave it, Hellcat. Now you have seen both parts of me." I confess, squeezing her tighter, hoping it wasn't too much.

"Eas, it was actually fucking hot, even if I was provoking you." She giggles and I look up at her. *She said that shit on purpose? This little bitch.* I tickle her sides and she giggles uncontrollably. *God, I love this girl. Hearing her giggle truly brings me life.* I slide off her and wrap her in my arms, cupping her gorgeous face as I kiss her and keep kissing her until those sexy lips are swollen and bloody.

"I love you Eas. I love you so fucking much." She whispers as tears pour down her face.

"Don't cry D, I don't like it when you cry. I love you so much too, baby." I assure her and she wraps a leg around my waist, reaching down to stroke my already hard cock. She lowers herself onto me and I moan.

"Make love to me, Eas." She whispers and I slowly push into her deeper, pulling her chest closer to mine as I kiss her neck, jaw, and lips. Slowly, she rolls her hips, pulling at the hairs at the back of my neck, never taking our eyes off one another. She kisses my face, biting my jaw as she shivers with every slow thrust I give her. I don't want to stop. I want to live in this moment forever. Being with her like this is something I've never experienced in my life. So much passion and love. Our heavy breathing and moans echo the small space as we both explore one another. I shiver as she claws my back while I continue to fuck her slowly, showing her how much she truly means to me, that nothing and no one, will ever compare to her. It has always been her and it will always be her. She tightens around my cock, drenching it as she ripples around me.

"I love you, Easton." She whines as her orgasm flows through her body. I tighten my hold as I feel that familiar tingle shoot up my spine, my balls tighten and I spill my load deep into her core.

"I love you too Dylan, always and forever, baby." I say breathlessly. We stay connected like this, with her head on my chest, and my chin resting on top of her hair. Light snores fill the room and I take a deep breath, shut my eyes, and drift to sleep with the girl I'm going to marry someday in my arms.

CHAPTER 31

EASTON

I wake up the next morning alone in my bed. Reaching over, I feel the spot next to me is still warm, so she hasn't been up long. Climbing out of bed, I walk into the bathroom and see my girl in the shower. I take a leak and get in with her, wrapping my arms around her waist, and inhaling her scent.

"Well, good morning to you, too." She giggles as I press my hard cock between her cheeks.

"Mmm, good morning it is." I groan, wanting nothing more than to slide my cock into her tight hole.

"One day, I'm going to fuck this ass of yours while my knife handle milks your tight pussy." I moan, getting myself worked up with that image. She turns her face slightly and smirks up at me.

"I might like that." She says, biting back a moan as I roll my thumbs over her hard nipples. She arches her back, clenching her thighs around my length and rocks against me. I shiver as she rubs the tip of my cock against her clit, using my precum to make it slide between her lips easier. I moan, biting at her shoulders and neck as she holds my cock where she wants while rocking faster along my length.

"Fuck, Hellcat. You're so fucking wet, baby." I pant as my dick continues to leak against her clit. I pull at her nipples as her moans get louder the faster she rides along my cock.

"I'm so fucking close, Eas. So fucking close." She whimpers as her body trembles the closer she gets. Her fingers swirl over my tip, causing me to jerk as she rubs my head furiously over her clit. Her thighs clench as her movements become erratic.

"Fuck, baby. You're going to make me cum with you." I groan as she rubs faster, gripping me hard as she screams.

"Fuck, yes, yes. I'm cumming." I feel her clit pulsating against my length as she pulls at my piercing, causing my cock to nut all over her clit. I pull away and spin her around, getting on my knees and shoving my face into her messy pussy, lapping up both of our releases.

"It's too much, Eas. I can't." She exhales on a shattered breath. I stand and grab her face, pinching her cheeks so her mouth opens and I slowly spit our cum onto her waiting tongue. Then I kiss her, reveling in our taste as we both moan and try to come down from our intense orgasms. Pulling back, I smile as she looks at me with a grin.

"If we don't get out of this shower, my cock is never going to go down. He already wants to take you against this wall and feel you shatter around him. Fuck, Hellcat, I can never get enough of you." I confess with a warning. She smiles with mischief in her eyes and jumps up. I catch her easily as she slowly sinks down onto me. We both groan as I fill her.

"I don't think I'll ever get enough of you either, Eas." She exhales as her skin prickles with goosebumps.

"Looks like we have quite the problem here." I laugh as I press her against the wall.

"What are we going to do about it?" She challenges.

This girl is going to be the death of me.

Later that night, and many more orgasms later, we head out for our next kill. I was told to meet at a club named Enthralled. Apparently, George frequents this place a lot. Putting my name on the list got the attention of the owners and I received a call with the details that helped in the end. I didn't tell them why I was killing him, just that it was a must. If they wouldn't have been able to help, I would have had to do it elsewhere, but because Jameson is the owner, and Dylan is his family, he insisted it be done there. We park across the street and get out. I grab her hand and give it a kiss.

"You look ravishing tonight, too bad this pretty dress will be stained with blood." I quip, as a blush crawls up her cheeks.

"You look hot in a suit, baby. You should wear them more often." She winks.

"Not a chance in hell, I'm more of a ripped jeans and white tee kind of guy." I laugh as we cross the street and step up to the security guard.

"Easton Daniels." I say and he opens the door to let us through. Entering this place, we are immediately hit with red and black hues, low lights, soft sensual music and the smell of sex. I look down at her as she takes the place in.

"We should come here one night for some fun." I say, and she smacks my chest, shaking her head.

"Not if my uncle owns this place. That's fucking weird." She retorts as we step up to the bar. I order a beer and she orders a mixed drink. While waiting for our order, we both check the place out. A lot of men of power sit around tables talking as girls dance in cages. A few minutes later, our drinks are placed in front of us. I pay the bartender, giving her an extra tip, and check the time.

"It's time, Hellcat. You ready?" I ask, and she nods. Taking her hand, I lead us towards the back where all the rooms are. Jameson told me room number nine. I turn the knob and enter the room after Dylan, shutting and locking the door. A gasp leaves her lips as we see Jameson getting his dick sucked by George. *Jesus fucking Christ. He could have warned us.* He groans as George gags on his cock. Dylan can't seem to look away and she better not get any ideas. It's one thing to watch her with Hazel, but it's an entirely other thing if she expects me to hook up with a guy. *Ain't fucking happening.* She grabs my hand, squeezing it as she rubs her thighs together. I clear my throat and

Jameson locks eyes with me, a smirk on his face. *Nope. He better get that smirk off his face.*

"Ahh, perfect timing. Sorry for the show, niece." He winks and she laughs.

"Thank God you're not my blood uncle because that would be some shit." She says and I grunt. Jameson doesn't let go of George's head as his eyes go wide looking at us through his peripherals.

"Is this your kill or hers?" He asks, and she steps up.

"It's mine." She says as her eyes are still glued to Jameson controlling George's head on his length. I shake my head and let her do her thing as I lean back against the door trying not to listen to Jameson's moans.

"Come here, Little Creature. Let's see if you're a good listener like your Uncle Spade. Shall we?" He summons, and she walks over to him waiting for her next instructions.

"Suck harder, Little Pig. You asked for this. Now do it correctly." He growls at George and looks up at Dylan with a smile.

"Some men can't suck dick for shit. This is one of them." He laughs before pointing over to the bedside table.

"See the scalpel over there? Go get it and bring it over here." He orders as he thrusts harder down

George's throat. Dylan does as she's told eagerly and I laugh. *She's such a good girl.*

"This may be weird to you, but it's not to me. People are just bodies. Unless they are the ones I love, they mean nothing to me. They all have the same worthless face; man or woman, it doesn't matter. I want you to pull his head back by his hair at an angle without letting my dick fall. If it does, you fail and I get to kill him." He instructs, and she nods, pulling George's head back slowly along his length. My dick should not be getting hard watching this, but anything Dylan does gets me aroused. She stops just as the edge of his head starts to show. *Jesus, this guy is huge, and thick as fuck. Way to make another man feel like the tiniest person in the room.*

"Good girl, Little Creature." He praises, causing me to growl, and he looks over at me.

"You shut up or you'll be on your knees next." He threatens, and I swallow hard. *Fucking psycho.*

"Now, as I was saying before I was so rudely interrupted, I want you to hold his nose–" He goes to say, but George starts to struggle and head butts Dylan in the stomach, causing Jameson's cock to fall from his mouth. He growls, tucking himself away as George tries to stand but Dylan kicks him in the back, causing him to fall on his face. I walk over and step on his spine.

"Thank you, Easton. This little pig has been a bad boy. Dylan, straddle his shoulders and lift his head back towards you." Jameson instructs. She does as she's told.

"Keep pulling until you hear the first crack." He tells her and she pulls harder, moving back towards me the more she pulls. George screams and Jameson laughs sinisterly as we both feel the first pop in his neck.

"Perfect, now reach over and feel where his Adams Apple is with your fingers, push it, make sure it's the right place." He tells her. I watch as she reaches around, finding the spot with ease causing him to choke a bit. She looks up at Jameson, waiting for her next command.

"Take the scalpel and slice right below it with one clean slice, just make sure you apply enough pressure to cut through the flesh and muscle to hit the artery. You will feel a pop when you hit it. You should pre-pare yourself for the sprayback as well." He informs. She looks up at me with a smile and I blow her a kiss as she takes the scalpel and does exactly what Jameson instructed her to do. Blood ricochets off the floor, splattering up at us, but not as bad as I expected. George gurgles as he chokes on his own blood. She lets his head go as it smashes against the marble floor. I step off his spine, putting my hand out for her as his body begins to tremble and seize. Jameson claps like a psycho.

"Well done, Little Creature, I'm so proud of you." He smiles, and she gives a little curtsy. I just shake my head.

"You crazy kids get out of here. This was fun, we should do it again some time." He laughs, and we bid our goodbye. We leave the room and head straight out the doors to the parking lot. Dylan laughs as we walk to the car.

"My uncle is nuts. That was absolutely insane! I fucking hate that my mom kept me and Benny from all the fun our entire life." She says, laughing as she gets into the car. I get in after her, light a cigarette, and continue shaking my fucking head at the whole experience.

Three down, two more to go.

The next morning, I'm jolted awake by pounding on my fucking door. I climb out of bed and swing it open. Bentley rears back and punches me in the jaw, my face snapping on impact as I stumble back into my room. Righting myself, he throws his phone, hitting me in the chest with it. I catch it before it falls to the ground as I rub my aching jaw. "What the fuck, Bentley?" I growl and his eyes narrow at me.

"Be grateful that's all you got so far. Fucking press play." He spits venomously. I press play seeing a compilation of all the moments me and Dylan had together: her bedroom, the window, my car, even my bike. Then it switches to the academy. The cameraman zooms in as Dylan lies on the bed while I touch her with the sex toy, making her cum with the sac over her head, then punching her in the face and raping her. I look up as my heart drops when my eyes connect with his.

"Listen, let me expl–" I don't get the chance to finish before he lays punch after punch, knocking me to the ground so hard that my knees crack on impact. Dylan screams in the background as Bentley pushes my head back by my hair and continues to punch me. I don't fight back. I take it. I take hit after hit, knowing I deserve it. I deserve all his anger.

"You fucking lied to me, and you lied to her. How the fuck could you do that? I trusted you!" He spits.

"Just let me explain." I rasp, but he doesn't let up. His rage has taken over logic and there's no stopping him when it gets to this point. He's my best fucking friend. I can predict his every move, but I do nothing as he continues his attacks.

"Fight back, you pussy!" He yells in my face, but I won't. This was inevitable. I always knew this day would come. I just didn't think it would be like this. I wanted to tell her myself.

"Benny, stop. You're going to fucking kill him! Stop. Stop. Stop!" She screams. He hits me once more and my head lulls to the side. He chucks his phone at her and my heart drops when she looks at the screen and gasps, covering her mouth with her hand as tears begin to stream down her face; the face I'll never get to touch again. Her eyes collide with mine and a tear leaves my own.

"You were there? You knew this whole time and never told me?!" She yells, but I shake my head.

"Dylan I-I," I stammer, trying to get the words out, but the look of disgust on her face breaks my heart into pieces. Her eyes scream at me with hurt and betrayal. I just need a second for her to listen to me. I just want to hold her and tell her everything.

"No, fuck you! How could you do that to me? After everything... how–" she screams as tears continue to pour down her face. She wraps her body tight in the blanket for comfort. Bentley punches me again and again as blood leaks down my nose and mouth. I can barely see anyone in the room.

"Take Dylan out of here." Bentley orders and Ace comes in to take her away.

"Please, let me explain. Please don't fucking leave! Just let me explain." I roar with the last ounce of energy I have, but she shakes her head, walking up to me.

"The time to explain has come and gone. You're fucking dead to me." She spits in my face and lets Ace lead her from the room. The others enter and surround me. I take a deep breath before they do what they do best. I block out the pain and let all the stolen moments I had with Dylan flood my mind. That's what they are. All the moments I stole from her. I don't feel the kick to the jaw or the punch to my stomach, cracking a rib. I just keep seeing her face, wishing that I would have come clean when I had the chance. Darkness starts to take over as her face fades away and the last thing I spew from my lips before a blast to the head knocks me out is, "I'm sorry, Hellcat."

CHAPTER 32
DETECTIVE ELEANA ST. JAMES

We got a call from some fisherman who found a head, and now I'm standing a few feet away from the cursed lake at the old academy, where divers pull out a beheaded body. April took the head to the CSI forensics department to see if we can get an identity. Lately, evidence has been tampered with, documents have gone missing and we are now under investigation.

There have been so many murders lately that we aren't even sure how many killers we are actually dealing with. Some are definitely a copycat of The Carver, but others look like The Carver himself. And now there's this new one. None of it makes sense though, none of it connects, so we are at a standstill. The only slight connection is that the last two bodies were boys from the swim team at Stonedge University.

Other than that, we keep hitting a dead end. Looking at the body, everything is intact, other than the places the fish have started to eat. So this person was beheaded and thrown in the lake. That's it? There's no sign of where this happened.

The lake is huge. This could take weeks to find any sort of evidence. I'm really at my wits-end with trying to figure this shit out. I take my phone out as I walk up the hill and shoot April a quick text to let her know I'm heading home.

It's not a long drive home, but I spend it thinking about where to go with these cases. I've never been one to give up, but we have no leads, just ghosts walking the streets and getting away with murder. The house is dark which means neither of my kids are home. They've grown up and spend more time out of the house than actually in it. I think it's time to tell April who I am. I want to ask her to marry me, but she needs to know the secrets I hold, and if she can accept me for who I truly am, then I want to make her my wife. It's time to be happy. I deserve happiness and to stop all this hiding.

When I make it home and up the steps, I key in the code, shut the door, lock it behind me and head straight for the shower, leaving my badge, belt and holstered gun on the table in the foyer. As I climb the stairs to my room, I start to unbutton my shirt and take off the rest of my clothes once I walk into the bathroom and turn the shower on.

Standing under the cascading water and washing the day off, I think about all of the scenarios that could happen when I tell April my story. What if she thinks less of me? At that thought, I turn the water off and grab a towel before doing my nighttime skincare and brush out my short hair, that's when I notice April standing in the doorway staring at me.

"Couldn't wait for me to get here?" She smirks, and I shake my head.

"Not tonight. I have to tell you something before I ask a certain question, but I need you to keep an open mind." I plead, as her brows furrow.

"Of course, Ele. What's wrong?" She asks, grabbing my hand and leading me over to my bed. I sit down, take a deep breath, and cup her face.

"I'm so scared to tell you because I don't want to lose you, so please, Love, please keep an open mind." I beg and she squeezes my hand.

"I promise Ele. You can trust me. Just spill it." She encourages as I take another deep breath.

"I'm not who I say I am, I mean, my real name isn't Eleana St. James." I confess, and she nods.

"Well, what's your real name?" She asks. This is it. She will either stay or run.

"Isabel Rodriguez." I confess, and her eyes go wide. I look down because I don't want to see the disappointment cross her face.

"*The* Isabel Rodriguez, as in The Rodriguez Cartel's long-lost daughter?" She asks and I nod slowly.

"I need your words, Ele." She orders and I look up at her.

"Yes, I'm the long-lost daughter of 'El Hefe', The Cartel leader is my younger brother Reid, but you know him as Spade," I say and she nods again, letting go of my hand and stands, pacing the room rubbing her thumbs over her temples.

"Wait, so you faked your death? How the fuck did you get into the Academy, let alone become a detective?" She asks, stunned as the information is finally starting to seep into her head.

"I didn't fake shit, that was all my father. I ran with Bentley and Dylan when he was four, with the help of my brother and his girlfriend. They gave me a new identity and enough money to start my own life." I say, covering my face with my hands.

"If you didn't fake your death, why did you run?" She interrogates. I deserve it, she's been sleeping with the enemy, so to speak.

"I've never spoken a word of this to anyone, not even my brother, but I need to start from the beginning." I say and she looks at me , sitting back down next to me.

"Women in my family are not wanted. We only live to bear children, specifically male heirs. The husband gets to decide how many you will bear, and once the youngest turns thirteen, you are strung up like cattle and killed by your own flesh and blood." I grit as her brows hit the top of her head.

"So Bentley would've had to kill you when he turned thirteen?" She asks as a tear falls from her eye and I drop my head, continuing.

"The boys then go through training to become ruthless killers. It's a sick and depraved cycle. So being that I'm attracted to the same sex, my father said I was an abomination and needed to fulfill the family's legacy by being impregnated by a man of power and produce an heir. Except I refused, and the more I said no, the more he used me as a sex slave for his friends. After the first time, I got on the pill, which I regret every fucking day," I say, taking a deep breath.

"Keep going baby, I'm listening." She says, taking my hand, encouraging me to continue.

"It didn't take long for him to find out. He forced me to stop taking it. He replaced them with pills to help me get pregnant easier. One night, he had a man come over and rape me but I cut his dick off. As my punishment, my own father held a gun to my head and raped me, repeatedly, for hours. Just when I thought he was finished, he came for more. I was left tied to a bed for days as he came in almost every hour to drop his seed into me, and a month later, I was pregnant with Bentley. I kept my pregnancy a secret from everyone but him because he would keep coming until a test came back positive, then he left me be." I sob as tears run down my face. April hugs me as I cry into her chest.

"I tried to get an abortion, but everyone turned me away. In this world, his reach knows no bounds. A few weeks after Benny was born, I wasn't even fully healed when he sent another man to rape me. I don't know who the man was, but that's how Dylan was conceived. After that, I ran. I tried to stay hidden for as long as possible, but he found me four years later and I went with him willingly, trying to come up with a better plan of escaping and once he went away for business, I called my brother, told him that I needed to run to keep Benny and Dylan safe from our father and he came through. I'm so thankful for Reid and I owe him my life. It hurts that my kids don't know their uncle and how amazing he is. And I'm so sorry I lied to you, but I need you to understand that I've never repeated this story to anyone, it was just easier to act like it never happened rather than deal with it head on." I plead and she nods.

"I understand. That's a lot of trauma for one person to hold all these years." She says, running her hand up and down my back.

"It is, and I'm done with the secrets, but most of all, I'm done hiding us. If you still want me." I say, cupping her face as she leans into my touch.

"I'm not going anywhere, babe. I'm here and I love you. Always." She whispers and I kiss her sweet lips. She deepens the kiss, unwrapping my towel, pushing me back onto the bed. She pulls away and slides to the floor between my legs.

"Let me show you how much I love you." She breathes, licking my clit. I moan and writhe against her face as she eats my pussy until I cum all over her face. She stands as I sit up, pulling her by her belt towards me.

"Kiss me." I beg as she bends down, placing her lips against mine as I lick my cum from her mouth.

"Fuck, I taste good. But you taste better." I smirk. I pull her onto the bed and stand, walking over to my dresser. I grab the small box from my top drawer, hiding it behind my back. I turn to face her as she sheds her clothes and is laying against my pillows in nothing but a G-string. I crawl up the bed between her legs and suck the silk fabric into my mouth. She whimpers as I bite her clit.

"I have a question, Love." I say, sliding the soaked silk to the side.

"Mmm, anything, Ele." She pants while I lick, suck and bite her lips and clit, making her tremble under my touch.

"Will you be my wife?" I ask, setting the box on her belly. She gasps as I suck her clit, flicking it repeatedly as her legs shake around me.

"Yes, yes, yes," she screams as I bite hard on her clit and slam two fingers into her core.

"I didn't quite get that. Will you be my wife?" I ask again, finger fucking her hard and deep as I rapidly lick her clit.

"Yes, fuck yes, I'll be your wife. Fuck, I'm cumming!" She screams as she soaks my hand and the bed, gushing her release. I remove my fingers, kissing her clit as I open the box.

"Are you sure?" I say with a raised brow. She sits up and licks my chin before grabbing the ring and sliding it on her finger.

"Yes, I'm sure. I fucking love you. Now go get that big dick in your drawer and fuck me like I'm your wife." She orders.

And I do just that. Now to tell the kids. Fuck.

CHAPTER 33

DYLAN

Ace leads me out of the room and I head straight for my car. *Fuck this.* "Dylan, wait!" He yells and I spin on him with narrowed eyes.

"Not now! Just leave me the fuck alone!" I spit as he takes his shirt off, throwing it at me. I catch it with ease, not realizing I was still wrapped in Easton's blanket. Nodding, I shake it off me, letting it hit the dirt as I shove my head in the shirt and climb into the car, wanting to get the fuck away from it all as fast as I can. *I'm humiliated, hurt, and pissed the fuck off.*

Peeling out in the mud, I get on the highway, pounding my fists against the steering wheel. *How could I have been so stupid?* I let out a blood-curdling scream as I speed through the streets. How could he? Why? Why would he do that to me? I feel so fucking disgusted. I let him touch me in ways no other man has touched me before. He violated me. He betrayed my trust. There's no coming back from this!

Tears stream down my face as I pull into my empty driveway. I lay my head back and let the tears flow freely. All the promises, the I love you's, were for nothing! Fucking nothing! I should have never given him my heart. I should have never gone to The Den the night I beat Bianca's ass! I should have just let her play him! Fuck, I'm so fucking stupid!

Wiping my tears away, I reach over to the glove box and open it to grab my clutch and phone. I slam it shut and get out of the car. Lightning cracks the moment I step out and slam my car door shut. Rain begins to fall from the sky, getting heavier with every step I take.

Opening the back gate, I toss my phone inside my clutch and throw it onto the covered porch, and walk deeper into the yard. I look up at the sky and let the rain lick my face as I sink to my knees and fall back onto the grass. I stay this way as thunder rumbles in the distance, getting louder the closer it gets.

It's not until lightning strikes the tree in the next yard, causing the branch to break and collapse, that I pick myself up and go into the house soaked, grabbing my clutch along the way. I move robotically as I strip in the laundry room, throwing Ace's shirt in the wash along with my panties, grab a bottle of water from the fridge, and head up to my room for a shower.

After berating myself some more, I pull out some sweats, a hoodie, and take some pain pills. As I climb into bed, I plug in my phone and scroll to Easton's name to block him before putting it on silent. *I never want to speak to him again.* A few texts come through from the girls, but I don't have the energy to deal with their questions, so I roll over and wait for the pills to kick in as tears pour from my eyes onto the pillows.

Taking a deep breath, I try not to think about anything other than the high from the pills, but Easton's battered face and the tears that dropped from his swollen eye as he begged me to let him explain, keeps haunting my thoughts.

Something is telling me I should have stopped and listened, but the proof is in the video. He forced me to cum when he violated my body with that sex toy. He made me feel good in that moment, when I fucking needed him the most, when I fantasized it was him doing all those things to make the situation less traumatic, and it was.

Then he punched me in the face, knocking me out. I don't remember him actually fucking me. I would know how he felt, how he smelled, but I saw it with my own eyes. Him rutting into me like a madman as the others in the room laughed. I just don't understand how he could humiliate me like that. How he could go against Fatal and let these monsters touch me, hurt me, fucking rape me!

Something doesn't add up. He always said he would never hurt me, he would always protect me, but after seeing that video, he's a liar. He didn't fucking protect me. He allowed it to happen, and that hurts the most. I laid there helplessly, wanting to fight back, but the drug wouldn't let me and you would think Easton, the man who confessed his love for me, would have tried to help me but he didn't. He went along with it and then made a fool out of me ever since.

I roll over facing the window and watch the rain pelt against the glass as my eyes get heavy and a dreamless sleep takes over.

Hours later, I wake up to a light shining in my window as nightfall bleeds the sky. I get up to shut my blinds and I freeze with a gasp as I see Easton beaten, covered in blood, struggling to get his clothes off. My heart breaks even more as I take in his appearance, then his battered eyes connect with mine and my hand covers my mouth. He's almost unrecognizable as he reaches a hand out to me, mouthing 'I'm so sorry' and I jump back, shutting the blinds.

Scrambling back to my bed, I don't know what to think. I've never seen him hurt like that. He's always so strong and resilient. My heart yearns to go to him, but my brain is telling me he deserved it, but fuck. I can't help but still fucking love him. And seeing him like that is destroying me, but I can't, I won't. He deserves to suffer just like I did. He's a liar and the ultimate manipulator. *Fuck this.* I reach for my phone and my clutch, grabbing another pill, washing it down with water as I text my uncle.

> **Me: Hey, can you have Hazel text me? I forgot to get her number when I was there.**

> **Spade: No problem, kiddo. She's texting you now. How's your rib doing?**

> **Me:** Thanks you're the best. The rib has seen better days, but it's fine. Nothing I can't handle.

> **Spade:** Good, I'm glad to hear it. Talk soon.

> **Me:** XOXO.

I pull open the next thread to Hazel.

> **Hazel:** Well, well, Skittle Pop. What can I do for you?

> **Me:** Wanna hang out?

> **Hazel:** Really?

> **Me:** Yea, unless you're busy, then I'll just go to bed.

> **Hazel:** Nonsense, I'll send you my address. Text me when you get here.

Me: Okay, see you soon.

She sends me her address and I climb out of bed, getting dressed in black leggings and a tank top. I grab all the things I need and head out. Getting into my car, I put the address into my GPS and it shows a thirty-five minute drive to her.

Maybe hanging out with Hazel will make me forget about today. Forget about how my heart is completely destroyed and there's nothing left but ashes.

Only one could hope.

CHAPTER 34

EASTON

Waking up in a cold sweat, I can't fucking breathe. My entire body aches from the beating I received. It was only hours ago that they dumped me on my doorstep with instructions to stay away from Dylan and to keep my mouth shut unless I wanted to die. Business will still be as usual, but that's as far as it goes. If I step out of line, they will leak this to Spade and I will be done for. There's no running from this or The Cartel.

Seeing Dylan in the window damn near killed me. I wanted to go to her and explain everything, but I couldn't even stand long enough, let alone take a breath to say a word. I should have told her, should have done so many things differently, but I was terrified and look where that got me.;shunned and hated by the ones I care about most. I lost the girl and my best friends who are more like brothers to me.

What hurts the most is none of them let me explain. Not a single one of them asked questions. The video was enough evidence to crucify me. I guess that says a lot about them and what they truly think about me. Have they always thought I was some loose cannon that would kill anything and anyone in sight? That I'm some kind of predator that goes around raping girls and video taping it for fun? All I've done over the years is train, kill, and be the best at what I'm paid to do.

Bentley has always told me, not the others, to protect his sister. When did that change? When did I lose his trust? I know the last couple of months we drifted a bit because I was keeping secrets and so far up Dylan's ass, but I have never given him a reason to think I was disloyal to him or to Fatal.

We still never figured out who set Bianca free from the basement. We keep getting hit from all sides. Almost like all of this is one huge distraction or an inner take down to something bigger coming. Am I the only one who sees what's happening here?

I reach over and growl at the stabbing pain running up my left side as I grind my teeth so hard to get my phone. I can't even take a breath without wanting to scream bloody murder. *Where are my pills? I need something to take the edge off.* I'm all about suffering the consequences of my actions but, fuck, this hurts so bad. Finally, after taking ninety million quick breaths just to get the phone, I pull up the thread with the guys. I don't fucking care if they hate me. If I'm right, and something bigger is happening, then they just left themselves wide open with me being down.

> **Me: I don't care how you all feel about me right now, but you need to put The Den on lock-down.**

> **Kingston: Too late.**

> **Ace: Why would we listen to you? Are you the rat?**

> **Bentley: I guess the beating didn't do you any good.**

> **Antonio: Enough you guys!**

Me: What do you mean too late?
And fuck you Ace, you know exactly where I was and what I
was doing the night we came
back from getting the job done.
So don't sit there and play
Mr. Innocent. HA. Maybe if you
didn't hit like a bitch Bentley,
the beating would have done
more damage.

Kingston: It doesn't matter,
you cannot be trusted anymore.

Me: Me? I can't be trusted.
Clearly someone let Bianca
out! Did any of you figure out
who that was? No. Don't sit
there and place blame solely on
me. None of you let me explain,
so fuck all of you. Some fucking
team you are.

Bentley: I'll show you a bitch. You're done!

Me: You are all blinded by the fucking video and not seeing what is happening here. Someone is purposely moving in and taking us out from within. Open your fucking eyes. Secure our shit before we all end up dead.

Kingston: We already did. That's all you need to know.

Me: So I should expect an ambush? You're all sitting ducks. We may all have our own skill set, but we work as a team. That's what we have always been, and they took out the silent killer, leaving you all wide open for the taking.

Bentley: We don't need you. We will be fine on our own.

Antonio: I'm sorry, but I agree with Eas. That video was sent anonymously at the perfect time. We were so busy worrying about him and Dylan that we left everything and everyone else unprotected. Amy was almost taken at the gas station. If it wasn't for that biker guy being there, she would be gone.

Bentley: Shut up Antonio. For all we know, he's working with the enemy. We all saw the video.

Me: You're a fucking idiot, Bentley. I'm done with this conversation. You don't want to let me explain? Fine, that's on you.

Bentley: There's nothing to explain. Everything we need is in the video.

Me: Whatever you say, man.

Kingston: I want to hear it.

Antonio: So do I, we may be a team but you don't speak for all of us Bent.

Bentley: I'm the leader. What I say, goes.

Antonio: Well, if that's the case. Fuck this.

Kingston: Same. This is not trial and execution. He has the right to explain. We are more than just a team. We've known each other our entire lives and that's been for a reason. We don't turn our backs on one another.

Me: It's fine, you guys. He's the leader. Follow what he wants. This should've never happened to begin with. You beat the shit out of me without thinking. We just blindly follow the leader into damnation and where did it get all of us?

Ace: This is bullshit! You hurt her, you raped her and you lied. What is there to explain? We saw it.

Me: You, out of all people, should know the answer to that. Think about it. Dumbass.

Bentley: Fuck this. It's him or me! Choose.

Me: Wow. You really are something else. I'm out. This was pointless.

Kingston: I'm not choosing shit. Everyone needs to cool down.

Antonio: I'm out.

Antonio Roselli has left the chat.

Me: You are all letting whoever is responsible for this win. I'm out! This is pointless.

Kingston Marks has left the chat.

Sighing, I grit my teeth, clenching my jaw so tightly as I roll out of my bed, dropping onto the floor, trying not to scream from the pain in my knees, neck, back, and ribs. Wrapping my arm around my middle hoping it would relieve some of the stabbing pain but it doesn't. I let go, gripping onto my mattress for support, trying to lift myself from the floor. I finally stand on wobbly legs and make it to the bathroom.

Turning the shower on, I let the water pelt against my bruised skin. I wash my body to the best of my ability without fucking screaming in absolute agony.

I need my fucking pain pills. I step out of the shower and wrap myself with a towel as I take in my appearance in the mirror. My face is all sorts of fucked up. The swelling in my eyes is going down slightly but not by much. I take a slow deep breath and instantly grab onto the sink. *Fuck, this hurts.*

Grabbing the cup from my vanity, I fill it with water and go to my desk, removing a few pills from the drawer. I take a sip and pop the pills into my mouth, swallowing them down. I stand in front of the window, looking at her blinds, wishing she didn't block me out.

As I wait for the pills to kick in before I can get dressed, I pull up the message thread with her and scroll up to the night of her rape, screen shotting the conversation as proof for later. To show I was lured out to the academy that this wasn't a plan I had any part of. Scrolling back down, I hover over the picture she sent me in nothing but a thong and my racing jacket. My dick twitches under the towel at the sight of her. *I need to get her back.* I just need her to let me explain.

> **Me: Hellcat, I don't deserve your forgiveness. I hurt you and betrayed your trust. You probably hate me, and never**

want to speak to me again, but you deserve to know the truth. All of it. The night you were taken, I was waiting for you to show up. Hours went by and you never showed. I stepped outside to text you in which you replied, luring me to the academy with your usual games. I didn't think anything was amiss other than you calling me big boy. Once I arrived, I was sent a video of them beating you and I ran into that academy completely blind, not knowing where you were, but knew that you were hurt.

Me: Once I reached the floor you were on, they held a gun to my head, beat the shit out of me, knocked me out and when I woke up, you were tied to a bed with a sac on your head. They forced me to do those things to you. They held the gun to my head, calling the shots. I didn't know they would take it as far as they did, so I knocked you out once they ordered me to rape you. I didn't want you to feel me. I didn't want you to experience our first time together like that. I would never hurt you. All I was trying to do was protect you from what little that I could. They ripped me from you and zip tied me to a chair and made me watch each and every one of them touch what didn't belong to them.

Me: You woke up at one point fighting back and I was so proud of you. I wanted to be set free so badly so we could take them down together, but you kept screaming and they couldn't have that, so they drugged you again and then drugged me. I woke up in my car and immediately tried to find you. Bentley had texted me as I pulled into my driveway, letting me know you were home and had been all night, and that's when I texted you and let you lie to me. I tried to come clean so many times, but I was terrified of losing you. And now look where that got me. You're gone and I'll never get to hold you again.

Me: I'm sorry Dylan. I'm so fucking sorry that I'm a coward and never told you. I don't know what else to say other than I'm so fucking sorry and I love you. I'll never stop fucking loving you. Now you know the truth, whether or not you believe me is up to you.

Me: I will leave you to live your life in peace and hope you heal from all of this. I wish you nothing but the best and know there will never be another love for me. You were it, until my dying breath. I love you now, forever and always. -Easton

I hit send and wipe the tears from my eyes. I've never cried over a girl before. Matter of fact, I don't ever fucking cry, but this, this hits emotions I didn't know I possessed. Taking a deep breath, the meds finally kick in. I get dressed and lay back down, shutting my eyes for a bit, hoping that one day she will forgive me, even if it is too late.

A few days go by and everyone has been radio silent. I keep taking the pills to function and adding a bottle of vodka with it. Tomorrow is race night with The Midnight Rider and some clowns from the new crew that rolled into town not too long ago. I haven't left the house other than to attend classes. I've watched Dylan come and go from my window and it's killing me that she won't even look up at me, nor has she unblocked me. She still doesn't know the truth, and it's starting to really piss me the fuck off.

Needing to clear my head, I take my bike out for a ride and gas up before tomorrow's race. One thing I've noticed on my drive is someone following me. At first, I didn't think anything of it until I purposely took us in a huge circle leading to the gas station. Shutting the bike off, I remove my helmet, heading inside, I ask the attendant for the key to the restroom to take a leak.

Before I leave the bathroom, I check for my knives just in case I need to protect myself from whoever it is following me. Feeling better knowing I'm armed, I grab a drink and snack, paying for them along with the gas for my bike. I notice how dead this usually busy gas station is. *Something isn't right.* I nod a thanks to the attendant and step outside to a gun being cocked and pressed harshly against my temple.

"Walk to the truck and get in." He says and I nod, knowing this is the end of the road for me. Taking out my phone as I walk to the truck, I send one last message, knowing damn well she will never get it, but needing to send it anyway.

> **Me: I love you until my last dying breath.**

Bang, bang...

CHAPTER 35

DYLAN

It's been a week since everything went down with 'He who shall not ever be named'. I was supposed to race the guys and ended up not showing which led them to running their fucking mouths about me, so I'm going to have to suck it up and make an appearance soon. I've been spending a lot of my time with Hazel when I'm not in class or in my bed crying. I'm a glutton for punishment, so late at night I'll peek through the blinds to get a glimpse of him. He's been drinking a lot lately. The other night, I watched him throw an entire bottle of liquor against his bedroom wall.

As much as I shouldn't care, I still do. I don't know if time will heal all wounds, but I dream about him nightly and wake up horny as fuck with my hands between my legs. I haven't spoken to my brother since it all went down. I'm too embarrassed and ashamed to face him. I've been in contact with the girls a few nights ago, but something happened with Amy and she has been quiet ever since. Ava has been with her sugar daddy, which I thought, or maybe I hoped, would have ended with how everything went down at the bar and the kiss she shared with Ace, but I was wrong. Everything has changed in such a short amount of time. The only person from Fatal who I've seen is Ace and he makes a point of talking to me to make sure I'm okay.

Sighing, I get out of my car and walk up Hazel's driveway. Her and my other cousins all live together in a house that has been in their family for generations. It's an old scary looking Victorian-style home, but once you walk inside, it's fucking gorgeous. There's three stories and an indoor pool with a theater room. It's so fucking cool. I guess when your parents are one of the most powerful criminal syndicates on the East coast, this is the type of luxurious life you live.

As I reach to ring the bell, the door swings open and Prince greets me with a huge smile on his face, his dark hair wild as ever and those big green eyes sparkling in the sunlight. The only indication that he's Spade's biological son is the smile, other than that he looks identical to Aunt Jade.

"You gonna stand there like a scared little doe, or you coming in? Hazel is waiting for you in the pool." He smirks, and I shake my head. Prince is the type of guy that will give you the shirt off his back if you need it. He's so fucking caring and hates to see a girl cry. I learned that the first time I came here crying. I wouldn't tell him whose fault it was, no matter how much he tried to con me. He steps aside so I can walk in. He shuts the door behind me and goes back to the couch, picking up the controller and putting his headset on, yelling into the mic. I laugh as I pass him and climb the stairs to the pool room.

I open the door and am instantly hit with hot air and the scent of weed. Hazel is standing in the shallow end smoking a joint, wearing a black bikini, with her hair flowing down her back. It's absolutely maddening at how attracted I am to her. We haven't hooked up past kissing since that night at the warehouse, not for the lack of trying, but we seem to always get interrupted. I walk over to her and she smirks as I take her in. It seems she added another tattoo to her body. I see a peek of roses on the top of her thigh but the water blurs the rest.

"Hey my Little Pet. How was your day?" She asks, taking a hit of the joint.

"Boring as usual, how was yours?" I reply, taking my shoes off and sitting on the edge, sinking my feet into the cool water. I throw my head back and moan as I look up at the sun beating down through the ceiling window. I've never seen a pool room have nothing but windows including the entire ceiling. What's even cooler, is you can be in here naked, and no one can see in from the outside. It's mirrored.

The first time I was here, she took me on a tour of the grounds, including the cemetery beyond the fence. I didn't ask questions when she picked roses from different vines as we walked and laid them down on a few graves. On our way back up the hill, she stopped at a tree that had three names carved into the bark, little stone paw prints and dog statues. Each one had a different color collar with their names engraved. It was so freaking cute but sad once she told me the story of her mom having three Dobermans known as Triple A. Auggie, Apollo and Atticus, were killed by the Russians a long time ago.

Apparently, Uncle Spade is still not over it after all this time. I've never had a pet, so I can't sympathize with how it would feel. Smoke being blown in my face takes me out of the memory as Hazel stands in front of me, sliding her hands up my legs to my knees, opening my thighs to step between them. My eyes collide with hers and I'm stuck in a trance with her. She tilts her head to the side and smirks.

"Open." She commands. I open as she takes a deep hit of the joint and blows it into my waiting mouth, licking my bottom lip. I inhale, holding it as I grab her chin, pulling her closer and releasing the smoke back to her. She groans as I suck her bottom lip, flicking it with my tongue. She runs her hands up my outer thighs, gripping the top of my shorts. I lift as she pulls them off without getting them drenched in the water and tosses them behind me.

She takes another hit off the joint, placing her lips gently against mine as I suck the air from her lungs. Her tongue caresses mine in a slow, seductive dance for dominance as we both deepen the kiss. Her hands slide between my legs, toying with my clit over my thong as I pinch her hard nipples. I groan into her mouth when she slides the soaked cotton to the side and sinks two fingers into my soaked pussy. She pulls away, taking another hit as she watches her fingers slide in and out of my hole. The more she watches, the wetter I get.

"So responsive, Skittle Pop." She moans as I tighten around her. She removes her fingers and I growl.

"Tsk, tsk, Little Pet. You get what I give you without complaint. Now shut up and move closer to the edge." She commands, and I inch forward, leaning back on my elbows. She raises one leg onto the edge, opening my thighs wider for better access as she takes another hit off the joint, spreading my lips and exhaling on my aching clit, rubbing her thumb up and down slowly, watching as it pulsates from her touch.

Goosebumps litter my skin as she takes one last deep hit off the joint, blowing the smoke on my clit again and sucking it into her mouth. My back arches as I try to bite back a moan, sliding her black hair to the side so I can get a better view. The need to see everything she does to me, makes me want her even more. She sucks my clit so hard as she brings the still lit joint to the bottom of my thigh, so close to my entrance and presses it into my skin as her other fingers sink into me while flicking my clit with the tip of her tongue. I cry out from the burn but revel in the pleasure she's inflicting, causing me to ride her fingers as they pump in and out of me. I dig my nails into her hair, causing her to moan as I pull her closer, wanting to ride her face until I cum, but she pulls away with a grin.

"Let's go. I want you in my bed." She orders and I try to stand on shaky legs as she climbs from the pool, handing me a towel and picking up my shorts from the ground. I push my thong back into place and wrap my bottom half with the towel, following her from the pool house. Her room is only down the hall from where we were. Once inside, she shuts the door and presses me against it. I groan as she lifts my tank over my head and sucks a nipple into her mouth.

"No bra? Smart girl." She praises, taking turns biting each nipple. I reach behind her, untying the top strings, pulling down the triangle cups, squeezing both her tits in my hands, pinching her hard nipples. She moans as I pull her closer to me, gripping her hips tight as she flicks my nipples relentlessly. I slide my hand into her bottoms and rub her clit hard and fast, causing her to growl.

She stands with hooded eyes, kissing me hard, biting my lips, sucking my tongue as I continue to rub her clit faster. Her hands grip my ass so fucking hard, spreading my cheeks wide as her nails skim both of my aching holes. *Fuck, this girl.* She pulls away and I lick my fingers, loving the way she tastes. I step into her space, but she takes a step back.

"I've never eaten pussy before, but your taste has me begging for more." I smirk as her breath hitches at my dirty words. I take another step and push her onto the bed, untying both strings from each side of her hips, removing the fabric from where I want to be.

She leans back onto her elbows as I sink to my knees, running my tongue along her inner thigh. Her body quakes under my touch as I reach her lips, sucking them into my mouth. I release them with a pop and lick her from cunt to clit, moaning at the taste of her.

"You're so fucking wet." I groan, sinking a finger into her tight entrance. Her thighs shake as I milk her walls slowly and flick her clit repeatedly. I pick up my pace as she begins to writhe beneath me. I write the abc's with my tongue, causing her to cry out and shake uncontrollably.

"If you don't let me cum, I'm going to cut that pretty body up." She threatens and I laugh, flattening my tongue against her clit and she pulsates, gushing down my wrist as she screams through her orgasm. I pull back, licking up the mess she made, but she stops me.

"For someone who's never eaten pussy before, you sure as fuck knew what you were doing." She smirks, sitting up.

"Get on the bed on all fours." She commands, climbing from the bed and walking over to her dresser. She pulls out a strap on and I swallow hard at the size of it but rub my thighs as the anticipation has me drenched for more. Doing as I was told, I get on all fours as she comes to the side of the bed and pokes my lips with the dildo. "Open and suck. Get him nice and wet for me." She orders and I take it down my throat, gagging a few times getting it nice and wet for her.

She pulls out with a pop, walking behind me and pulling my hips to where she wants before she finally slams inside me. I moan, pushing back against her as she pulls out and slams into me again. I reach down between my legs and rub my clit hard and fast. She slaps my ass with every thrust, rolling her hips to fuck me deeper. It doesn't take long for my orgasm to build as she continues to slam into me, but someone walks in the door.

"What the fuck Hazel? She's our cousin!" Preston yells.

"Only blood related to Prince. Now either come join or get the fuck out." She yells and his eyes go wide, taking a second to think about it.

"Ewww, you're my sister. Asshole. I'm not sharing a girl with you. Get fucked." He yells, slamming the door. She giggles and I can't help but laugh too. She slams into me a few more times as I pinch my clit and gush my release all over the silicone toy. She pulls out and shoves her face into the mess I made, sucking my clit until I cum down her neck. I collapse onto the bed, unable to move as I take ragged breaths.

"Damn, Haze. That was hot, and I totally needed it." I confess. She kisses my ass cheek, removing the strap-on and laying down beside me.

"You ever going to tell me what happened with your boy-toy?" She whispers. And there goes the mood.

"One day, but today ain't that day. What time is it? Your Dad summoned me tonight. I don't want to be late." I say, forgetting all about having to go see him. Hazel is a great distraction for all the bullshit in my life. I just hope she doesn't think we can be anything more than a hookup.

"It's 6:30. What time do you have to meet him?" She asks.

"8." I reply and she nods her head. We lay there for a bit in silence before getting up to get dressed. She walks me out and I give her a kiss on the cheek, promising to come see her soon. Now we go see what good ol' Uncle Spade wants from me.

CHAPTER 36

DYLAN

Sitting in my uncle's office waiting for him to arrive, leaves me wondering what I'm even doing here. Usually if it's a race, he will just tell me over text, but I'm guessing that's not what this is about. Gio let me know he was running late and to make myself comfortable in his office. I've never been in here before. It's very big and luxurious, with a desk tucked in the far back and a large oval table, much like the one Fatal has in their "No one is allowed in here" office. I've only seen glimpses of it during passing if one of them happens to come in and out.

I fidget in the leather chair as I go through all the reasons why he would call me here. I hope this doesn't have anything to do with Hazel. He shouldn't be privy to what we get up to but that doesn't mean Preston didn't open his big ass mouth ratting us out.

The door opens and the man of the hour walks in dressed in a suit. This is a sight to see considering in all the years I have been sneaking around to spend time with him, not once have I ever seen him dressed in anything but jeans and a tee.

"You look dashing this evening, Uncle." I say with a big smile and he rolls his eyes, loosening the tie and pulling it over his head, tossing it onto his desk. He takes off the jacket and tosses that as well, but he doesn't stop there as he unbuttons the dark charcoal gray dress shirt, ripping it from his body. I laugh because you can totally tell this is not his doing or his style.

"Ahh, that's better. You're lucky you're my niece, otherwise I'd be stripping down to my boxers. I fucking hate suits, but your uncle insists I wear them to meetings. I'm the fucking boss. I should be able to dress how I like, but noooo I have to be professional. Fucking crock of shit if you ask me." He rants and I laugh harder as he continues.

"Have to be professional in front of a bunch of gangsters and criminals. Please make it make fucking sense." He mocks and I have tears running down my face as I continue to laugh at his charade.

"Laugh it up niece, laugh it up!" He smirks.

"Okay, okay, I'm finished. What's up? You summoned me here and I know it's not for a race. So spill it." I say as he grabs a folder and sits opposite of me.

"Why are you so fucking far? Can't we sit at your desk?" I whine and he laughs, shaking his head.

"Jameson will be here momentarily, then I'll explain everything." He says and now I'm suddenly nervous as my hands begin to sweat.

"Am I in trouble or something? Is this what it feels like for a dad to sit their daughters down and have 'the talk'?" I ask with a raised brow.

"Oh, no, no, no. I only had the talk with my boys, who then threatened to kill any guy that touched their sister." He laughs and I shake my head, thinking the apple doesn't fall too far from the tree. Bentley is the same way. The door swings open and a heaving Uncle Jameson barrels his way in. Uh oh, he doesn't look fucking happy.

"You." He points at his brother and my eyes widen as my uncle sits back and folds his arms over his chest with the biggest smirk on his face.

"You ever do that shit again, I swear to god–" Uncle Spade clears his throat and looks over at me then back to his brother whose eyes connect with mine and he smiles.

"Hello, my Little Creature. Sorry for the outburst." He says, then looks back to his brother.

"You will be dealt with later." He growls and Uncle Spade just laughs.

"Sit the fuck down and shut up already." He orders and Uncle Jameson takes a deep breath and sits, shaking his head as he gets himself situated. I wonder why he shakes his head. I almost ask but Uncle Spade clears his throat.

"I asked you to come here so we can talk about something that fell into my lap. I need you to answer truthfully. We would never judge you or think less of you. My blood runs through your veins, that means you are mine to protect, love and cherish. Family and loyalty mean everything to me." He confesses and I nod, waiting for the interrogation to start. He's not like my mom though. He isn't pressing me like she does. Anytime in the past that I have confided in him, he's always listened and gave me advice if I wanted it. He's never raised his voice, or called me a liar and most of all, he's never been down right mean and malicious. If anyone has been a parental figure in my life it's him.

"When was the last time you spoke to Easton?" He asks and I freeze. *Shit.*

"Umm, it's been awhile. A week or two." I answer truthfully.

"Why is that? Did something happen? You two were very cozy not too long ago, and then the shit you pulled at the bar, is the last time you two were seen together." He says with a raised brow and I look over at my other uncle with narrowed eyes. *Little rat.* His eyes connect with mine and he shakes his head.

"I didn't snitch on you. Slash called Spade, and I was sent to see what was going on, so put the claws away, Little Creature. Have faith in your old uncle." He laughs, shaking his head again. It's seriously on the tip of my tongue to ask him what the fuck is up with the shaking but Uncle Spade clears his throat, clearly waiting for answer, so I take a deep breath and cringe in my seat as I speak.

"For one, I didn't pull anything at the bar. Me and the girls got litty titty and we had a great time. I didn't know asking for a cigarette from some guy would cause such a scene, thank you very much." I say and they both laugh.

"Just like your Aunt, I swear if I didn't know that you are my sister's kid, I could put my life on it that you were Jade's." He says with a grin. I clearly can't avoid this any longer. Fuck. My. Life.

"The morning after the bar incident, Benny came barging into Easton's room at The Den with a video compilation of me that was sent to him. I don't know who sent it, but it wasn't good and put Easton in a very compromising position which caused my brother to flip out and kick his shit in. Apparently, after I walked out with Ace, the rest of Fatal beat the shit out of him." I say answering with half truths.

"Did he try to explain or come clean during or after?" He asks and I am not liking where this is going.

"He asked Benny to let him explain but he was too far gone to stop. When I approached, he asked me the same thing and I told him he was dead to me and that was the last time I saw him, other than from my window later that night." I answer as my hands become clammy gripping the leather arm rests.

"We know what happened to you at the academy. We also know Easton was there and everyone else who's responsible for hurting you. I don't take this shit lightly and I'm a little pissed off you didn't come to me about it. I would have taken care of it and no one would have had to know." He confesses and my eyes widen at the revelation as embarrassment creeps up my spine, making me want to crawl away and hide.

"I didn't tell anyone, I buried it acting like nothing happened. Even as they continued to taunt me. It wasn't until a month or two later that I told East-on after beating the shit out of that girl Bianca for claiming she was carrying his baby, meanwhile she was playing him from the st–" I say but Jameson interrupts.

"Bianca who?" He asks.

"Bianca Pierce," I growl and he slams his fists down onto the table.

"I knew I smelt a fucking snake. Can't they all just fucking die and stay dead. I fucking told you Spade! This shit reeks of them." He seethes as my uncle nods with furrowed brows as he thinks. I take a deep breath trying to center myself but my hands shake waiting for the ball to drop.

"What if I told you, because of your actions and deceit, you killed an innocent man?" He says and I gasp, covering my mouth with shaky hands.

"What do you mean killed an innocent man? Me and Easton killed Garett and George together and he killed Bryce alone. None of them are fucking innocent!" I yell, slamming my hands on the table, but he shakes his head, sliding a folder down to me. I catch it before it flies off the table and open it.

"Easton is dead because of you. You didn't let him explain that he was lured there by someone texting him impersonating you from your fucking cellphone." I gasp, reading the text messages that are blown up.

"Once they got him inside the academy, they sent him a video of you being beaten, hanging from the ceiling by chains." He growls as he plays the video on the big screen TV. Tears stream down my face as

I watch my dangling body swinging as they lay hit after hit.. The video stops and I read the rest of the messages.

"Easton ran up those stairs trying to get to you, unarmed and alone, knowing he could very well lose his life trying to save the one he is ordered to protect; the woman he loves. They cornered him but he still fought to get to you, until he couldn't, taking a pistol to his head. When he woke up, you were strapped to a bed with a sac over your head–" he continues and I interrupt.

"I know. I remember bits and pieces. They kept drugging me, except they said it was supposed to knock me out fully which it didn't, I could feel or hear everything, but I couldn't move to fight back or scream either. I was even hallucinating at times." I say and Jameson chimes in.

"Wait, you weren't asleep, but you could still sense everything, even though you were paralyzed? And you couldn't scream either, did I get that right?" He asks and I can only nod my head.

"Words, Dylan. I need your words," he commands.

"Yes, when I was hanging I was able to open my eyes, but what I saw was a hallucination. I saw all of Fatal in front of me but the voices didn't match the distorted faces. When I was strapped to the bed, I had the sac blocking everything out, thank God, but I was still able to open my eyes. It wasn't until Easton placed that blow to my head knocking me out, that I was actually asleep because once I came to, I was able to fully move and scream and that's when they drugged me again." I admit, taking a deep breath as Jameson sits back in his seat, tapping his finger on the table.

"This is a bigger problem than I originally thought. Too bad she didn't see the color of the syringe. That formula is either off or she's susceptible to the injection. I really wish you would have come to us. I would have taken a blood sample to see exactly what you were drugged with." He says with a look of worry.

"I agree, I think this goes much deeper than we originally thought. The Maker has a copycat who's sloppy and using multiple formulas into one injection, which can kill a person. That's not what they were created for." Uncle Spade grits.

"It's like Acid Dreams and Violet Lucies had a deformed baby," Jameson growls, his voice laced with disgust.

"Hazel is already on the hunt for him. Nothing more we can do but leave the bait and hope he's stupid enough to take it." He responds.

"Operation: Catch a Rat just got a whole lot more sinister." Uncle Jameson grins.

"Okay, back to what we were saying. Easton was held at gunpoint and forced to harm you and after knocking you out, he was zip tied to a chair and again forced to watch those men defile you." Uncle Spade says getting back on track and I shake my head.

"I saw the video—" I grit, starting to get real fucking angry with the accusations.

"Yeah you saw an edited video to paint Easton as a predator. You never took a fucking second to think. Neither did your brother and the rest of Fatal. You all assumed the worst and because of that, he's fucking dead." My uncle spits and I keep shaking my head as tears stream down my face.

"He's not fucking dead. Stop saying that!" I scream.

"Turn to the next picture." He orders and I flip the page seeing a man with a bullet hole in his temple. His face is barely recognizable. Curly dark hair caked in blood. I think I'm going to be sick. I turn and vomit all over the floor beside me. A napkin is slid in front of me but I don't move as the tears continue to fall down my face. *No. This can't be happening.* I-I killed him. I did this. All because I didn't give him a chance to explain.

"You knew this man your entire life and he never once harmed you! He took a fucking oath to protect you, on my fucking orders, and never once has he ever gone against my word! He was like a son to me. I saved him from the life me and your uncles had. How could you ever think he would do something like that to you?" He spits as I shake my head, never taking my eyes off the dead man in front of me. I run my fingers over the picture, wishing I could have handled this differently. Now he's gone. I can't, I fucking can't. I shove the folder away and look up at my uncle, his face riddled with disappointment. My heart hurts so fucking bad.

"Answer me!" He yells and I jolt from his tone.

"I-I don't know." I stammer and he slams his fists against the table.

"You don't know? You don't fucking know. That's not a good enough answer." He growls.

"I-I was so hurt, embarrassed and ashamed. I watched the video and saw Easton doing those things to me. I wasn't thinking logically, I wasn't thinking at all. Why didn't he come clean? Huh? Why is this just my fault? He had plenty of time to come fucking clean and just tell me the truth!" I yell.

"Men do stupid things and make irrational decisions for the ones they love. Would you have actually listened? Or just block him, writing him off like you did the first time, instead of dealing with the problem head on. You run and hide like a little rabbit. You're a fucking Rodriguez! We don't fucking run, nor do we cower!" He yells and I jump again at his tone.

"I don't know what you want me to say. I'm sorry. I don't fucking know!" I yell. This can't be real. It just can't be.

"There's nothing left to say. A young man's life was taken too soon because you reacted first instead of taking a beat and using the brain God gave you. I'm disappointed in you. As your punishment, the next race will be your last one. You will reveal your true identity to Fatal and let the cards fall where they may. Now go home. I'll be in touch." He says, dismissing me. I get up on shaky legs and leave as fast as they will carry me.

Getting in the car, I start it up and leave the same way I always come in. Once on the highway, I break, letting the tears pour down my face. I sob so hard I can barely see anything in front of me. A horn honks and I veer to the side of the road, skidding in the dirt as I slam on the brakes.

I'm so sorry Eas. I'm so sorry for not letting you explain. This is all my fucking fault. I'll never fucking forgive myself for this. I slam my fists against the steering wheel, screaming bloody murder. I can't. I just fucking can't. I close my eyes for a moment trying to calm down but I can't, I keep seeing that picture of him over and over again. It won't leave my mind.

It's fucking torture. I don't want to remember him like that. I scream again. I need to get home. I-I just need– *HIM.*

Two months later, I'm a shell of a person. I refuse to speak to anyone, including my mother and brother. I've just been silent. Carter came out of hiding and has been texting me, threatening to come hurt me again, but I don't care. They could kill me and I could care less. I actually pray for it nightly. If it brings me closer to Easton, then do it already. He's been a missing person for the last two months, his body never found. April has scoured the earth for him with my mother by her side. I refuse to accept it. Not until I see his body in front of me. I've spent numerous nights in his room, sleeping in his bed, inhaling his scent. Last week his smell started to fade and I broke down, trying to find it. I wear his shirts to bed praying the smell never fades but it does. I imagine seeing him from time to time in the crowds at school but once I blink, he's gone.

Tonight, I was summoned for my last race. I went to the warehouse and retrieved my bike. Now I wait on the starting line for my brother and the rest of Fatal. There's a few newcomers tonight that I've never seen before but I don't care. I'm not in the mood to even be here, but orders are orders. As the other racers line up, some girl in a bikini does her thing with the flag and off we go. I hit the throttle taking off, speeding down the same road we always race on.

All I can think of are the times I would get a rush beating Easton on race night. He always wanted to be the best of the best, but he could never beat me. Now I'll never get to race beside him again. After tonight, I'm selling my bike and gear, there's no fun in it anymore. Not with him being gone.

One of the new guys comes real close to my bike, taking me out of my thoughts as we hit our first turn. He skids in front of me trying to veer me off the road but I handle my bike with precision and whip ahead of him, hitting the throttle at full speed. I shift gears getting ready for the straight run to the finish line. This fucking guy is on my tail again. I hit the nos and he can eat my dust as I cross over the finish line and circle around.

I stop at the roadmaster to collect my winnings and head back to where my brother and the others stop. Just as I hit the kick stand down and climb off my bike, I see a crowd forming. I think nothing of it and walk over to my brother and stand before him with my hand on my hip.

"This is a turn of events. Usually you dip out and we never get a chance to meet the infamous Midnight Rider." He mocks with a laugh. Oh, he better laugh it up now because he's about to lose his shit. I take my helmet off and shake out my hair.

"Surprise, brother." I say with a grin as his mouth drops open and 'what the fucks' are being thrown around by the others.

Surprise, surprise.

CHAPTER 37

DYLAN

"Never thought you were being beaten by your little sister, aye?" I ask, doing a little dancy dance which he doesn't find remotely funny.

"Oh, shit." Ace says, his face dropping as he cups his junk.

"You're a fucking pig, asshole." I grin but he shakes his head.

"Do you know how many times I jerked off to you, not knowing you were YOU? Now my spank bank is ruined!" he yells, throwing his hands in the air.

"Good, you idiot." I laugh. Benny still hasn't said a word but the questions start flying.

"Where did you get the bike?" Kingston questions as he runs a finger along my ride.

"Who taught you to ride like that?" Antonio asks.

"This bike is fire. There's no way you did all the work yourself. God forbid the Ice Queen breaks a nail, let alone get her hands dirty." Ace accuses and I narrow my eyes at him as Benny finally decides to pick his chin up off the concrete and use his mouth to form words. After throwing his helmet across the ground, he moves in front of me, getting in my face.

"You've been playing us the whole time?" He accuses and I grin, thinking *fuck it.* It's time to lay all the cards on the table.

"You can thank your boss for that!" I spit as he jumps back like I hit him or something.

"Run that back to me." He orders, and I smirk.

"I fucking said you can thank your boss." I grin, not backing down as his eyes narrow on me.

"And who's my boss, Miss-know-it-all?" He asks, rubbing his thumb under his scruffy chin.

"Oh, Uncle Spade." I reveal, and his face pales. *Got 'em.* Gasps can be heard all around us but Benny remains like a statue, unmoving.

"He's mom's younger brother. She's been keeping this little secret our entire lives. Ain't it fun being left in the dark?" I sass and he slaps me across the face. I'm stunned into silence. He's never put his hands on me like this before. I cup my face feeling the heat radiate from my cheek. I rear back but a familiar voice stops me.

"Back the fuck up, Bentley," comes from somewhere deep in the crowd. I'm frozen for a second but I don't see anyone. Fuck it. I slam my fist into my brother's face, causing him to stumble back. Kingston tries to get a hold of him but he slips right past his reach, grabbing me by my hair, and pushing me hard to the ground. I cry out, feeling my tailbone crack as it hits the pavement.

"You're a fucking liar," he spits, wrapping his hand around my throat, squeezing roughly. Everything happens so quickly, one minute I'm being choked out and the next Bentley flies onto the pavement.

"I told you to back the fuck up." There's that fucking voice again. I look over and see combat boots but I can't fucking see who it is. There's too many fucking people surrounding them. I try to get to my feet but the pain that radiates up my back puts me on my ass.

Fuck, something isn't right. I lay on the concrete as I hear yelling and skin hitting skin while I look up at the sky as tears fall from my eyes. *There's no one here to help me. I'm all alone.* They don't care that I'm laying here unmoving staring at the sky as it starts to spin. I close my eyes hoping the spinning would stop, but when I open them again it's worse. Then I hear, "Hellcat, talk to me. Wake up. Please wake up," and a smile litters my face.

"Always saving me, huh, Crow?" Then darkness takes me from a dream to a nightmare.

Jolting awake, I scream for Easton, but it's so quiet. A dull beeping hits my ears and the smell of disinfectant assaults my senses as I try to sit up but my wrists and ankles are strapped to the bed I'm laying in. I peel my eyes open, which instantly water from the harsh brightness of the light above me. My heart rate picks up as I thrash against the restraints trying to get myself free. I don't know where the fuck I am.

What is happening? I scream as I continue to pull and kick as hard as I can. *Why am I restrained? How did I get here? Wherever here is.* It hurts so fucking bad to open my eyes, it's like I have been asleep for so long and they refuse to adjust to the light beaming down on me.

A door opens and footsteps squeak against the floor, getting louder the closer they get. Fingers run down my face and along my jaw. "Shh, settle down sweet child. No need to scream," he soothes as he caresses my face. His sinister voice and strong cologne are vaguely familiar. I want to open my eyes so bad and see who he is but it burns so fucking bad.

"W-who are you?" I rasp, needing a drink to put the fire out in my throat.

"You know who I am, I've just been hiding deep in your memories. It's almost time for you to come out and play with us," he says, tightening the straps on my wrist.

"I don't want to play. I just want to go home. Let me go." I yell and he slaps me across my cheek. Tears instantly leak from my eyes.

"Be a good girl and hush. The more you scream, the more you will be stuck in the abyss, and I have plans for you so I need you to behave." He threatens and I take a deep ragged breath.

"What is it that you want with me? I'm just a girl in college. What can I possibly have that you want?" I ask, and he laughs sinisterly.

"An heir, my sweet girl. Your mother failed with her abomination of an incest baby and we cannot have that. He's useless. You, on the other hand, have the perfect bloodline to give me an heir who will reign true power in the future. My legacy must live on," he confesses.

"A son? Incest baby? What the fuck are you talking about?! I'm not giving you a child. Get fucked." I spit, pulling against my restraints wishing I could get myself free.

"You don't have a choice. Ya see, while you were asleep, I had your IUD removed and administered hormones into your IV to get your eggs ready." He laughs as I continue to try and free myself.

"Fuck you. You're sick." I spit, hoping he's fucking lying.

"Tell me something I don't already know. I'm just not as sick as your grandfather who raped your mother because he so desperately needed her to fulfill her legacy." He confesses and I gasp. No. That can't be true.

"You're a liar." I growl and he slaps me again, this time my face whips to the side from the impact. I cry out from the sting that radiates my cheek.

"Am I? Guess only time will tell my dear. Now, back to sleep you go. I have more tests to run on you, my Little Puppet. Your blood rejects the molecules in these injections. You were supposed to die the night those idiots took you and I need to know why you didn't. Plus, plans have changed and you might be my ultimate weapon. Hopefully, this next injection doesn't kill you, sweet girl." He whispers as I feel the sudden rush of heat flow through my veins. I thrash, wanting to get out of here and as far away from this man as I can get.

"No, please no. Let me fucking go." I scream.

"Hush little baby, don't you cry," he sings and I immediately stop as tears spring from my eyes and a burst of white floods my vision pulling me into a memory of a tall blonde man with piercing blue eyes holding me as a little girl singing me that lullaby as I cry out for my mother. I remember Bentley huddling in a corner with duct tape covering his mouth as he cried, watching as this man held a knife to my throat. A sinister laugh follows the end of the song as the man whispers in my little ear.

"Poor little mommy isn't going to buy you anything, she's too busy chasing a ghost she'll never catch, but she will never hide from the big bad wolves." Then I'm pulled into another memory, as I run through the grass, my pigtails whipping me in the face. I look back to see if Benny is still chasing me, but I slam into strong legs. I look up and see the tall man who sang me to sleep. "Hello, sweet girl," he whispers, smiling down at me as he takes a bright green needle from his pocket. Before I could scream, he stabs me in the neck and I fall to the ground, causing my vision to spin, bringing me back to reality as the same man whispers in my ear.

"Give me what I want and no harm may come to the ones you love. When you wake up, be a good girl and I'll let you go. Tick, tock, Little Monster!" Tears stream down my face at the realization of who he is as the drug fully hits my system warping my brain into a spiral of colors and shapes before I see a tunnel of light and Easton standing at the entrance with his hand out waiting for me. Before I fall deep into the abyss I whisper,

"Yes, father."

CHAPTER 38

EASTON

I've been gone for months, sent away as punishment for what I did. We were all punished for our actions, but now I'm back and nothing will stop me from getting my girl. It's been brutal to watch from the sidelines as she dealt with my fake death all alone. I wasn't in agreement with that part of the punishment but Spade and the others insisted. Again, I was left without a choice.

Arriving at the race last night, I did not expect the Midnight Rider to be Dylan, let alone their family secrets spilled for everyone to see. After punching him in the face for laying hands on my girl, I immediately noticed she wasn't moving and something was seriously wrong.

Despite all the guys yelling, I scooped her in my arms, placed her in my car, and took her to the

ER. Once we arrived, they took her straight back, concerned she could be suffering from a spinal cord injury. I was beside myself with worry for her. I kept going up to the nurses asking for any type of updates. All they would tell me is that they were running tests and placed orders for X-Rays and a CAT scan.

My leg constantly shook as I sat, nervously waiting for what felt like hours until finally a Doctor came in to let me know she has a broken tailbone and a concussion with swelling in her brain, meaning they have to put her into a brief medically induced coma in order for the swelling to go down. After she was stable, they moved her to a private room while we wait for the swelling to go down.

I left for a few hours to go see my mom because I knew she'd been scouring the earth looking for me. I'll give it to her, she never stopped, never gave up. I needed to show her I was alive and well. Did I tell her the exact truth? Fuck no. But Spade and the others concocted a solid story for me to feed her. It worked after a lot of tears and her hitting me, but needless to say, she's calm and happy that I'm home. I felt bad for making her think I was dead, but it had to be believable in order for the plan to work. I just hated that the two women I love the most suffered from it, but I vowed to myself that I will make it up to them for the rest of my life.

Taking out a cigarette, I light it and inhale the minty smoke as I drive back to the hospital. The need to be by her side when she wakes up, to hold her in my arms and feel her sweet lips against mine, is all I want right now. *I've missed her so fucking much.* I just hope she forgives me for making her think I was dead. There's no way I can spend another moment without her, it's already been too long. Plus, we have two more fuckers to kill and I refuse to do it without her.

Arriving at the hospital, I shut off my car, grab the bouquet of flowers from the dash and climb out as I take a deep breath of fresh air, letting the sun kiss my skin while I walk to the entrance and head straight to the elevators. Hitting the button, the doors slide open and I get in, hitting the eighth floor. The car takes me up and dings once I reach the correct level.

Stepping out, I make a left down the hall, bypassing the nurses station, right to her room. Opening the door, I see an empty bed and think, do I have the wrong room? I back track and look at the plaque on the wall with the correct room number. *What the fuck?* I spin and hit the nurses station. Clearing my throat trying to gain someone's attention, an older lady looks up at me with a smile. "Can I help you, young man?"

"Yes, ma'am, my girlfriend is supposed to be in room eight-oh-eight but it's empty. Did they take her for more tests?" I ask, impatiently waiting for an answer.

"What's her name, dear?" She replies, typing on her computer.

"Dylan St. James. She was admitted last night." I blurt, and her eyes furrow.

"Um, I'm sorry dear, there is no one by that name registered here." She says with a frown.

"Are you sure? I brought her in myself. She had a broken tailbone and a concussion." I grit, getting angry that they lost my girl.

"Nope, I'm sorry. No one by the name Dylan or St. James has been here in the last twenty-four hours." She apologizes and I nod my head in thanks. Gripping the flowers tightly, I walk back to the elevators, wracking my brain at how this could have happened. *A girl just doesn't fucking disappear into thin air.* Taking out my phone to text the guys, I smack the button for the main floor.

Me: Was Dylan discharged this morning?

Bentley: The ghost has risen and is gracing us with his presence.

I roll my eyes, we have unfinished business to handle but that can wait until later.

Me: Well?

Ace: I haven't seen her since last night. Been waiting for an update.

Kingston: Same.

Antonio: Me three. Lol.

Me: Seems to me the prince of darkness has his thumb up his ass and could care less about his fucking actions.

Bentley: Preaching to the choir, my guy.

I slide the phone into my pocket and step into the elevator. That was fucking useless. I can't text Eleana because she has no clue what has happened and I plan on keeping it that way for now. Finally, making it to the main floor, I walk out of the elevator and through the front entrance to my car, nearly getting hit by an all black SUV speeding through the lot.

My phone rings as I reach my car and see a piece of paper lying on my windshield under the wipers. Letting the call go to voicemail, I remove it from the glass and read it, "It's time to come out and play, Little Puppet." I crumple it in my fist and let out a roar. "Mother fucker!" I scream, ripping my door open and climbing in, taking my phone out and pressing the call button as I lay the flowers on the passenger seat.

"What's up, Eas?" Spade answers, sounding way too chipper for my liking.

"He has her!" I growl as I hear shuffling and a door close. I don't have the patience to wait for him to get his thoughts together.

"This was not part of the plan! She is not the fucking bait, Spade!" I yell.

"How do you know it's him? We have a lot of enemies, Easton, fucking think!" He growls as I tighten my grip on the phone.

"Think?! You want me to think while my girl was fucking sedated, with a swollen brain and broken tailbone, who disappeared into thin air without a trace... and you want me to fucking think?" I yell, clenching my jaw so hard I'm surprised my teeth don't shatter from the pressure.

"Again, how do you know?" He spits down the line.

"Are you not hearing me? She's gone, helloooo, big fucking red flag, on top of the note found on my windshield!" I seethe and he takes a deep breath.

"Why didn't you lead with that, dipshit?" He yells. For fucking Christ sake.

"You know the answer to that!" I growl.

"What did the note say?" He asks.

"Time to come out and play, Little Puppet." I reiterate and something crashes down the line as Spade yells, but I can't make out what he's saying because the signal starts to fade, making him sound like he's underwater, then the call fails.

A text immediately comes through with instructions to meet at The Den. I hit Dylan's contact hoping *maybe* she unblocked me and has her location turned on. *Bingo!* There's that little blue dot on the move! *Fuck yes! I'm coming for you, Hellcat!*

Starting my car and putting it in gear, I pull out of the parking lot onto the main road and shoot a text to Spade letting him know I got her location! My phone immediately rings and I pick it up, putting it on speaker.

"Eas, don't fucking follow!" Spade screams down the line.

"I can't do that, Spade! You know I can't." I say, shaking my head as he sighs.

"I know man, but you're alone and unarmed. It's a suicide mission. This is exactly what he wants!" He spits.

"I have to at least try! He can't fucking have her!" I yell, pounding my fists against the steering wheel. I hear shuffling before Jameson's voice growls through the speakers.

"I know the monster better than anyone else. I've been his puppet for far too long. My father is smart and always ten steps ahead. I order you to stand the fuck down and get your ass to The Den! Now, Easton! Or you will be signing a death warrant for you both! Is that what you want?" Slamming my fists again, I know he's right, I'm playing right into his hand.

"No, that's not what I want, but we need a plan! I've done everything asked of me and now I need all hands on deck to save her. Please grant this to me." I beg as shuffling comes down the line.

"Done! Meet you at The Den in twenty." Spade says, and the line disconnects. I take a deep breath, wanting to continue following the blue dot, but I won't risk her life doing so. I take a left as I drive the opposite way from the girl I love. Clicking over to the group chat, I give them a heads up.

> **Me: The Kings are coming! Be there in 5.**

Bentley better get the fuck over himself real fucking quick because The Kings won't tolerate his bullshit today. Him and Spade have their own hashing out to do.

"Fuck!" I yell. I forgot to warn Spade that Bentley knows. Shit!

Welp, it is what it is at this point. I pull into the parking lot of The Den and Kingston is standing outside the doors yelling at someone on the phone. Shutting my car off, I climb out and raise a brow at him. He shakes his head, giving me that 'Not now' look as I head inside. *No one is in sight which means everyone is in the office.* I walk down the hall and enter the room. Bentley snarls at me and I've about had enough of his bullshit.

"Grow up, Bentley. This shit isn't about you or us! Now get your head in the game before The Kings arrive." I spit. He pushes against the table and stands, causing the chair to fall back.

"Who are you to bark orders at me?" He points and I laugh.

"Look at you. You're acting like a fucking wounded child. Why? Because I'm in love with your sister and lied about it?"

"That's enough!" Spade yells, scolding us like children as he enters the room with Jameson not too far behind.

"Anyone check the room for bugs?" Spade asks, and no one says anything.

"Kingston usually does that." I answer and he rolls his eyes.

"Well, get his ass in here. Our phones were compromised and I'm betting so is everything here. We need to sweep everything and everyone." He orders.

"Why everyone?" Antonio asks, and Jameson chimes in with a huff.

"Because you idiots don't know who the fuck you're dealing with. My father is a ruthless fucking man who will stop at nothing to get what he wants.

He'll go as far as administering a tracker and listening device in the human body. We know from experience." He says, taking out a wand from his jacket pocket that looks similar to Kingston's.

"What the fuck is actually going on?" Bentley says, pounding his fists on the table. Jameson doesn't hesitate rounding the table, grabbing him by the scruff and slamming his face down into the wood. A crunch reverberates through the room.

"Watch your fucking tone! This is not a fucking game. Shut the fuck up and wait until we sweep the room." He growls as he lifts up the chair, throwing Bentley back in it. Kingston finally barrels into the room, shutting the door behind him.

"My apologies, my mom was trippin'." He says exasperated.

"How is Ophelia holding up?" Spade asks.

"She's managing with Dad being inside." He says with a shrug.

"Let her know I'm working on getting him home. In the meantime, let's get this place swept." Spade orders and Kingston nods, walking over to the desk, retrieving his device and getting to work. Jameson goes around the room, running the wand over everyone. The instrument chimes when he gets to Bentley and his eyes widen. He runs it over the back of his neck and it lights up, then again over his groin. *Fuck.*

"This is going to sound weird but, do you have a bump on your shaft?" Jameson asks not giving a fuck how awkward this shit is.

"What the fuck? I-I don't know." Bentley stammers.

"How do you not know? Take your dick out. I'm pretty sure you have a device on it." Jameson says and Bentley shakes his head.

"You either do it or I'll do it for you and you won't like how." Jameson threatens. Bentley stands taking a deep breath, unzipping his jeans, taking his dick out.

"I'm going to need you to make it hard for me." Jameson says and Bentley's eyes go wide.

"How? I'm not gay and there's a room full of dudes," he panics.

"Call Amy in. Put her on her knees and get it hard." Jameson orders.

"What? No, I'm not having my girl come in and do that in front of everyone!" he yells, but Jameson grabs it and starts pumping.

"Jameson!" Spade yells, but he ignores his brother.

"It's either I do it or she does it. Don't fucking embarrass yourself, team leader!" Jameson growls.

"Fine, just get your hand off my junk!" He spits. Jameson pulls away and Bentley takes out his phone, calling Amy to come in here. Seconds later, there's a light knock on the door and Antonio opens it, letting her in. Her eyes widen at all the men in the room. Jameson steps up and grabs her hand, placing a kiss on it. A blush crawls up her cheek and Bentley growls.

"Hello, new Little Creature. We need your assistance. Your boyfriend can't seem to get it up for us. I'm sure you have been down there more often than not. Do you know where the bump is on his shaft?" He asks as Bentley continues to growl while Jameson runs his finger down her jaw.

"Uh, yes. I know where it is." She answers with a smile.

"Good, can you get on your knees for him? Get him nice and hard and show us where it is." He whispers.

"Right now?" She responds with wide eyes.

"Yes, please. Be a good girl and maybe he will give you a treat?" He says as they walk over to a very pissed off Bentley. *He better keep his shit together because Jameson is one scary mother fucker when pissed off.* She gets on her knees as instructed, taking Bentley into her mouth. He groans as she sucks him hard and fast. Jameson removes her head with a pop and she shows him exactly where the bump is.

"Such a good girl, Little Creature. You are dismissed. Run along now." He warns, and she scampers out of the room.

"Don't lose the spot. We need to remove it." Jameson orders and Bentley pales. *I grab my own junk because fuck that.* Spade takes the first aid kit out of the bottom drawer of the desk and pours disinfectant on Bentley's shaft. He hisses and damn near goes soft as Jameson takes out a bag, unzipping it and laying it out on the table. Bentley passes out at the sight of all the different scalpels. *I would have passed out too.* Jameson takes one and pours the same liquid on the metal and slices a small cut along Bentley's shaft, pushing the device out. He does the same with the one on the back of his neck and comes over to me after discarding the tiny rods, waving the wand over my body. He smiles once he's finished. Kingston finally gives the all clear and now we can talk fucking business.

It takes hours to come up with a solid plan to get Dylan back. Kingston showed Jameson his set up which impressed the guy and they have been using both of their programs and contacts to hack into Dylan's phone. The blue dot finally stopped about an hour north of us. We just don't know if it's a set up or not, so Spade sent some men to scope it out before we suit up.

Bentley finally woke up and was glad he passed out, not having to witness the bloodshed. Him and Spade left to go talk. Hopefully, they don't kill each other. I leave the office and head to my room while we wait. I was so close to getting my girl back and then this. Why? What the fuck does she have that he wants so bad? I don't fucking understand. Is she even sedated? Was anything the doctor said true? Was I fucking played that whole time and didn't realize it? So many fucking questions. I just want her back. My phone pings, taking me out of my thoughts and I reach into my pocket opening it. It's a text from unknown.

> **Unknown: Meet at this address if you want her to live. Multimedia video attached. Click to open.**

I click it and watch as my girl struggles against ropes that tie her legs together in the corner of a van. Her arms are behind her back with duct tape covering her mouth as tears stream down her face.

> **Me: You have my attention.**

> **Unknown: Good. Come alone and don't alert the others. If I even see anyone but you, she dies and the blood will be on your hands.**

> **Me: Send me the address. I'm leaving now.**

> **Unknown: Such a good Little Puppet.**

I leave the prick on read and grab my racing jacket, hiding my holster underneath it. Leaving my room, I tell the guys my mom called and needs me to come home real quick. They all nod except for Jameson. He eyes me down, reading the deceit on my face. I school my features and assure him I'll be right back. He nods and I leave.

Getting into my car, I plug in the address on my phone, seeing it will take forty-five minutes to get there. An idea pops into my head and I make a call I didn't think I'd have to make.

"Hello, Boytoy. How's my Little Pet doing?" Hazel greets.

"Not well, Haze. I need your help. Think of it as a job. A solo job. You in?" I ask.

"First, I need to know what's wrong with my Skittle Pop and that will lead me into whether I'm in or not." She quips and I shake my head.

"She's been taken and I'm going to get her. What I need–" I don't even get to finish before she's yelling down the line.

"What the fuck, Easton? You should have led with that. Where and when? No one takes my pet and lives to tell the tale."

"She's mine, Hazel. Don't get it twisted." I growl.

"Maybe so, but she loves when I make her cum." She laughs sinisterly.

"I see you've been keeping my girl nice and warm for me." I say with a grin.

"Something like that, but anyway, where and when?" She growls.

"Now. I'll send you the address, but here's the catch. I need eyes up high. You know what to do." I say and she laughs.

"Finally I get to use my mom's sniper rifle. I'll be waiting for your text." She says.

"Thanks Hazel. I owe you."

"Nonsense. Just let me borrow her every so often or you can watch. That's payment enough for me." She giggles, ending the call.

I send her the info she needs, feeling better about going alone than I was before. I'm glad I made that call. Hazel is a sharp shooter, so if this is a set up, she will be my eyes in the sky. Getting on the highway, I gun it.

I'm coming for you, Hellcat. Just hang on for me, baby.

CHAPTER 39

EASTON

It takes me less than forty-five minutes to arrive at this deserted lot. Hazel texted me about twenty minutes ago, letting me know she was in place. I told her to only shoot on my signal. She wasn't pleased, but we have to do this strategically. There's a black van and SUV parked in the distance. I get out of my car and lean against my hood, tapping the holster strapped to my belt.

The SUV door opens and a tall man with dark hair, dressed in a suit holding papers and a tablet, walks towards me as two men spill out of the van. Both armed heavily with guns. I take a deep breath as one of them opens the sliding door retrieving the girl I love by her hair. I reach into my holster for a throwing star but the other man lifts the AK strapped to his chest, pointing it at her head as they all walk towards me.

A shot rings out, colliding with the man's skull, exploding his head wide open. *Fuck! Hazel.* Dylan screams as the blood and brain matter ricochet off her face. Another shot rings out in the distance, but it doesn't make contact. A knife is suddenly pushed against Dylan's neck as I reach for my sais.

"Enough!" is yelled through the tablet the suit guy is holding.

"One more fucking move and you both are dead. This is a simple fucking transaction." The voice commands.

"Let's get this over with. What the fuck do you want?" I spit and he laughs.

"Clyde, hand the Little Puppet the papers." He orders and Clyde lays them on the hood of my car.

"You both are to sign over your first-born son to me. You will care for him for the first thirteen years and then he's mine to do as I see fit. You will be paid a substantial amount of money throughout this contract. You have two years to fulfill it or you both die." He says like this is a no brainer. I look over at Dylan whose eyes are wide as tears pour down her face.

"And if I don't sign this contract? Who's to say I don't just kill everyone here and take her home?" I ask, because fuck this, I'm not signing my unborn child over to this psycho.

"I figured you would ask that. Clyde, press play on the video." He orders and the screen lights up to our sleeping mothers with guns to their temples. *He fucking knew this would get me. Using our moms as weapons to get what he wants. Fuck.* My eyes collide with Dylan's and she nods her head as tears pour from her eyes. *Fuck!* I take the pen from this clown and sign my name. The papers are snatched from the hood and brought over to Dylan as her hands are untied, taking the pen with shaky hands, she signs on the dotted line. My heart drops at what this means for our future. *We are fucked!*

"Now you are free to go. Your mothers will be released by the time you get home to insure you don't try to kill the rest of my men. It was such a pleasure doing business with you both. See you soon, Puppets." He laughs, and the screen goes black. I grab Dylan and pull her in for a hug as the men back up, never taking their eyes off of me, dragging the dead body as they go.

"Eas, is it really you?" She rasps, squeezing me tighter.

"Yes, baby. It's me. Let's get in the car and get the fuck out of here." I whisper, kissing the top of her head. She steps back and climbs in the car and I follow suit. I'm not ready to take her home. I want to be alone with her for tonight as long as she will have me.

"Can we go get a hotel and be alone tonight? I don't want to take you home just yet." I say, nervous she will reject me.

"Yes, please. We have a lot to talk about." She replies and I nod, putting the car in gear and whipping out of the deserted lot. I click over to the text threads and see I'm cooked. *The guys know what I did. Fuck. I'm definitely not going back tonight.* First, I text hazel to see what the fuck happened.

> **Me: What happened to waiting for my signal?**

> **Hazel: It wasn't me and I'm handling it.**

> **Me: What the fuck do you mean it wasn't you?**

> **Hazel: I'll explain later. Tell my Skittle Pop I said hello.**

> **Me: Jesus Christ, fine!**

Switching over to the group chat, I send out a text.

Me: I got her! We will be back tomorrow.

Kingston: The Kings are not fucking happy.

Me: I can imagine.

Antonio: You both good?

Me: I don't know, man.

Bentley: What do you mean you don't know?

Me: Oh now you give a shit?

Ace: Can we not fucking argue? This is a good thing. Everyone is alive, right? Dylan's safe?

Me: Yes and yes. Let Spade know I'll call him momentarily.

Bentley: Roger that and thanks, man!

Me: Shut the fuck up. You can be in your feels tomorrow. Them pain meds did you right, huh?

Bentley: Listen, I'm sorry. I was fucking wrong.

Me: Save it for tomorrow. Can someone swing by the houses and check on our moms? Don't ask questions, just do it. Plus, we are summoned there in the morning.

Bentley: Fine. Jameson is going to check.

I roll my eyes. He's such a crazy mother fucker. Hopefully, he gets in and out undetected, otherwise a bullet will meet his head.

Me: Okay. I'll see you guys to-morrow.

They all respond with their okays, and I take a deep breath, looking at Dylan. Her hair is a fucking mess and she seems so fucking sad.

"I hate the look on your face and it's my fault it's there." I say, catching a stray tear running down her cheek.

"I spent the last two months thinking I killed you. Then all this happened and I'm just fucking numb. Is this real? Am I going to wake up from this dream and still be locked in a nightmare where you're fucking dead? Because if that's the case, I don't ever want to wake up. I can't survive this life without you. I just fucking can't. I tried and I don't want to do it." She sobs.

"Please don't cry, Hellcat. I'm not going anywhere. This is fucking real." I say, taking her hand, placing it over my rapidly beating heart.

"You feel that, baby? You feel how fast it beats for you? I'm real. This is real. I promise you that." I whisper and she sobs, pulling at my shirt. If I wasn't driving, I would scoop her in my arms and hold her forever, but I need to get us to a hotel.

A few hours later, after arriving to a hotel close to home and being threatened by Spade, we both shower separately and lay in bed. I hold her in my arms as she wraps her naked body around mine and lift her chin so I can see her gorgeous ocean blues.

"I'm so fucking sorry for lying to you, baby. I should have come clean after it happened." I whisper, and she places a finger over my lips.

"No, Eas. You did what you had to do. I'm the one who's sorry for not letting you explain and assuming the worst. I know deep in my soul you would never fucking hurt me. Anger and rage blinded the truth and I will never forgive myself for that. I'm so fucking sorry." She rasps against my lips.

"We both fucked up, but I can't live in a world where I don't get to be with you. You are all I want. All I fucking need in this life. Please forgive m–" soft lips interrupt me and I moan into the kiss, deepening it as my tongue sweeps hers. *Fuck, I missed her taste.* She groans as my hands grasp both ass cheeks, squeezing tightly. Our hands roam each other's bodies as we get lost in the kiss. She pulls away panting, reaching down to line my cock up with her entrance, pushing me on my back to straddle my hips and slamming down onto me. "Fuckkkk, Hellcat! So. Fucking. Wet." I groan as she rides my cock, whimpering.

"Jesus, Eas. I fucking missed you," she whines as I grab her hips tightly, thrusting up into her, watching her tits bounce. I go to sit up, but she pushes me back down, shoving her tits in my face as her ass bounces on my cock. I slap her ass hard as I suck a nipple into my mouth, biting it then switching to the other one as she moans, riding me faster.

"Just like that, Hellcat. Fuck Daddy's cock." I command.

"Oh god, Eas. You feel so good." She moans. *Fuck this.* I flip us over and slam into her relentlessly. It's been way too long and I want her to shatter all over me. I kiss her face, sucking her bottom lip as she meets me thrust for thrust. I sit up and press my thumb on her clit, pulling it up as I spit on it and rub tight circles. She tightens around me as her body starts to tremble.

"Let me hear it, Hellcat." I command.

She screams her release as her body spasms under me. Flicking her clit hard and fast, she gushes on my cock as I feel that familiar tingle creep up my spine, I pull out and paint her pretty swollen pussy with my cum. "Fuck, baby." I growl, lifting her hips up high to lick our cum from her cunt. I gently place her ass on the bed and grab her by the neck, pulling her up to me as she opens her mouth like the good fucking girl she is, and I spit our release onto her waiting tongue. "Swallow us." I command and I watch her throat bob.

"Such a good fucking girl." I praise. She pulls me down onto her, biting my bottom lip. I kiss her, loving the way we both taste and before I know it, my cock is sliding into her wet cunt for round two.

"I fucking love you, Dylan. You are it for me. Forever and Always." I whisper against her lips, looking deep into her eyes as my hand cups her face and my dick slowly milks her walls.

"I fucking love you too, Eas. Ride or die baby." She smiles. We make love until the sun comes up and reality sets in of what we had to do and what's to come.

Now we have to go see what our mother's want and check in with Spade.

If only we could stay in this love bubble forever.

CHAPTER 40

DYLAN

Sitting on my mother's couch waiting for Bentley to arrive is really fucking nerve wracking. Thank God for the anchor next to me, otherwise I would have left already.

"Is Benny on his way? Because I'm over this." I whisper to Eas and he shakes his head yes.

"He should be pulling up any second." He whispers back, running his nose on the shell of my ear.

"I'm over it too. I'd much rather be stretching out your pussy than sit here and listen to whatever it is they need to tell us." A blush creeps up my cheek and I smack his chest.

"Behave, our mothers are only feet away." I laugh as a throat clears.

"Took him long enough." My mother snides as Bentley walks into the house and plops next to me, giving Eas a fist bump behind my head.

"I'm here. What's this about?" Bentley asks and April steps up.

"So I'm just going to say it. Your mom and I have been seeing each other for years." She admits, and I roll my eyes.

"We know." Both Eas and Benny say at the same time, and their eyes widen.

"Oh? Well then, I've asked April to marry me and we would like you all to take a trip with us to Aruba next month." My mother states.

"So that's the only secret you want to come clean with?" Bentley growls, and I lay a hand on his knee. This is not the time to hash out this shit.

"What do you mean Benny?" My mother asks with a raised brow. She knows damn well what he's talking about, but here we go. He's going to pull it right out of her. He stands and starts to pace. *Fuck.* I look over to Eas and he shakes his head.

"Oh, how about we have an uncle who I've been working for all these years? Or, the fact that I have cousins I didn't know were my family because you kept this fucking secret? For what?" He yells and she gasps.

"I don't know what you are talking about." She replies, and April raises a brow.

"Bullshit! We all fucking know we are family members of The Rodriguez Cartel. Fucking admit it already." He yells, throwing his hands up in the air.

"I'm sorry. I kept this secret to keep you both safe. You don't fucking know the story. My story." She yells back at him and this time I chime in.

"But I do. I know it all." I confess and she turns to me with wide eyes.

"How? No one knows. I've never told anyone but April." She whispers, looking at her fiance with accusing eyes.

"It wasn't me. I didn't say shit to anyone so take that look off your face." April points.

"It doesn't matter how I found out, but you're not telling him the full truth." I say with a pointed look, and her face drops.

"I can't, not now!" she says, shaking her head.

"Tell me what?" He says.

"Dylan, don't!" she yells, but I shake my head.

"He deserves to know. No matter what his reaction is, he deserves to know the truth." I yell and she slaps me across the face. Easton immediately gets in front of me, but I pull him back by his shirt.

"Stand down, son." April warns.

"Don't fucking touch her!" He growls as I continue to pull him towards me. He grabs my face, looking at the damage, and takes a deep breath.

"What the fuck is this? Are you two together?" My mother asks accusingly, and I look her dead in her eyes and nod my head yes.

"Yeah, we're together. Is there a fucking problem?" Easton says and my mother narrows her eyes.

"Will someone tell me what I need to know so I can fucking leave?" Bentley chimes in, but no one says shit. Eyes are on me and Easton.

"Benny, just go. Fuck this." I say, walking towards the door. Benny leaves without another glance and Easton chases after him.

"It's bad enough you ran through the swim team and now you're fucking your soon to be step broth-er?" She says and I laugh.

"That's rich coming from a liar like you. Can't even tell your fucking son that he's a product of incest, nor tell me that I have to fulfill the legacy you couldn't. Get your fucking shit together before this is the last time you see us." I spit and she slaps me again.

"You're a product of rape too, you little bitch. I'm done protecting the both of you. Fuck you and him. Get the fuck out of my house you little whore." She yells and I laugh in her face, looking at April.

"I feel bad for you! You're marrying a fake and a liar. I hope the two of you are happy." I say walking out but my mother's next words stop me.

"I should have aborted you when I had the chance." Those words hit me exactly where she intended.

"Fucking useless little spoiled bitch you are. Get out. You're not my daughter anymore. Selfish cunt." She yells and I leave with a tear running down my face. I walk down the steps and out the fence and keep walking, despite my brother and Easton yelling for me. I don't stop, I just walk. Needing to clear my head alone, it's not until a familiar truck slows alongside me that I realize I'm close to Uni. I look up and my eyes collide with Carter's and he drags his finger across his neck in warning, then the revving of an engine behind him causes him to speed off. I look over and see Easton, waiting for me with a raised brow. He lights his cigarette, taking a deep pull.

"Was that who I think it was?" He asks and I nod.

"Get in. I want to show you something." He says, and I climb in the car with him, taking off into the sunset.

The next morning, I'm standing in my bedroom at my mother's house packing my stuff up. I sent her a text letting her know I was clearing out my room. Of course it's radio silence, but Eas told me she was kicked off the case and sent to California for the week on a new assignment. So while she's gone, I figured I'd get this over with. Last night, after everything went down, Easton showed me a little house that sits on Whitestone lake. When we pulled down the long driveway and the little white house came into view, I immediately fell in love. I wasn't sure why we were there. I thought maybe it was another Airbnb and he just wanted to be alone but that wasn't the case. He bought us a house. Our own fucking house. I cried happy tears in his arms and we made love against the stairs but we didn't stop there. It was one incredible night and I can't wait to get back there. Creaking of the stairs takes me out of my thoughts.

"Hello? Eas, is that you?" I yell waiting for a reply but nothing. I continue to grab all my stuff from my bathroom and shove it in my suitcase. My closet is already empty. Eas told me not to worry about furniture. We will go shopping later to pick out everything we need. *Ugh this man makes me melt into a fucking puddle.* I'm so deep in thought that I don't feel the presence behind me until it's too late.

"You've been a bad girl, Dyl." Carter whispers and I jump out of my skin, spinning around to face him. He holds up a knife pressing it to my face, trailing it down my jaw and over my breasts. I freeze.

"I've missed this tight little body writhing beneath me, baby." He whispers and I slam my knee as hard as I can into his nuts. Jumping back, he falls to his knees and I run out of my room and down the stairs, but I'm not quick enough. My face collides with the front door as he slams me into it. "You little bitch!" He growls, pulling my shirt back and throwing me against the bookcase, causing the shelving and books to fall onto the floor. *Fuck, that hurt.* I try to right myself but he lifts me off the ground by my hair. I punch him, slicing the side of my hand with his knife causing me to cry out. Blood pours down my hand and wrist onto the floor. "You ruined everything you dumb bitch! I was supposed to be a part of Fatal. You were the key to getting me in!" He yells and I laugh.

"You aren't worthy enough to be a part of them! Fucking loser." I spit blood into his face.

"Fucking cunt!" He yells as he slams my head into the TV along with the knife only centimeters away from my eyes. My vision blurs but I refuse to stop fighting. He walks away thinking he won, but I grab one of the statues next to the TV and slam it against the back of his neck causing him to stumble forward onto the couch. I spin, running down the hallway as blood drips onto the wood floor.

Getting into the kitchen I grab a knife but he slaps it out of my hand, slamming my face onto the counter. Blood spews as I knock over the vase of fresh flowers causing glass to shatter all over the floor.

"Can you just die already? Fuck!" He screams. Then I see the reflection of fluorescent blue before I feel the pinch in my neck as a sudden rush of heat fills my veins. The room spins for only a second before Carter drops behind me.

"Hellcat! Get up. Finish this mother fucker!" Easton orders and I take a deep breath, standing.

"No, take him to the basement. I'm not done with him yet," I spit and Easton grins. A voice echoes in the distance as he drags the body down the basement steps.

"It's almost time, my Little Puppet." I shake my head as I grab the railing. What the fuck is happening? My vision blurs and I miss a step but strong arms catch me.

"You okay, baby?" He asks and I nod. At least I hope I am. I step further into the room grabbing an old chair from the corner and some bungee cords, handing them to Easton. He rolls his eyes but takes them as I wrap Carter's legs around the bottom of the chair. The room starts to spin with different colors and shapes, clouding everything in front of me. I shut my eyes tightly and open them seeing everything is normal.

"Eas, call my uncle. Get him and Jameson here now. Something is wrong. I don't fucking feel right," I say in a panic as our eyes collide and next thing I know, I'm falling back into the abyss and darkness takes over.

CHAPTER 41

EASTON

Dylan's eyes roll in her head and she falls back onto the cement floor with a thud. Fuck.

"Dylan, wake up, baby." I yell, working faster to get this fucker secured.

"I hope she's dead! The stupid fucking cunt." Carter spits and I grab a hold of his throat, squeezing.

"You're lucky I can't kill you yet!" I growl, releasing him. I step away and immediately reach for her. Feeling her neck for a pulse. *Thump. Thump. Thump. Thump.*

Taking out my phone, I dial Spade and he answers on the first ring.

"What's up, Eas?" he asks.

"Get to Dylan's house now! Bring Jameson with you. Carter came here and injected her with some fluorescent blue shit and now she's passed out!" I blurt.

"Fuck! Okay, we will be right there." He says and the line goes dead.

I'm not sure what the fuck to do at this point, other than to monitor her breathing. A few minutes go by and she jolts awake with a roar.

I step in front of her as she gets up to stand.

"You good baby?" I ask but her eyes are void, almost white instead of the ocean blues I get lost in.

"Father told me I needed to kill you all. I have a list stored in my pretty little head. Check, check, check." She says sinisterly. *What the fuck?*

"Hellcat, you're not making any sense. I need you to lay back down." I order but she slowly walks towards me.

"I'm his secret weapon to get what he wants. Did you call my uncles? They die first." She giggles as she runs her fingers down my clenched jaw, over my chest and down my abs, cupping my junk. I grunt at how rough she grabs it. She slides her hands into my jeans but I grip her wrists tightly.

"No, Dylan. I don't know what the fuck is happening but you need to back up." I command. She grabs one of my daggers and slices my chest. I push her away as she laughs maniacally.

"The drug is working. You are all dead. Finally!" Carter spits but Dylan spins on him and straddles his lap.

"I knew in the end you would choose me, baby. He can't make you feel as good as I can." He smiles, gyrating his pelvis against her. She throws her head back, laughing like a maniac and drags the dagger across his neck. I pull her off him and she strikes me again on my arm, but I don't care, she's out of her fucking mind, I know it's the drugs causing this behavior.

"Get off me, you fucking prick!" She yells and I toss her onto her ass. *If she wants to play rough, let's fucking go.* I take out one of my daggers and her eyes light up. We circle one another, never taking our eyes off each other.

"So you're just going to go around killing people? Is that the plan?" I ask and she smiles.

"Oh, there's a much bigger picture at play. Father wants everything and everyone. No matter the cost. He has so many soldiers, or puppets, as he calls them. This idiot was one and that cunt Bianca is another. There's no saving the children. They all belong to him," she grins with a smile I've never seen on her before.

"Who is your father?" A deep voice from the stairs booms out. *Fucking finally.* Jameson and Spade take in the scene but don't say a word.

"Answer me, Little Creature. Who's your daddy?" he says, stepping closer to us.

"Ahhhh, hello big brother." She smirks and his eyes narrow.

"So you're the secret he's been keeping?" He asks and she nods.

"Looks like our daddy raped my mother and now he wants me to kill everyone. I'm the secret weapon. I've already sold my soul to the Devil. There's no saving the children. Hazel, Prince, Preston, they are all dead. Including the two of you." She yells, lunging for Jameson.

"Dylan, no!" I yell but Jameson is too quick. Wrapping his hand around her wrist, he twists and the dagger drops to the ground as he holds her by the throat.

"I have a little message for our dear daddy. Let him know, The Carver is coming for him! So he better crawl back into the hole he was hiding in, because I will stop at nothing to rip his fucking heart out with my bare hands. He's taken everything from me and now, I'm going to destroy him." He spits, slamming–

"Let her fucking go, Carver, or I'll put a bullet in your fucking skull!" Eleana spits.

Holy. Fucking. Shit.

CHAPTER 42

ISABEL RODRIGUEZ

Walking down the basement steps undetected, I am stunned to hear the revelations spewing from my daughters mouth, and even more horrified to know that the man who is about to plunge black substance into her neck is the infamous serial killer, 'The Carver'.

I cock my gun and point it straight at his head. My brother takes a step towards me as I threaten The Carver to back away from Dylan but the sick fuck smiles and pushes the plunger. I pull the trigger just as I'm tackled to the ground. My head bounces off the cement floor and my gun skids across the room. For a second, everything is quiet. It's not until Dylan's screams permeate the air, that I'm brought back to reality. Reid lifts me off the ground, holding my hands behind my back. I look over at Dylan who's holding Easton, blood splatters the side of his face. I gasp at the realization that I shot my fiance's son and not the mass murderer standing in my basement.

"Who the fuck taught you to shoot? You fucking missed even if the kid shoved me out of the way. What a fucking disappointment." The Carver says, shaking his head.

"Jameson, shut the fuck up!" My brother spits, letting me go.

"I have to call this in. There's a dead boy tied to a chair, my home is in disarray and finally, The Carver is here in my fucking basement." Reaching for my phone, my brother smacks it out of my hand and it smashes to the ground on impact.

"It's sad how far you really fell down the rabbit hole of your new identity. Do you know who this kid is? No? He's the one who orchestrated your only daughters rape!" He spits and I gasp, covering my mouth with my hand. I look over at Dylan who is helping Easton to his feet as he holds his shoulder.

"Is that true Dylan?" I ask and she nods, not even looking at me.

"Who did it?" I interrogate and Easton steps up but Dylan pulls him back.

"I did, I dragged the dagger across his throat." She admits and I nod looking at my soon to be step son.

"Easton, I'm sorry. I didn't mean–" I don't get to finish as he interrupts me.

"It's fine. Just a flesh wound. You need to practice on your aim, though," he laughs and my eyes go wide.

"Isabel. We will clean this up." Reid says, and I shake my head.

"I'm a detective. I have to call this in. I made an oath. I can't just turn a blind eye." I say in a panic.

"Mom, you're a fucking Rodriguez. Act like it! You're a fake fucking detective at best. Get your head out of your ass!" Dylan spits.

"Fuck, I'm not even supposed to be here. But I was worried about you, Dylan. Something told me to come home." I say as a tear falls down my face.

"It's fine mom, just go. We will clean it up, and by the time you return, everything will look as it did before you left this morning." Dylan retorts.

"Honey, I'm sorry for everything I said, I was-" but she interrupts.

"I know Mom but I need you to get the hell out of here. Go catch your flight. I'm fine, I'm safe. These men won't let anything happen to me, especially your stepson." She laughs winking at Easton.

"She's right, Isabel. We will get this done! Just act like nothing happened today. Get on your flight and call me when you land." My brother says, pushing me towards the stairs.

"Wait, where's my mom?" Easton asks.

"She's at the precinct. Apparently another body showed up without a heart. You wouldn't happen to know anything about that would you?" I smirk, looking him in his eyes

"No, ma'am. No idea what you speak of." He laughs. I turn to head for the stairs but arms wrap around my waist.

"I love you mom, safe travels." Dylan says and I wrap my arms around hers.

"Love you too, Dylan. I'll see you soon." She nods and I head up the stairs, closing the door behind me.

It's time to get on that plane and finally kill the ghost that's been haunting me for the last twenty-one years.

CHAPTER 43

DYLAN & EASTON

Part I: Dylan:

Two months later...

"Crawl to me." He commands. I get on my knees in the sand and give the man what he wants. Everyone is in the water but someone wants my attention, like he hasn't gotten enough since we arrived in Aruba, or any other day for that matter. Since the night in the basement, the dynamic between us all has been better than ever. My mother is trying to be more caring and not so cold, which is a breath of fresh air. I think moving in with Eas was the best bet for everyone. April sold their house and moved in next door. Easton is annoyed by that because he still likes to live in a fantasy world where we could get off watching each other through the window.

"Come sit in my lap, little sister." He laughs and I roll my eyes. Ever since finding out our moms were getting married, he's been soaking in the 'little sister' bit a little too much. I slide onto his lap and he automatically grabs a handful of my breasts, pulling at my hard nipples.

"Jesus, Eas. You're insatiable." I rasp as he takes my bottom lip into his mouth.

"Only for you, Hellcat. Can we just go back to the room? I want to fill you." He whines and I roll my eyes again.

"That's only because you're on a mission to make me fat." I huff as he pulls my face to look at him.

"Damn right I do. I want this belly filled with my babies. I can't wait to taste your milk." He growls, placing a tender kiss against my lips. I moan when he slides his hand between my thighs, applying pressure to my aching clit.

"You're not playing fair baby. You promised we would hang with everyone today. We can't spend the entire time here in bed rolling in the sheets." I scold and he growls.

"Says who? We are on vacation and I just want you to myself." He whispers, kissing up my neck, sucking the soft spot underneath my ear. I giggle at the sensation.

"You promised, Easton." I say with a raised brow and a little pout of my lips.

"Fine, but let me make you cum first, then we can go in the water and you can ride my cock without anyone knowing." He smirks as he dips his hand in my bathing suit bottoms, feeling how soaked I am for him.

"Deal." I giggle, then moan as he rubs my clit in tight circles, pulls at my nipples with his other hand, and sucks my neck. He knows just how to set me on fire and have me cumming hard against his hand. After flooding his fingers, he removes them from my bottoms and sucks his fingers into his mouth.

"You always taste so fucking good, Hellcat." He groans as I go to stand but he pulls me back.

"Not yet, I need my dick to go down, otherwise I'll be giving the whole beach a show." He says and I laugh.

"Welp, sucks for you now doesn't it?" I say, getting up quickly and running for the water. I look back as I run into the warm crystal blue water as it sprays against my thighs. Easton just shakes his head as he stands, adjusting himself. I walk deeper, reveling in the feel of the ocean. The smell of the salt water and the breeze against my face. This is paradise and I never want to leave. Right here, in this moment, is everything I could ever dream of. Everyone is safe, we're all together and most of all, Easton is alive and I get to keep him forever. My ride or die bad boy.

Part II: Easton

Hours later...

The way her body trembles as I eat her cunt like a starved man, I can never get enough of this girl. I've never wanted to be with someone day and night as much as I do her. I had a dream not too long ago of Dylan, pregnant with twins, and a little boy following her around the house as she was making pancakes. Ever since that day, I've been on a mission to get her pregnant. We thought she was last month but it was a false positive. I was devastated finding out she wasn't. It didn't seem to bother her as much as it did me. She keeps saying she's not ready to become a mom, but I think she's wrong, so any chance I get to fill her, I do. Her moans take me out of my thoughts and back in the game. She pulls at my hair as her legs shake the faster I lick her clit. I love making her shatter, so I flatten my tongue, pull her nipples and milk her walls slowly. It only takes a small flutter of my tongue for her to tighten and scream her orgasm. I sit up as she pants, flipping her onto her stomach, pulling her hips back and slamming hard into her soaked core. She moans as I give her long, deep strokes. I slam her ass making her yelp. "Fuck, Eas. Just like that baby. Fuck. You make me feel so good." She whines.

"So. Fucking. Tight." I growl as I pound into her, rolling my hips, causing her body to shake.

"Fuck, Hellcat. I need you to cum again. I'm so close but I need you to shatter on my cock, aby. Now give Daddy what he wants." I command with a groan.

"Yes, yes. Take it daddy. Harder. Harderr!" She screams as I shove her face into the pillow.

"That's right you little bitch! Take this fucking dick! Fuck! I'm going to cum so hard in this wet cunt! Fuck! Hellcat!" I roar as my balls tighten and spill deep inside her tight pussy. I slow down, milking her walls making sure all my cum stays deep inside her. I lift my hand off her head and she swats at me.

"I could've suffocated you dickhead!" she yells.

"You liked it. Shut the fuck up." I say, pushing deeper into her and she groans.

"Eas, we will never leave this room if you keep it up." She laughs.

"It's always up for you baby." I smirk, slapping her ass and she tightens around me.

"Well, well, well. It looks like I'm not the only feen around these parts." I drawl and she laughs, fully belly laughs. Damn, how did I get so fucking lucky with her? I finally pull out and lay next to her. She rests her head against my chest and throws a leg over my hips.

"You happy?" I ask, and she raises her head with a lifted brow.

"Of course I'm fucking happy. As long as I'm with you, I'll always be happy, Eas. Don't ever fucking doubt us." She says sternly and I kiss her nose.

"Okay, I was just making sure." I say and she gives me that look of 'I call bullshit' and I roll my eyes.

"Fine, I just want to make sure the life we have is everything you ever dreamed of." I say and she shakes her head.

"It's so much more Eas. So much fucking more." She smiles and I kiss her lips, she deepens the kiss but we are interrupted by her phone going off. She pulls away to read the text. She looks at me with a sad smile.

"I gotta go talk to Amy. Her and Benny are fighting and she needs girl talk. I'll be back in a few hours." She promises and I pull her back to me placing a kiss on her lips. She pulls away with a smile, climbs out of bed and walks over to the closet, swaying her hips as she moves. *Damn that's one fine ass.*

"I can feel you staring at me." She yells, looking at me over her shoulder. I remove the sheets and grab my dick, stroking it slowly.

"You are not playing fair Eas." She says as her hand travels over her breast and down her stomach to her clit. She rubs tight circles and moans as I pick up my pace. We watch one another as we bring ourselves to orgasm. Stepping on the balcony to smoke a cigarette, I inhale the minty smoke as the cool night breeze hits my skin.

"I'm leaving baby, I'll be back in a few hours or sooner." She yells from the door, but I grab her and fuze my mouth to hers, kissing her like I do everytime I leave the house. She's panting by the time I pull away.

"I love you, Hellcat. Tell Amy I said hi." I smile.

"I love you too, Eas." She blushes, walking away and leaving the room. I take another hit of my cigarette feeling like something is going to happen. Everything has been too good to be true. Unless it's my anxiety of being so far away from home, not knowing what's going on with the business. My gut feeling is telling me the ball is about to drop, but I try to focus on the happy things in my life. There's so much danger surrounding all of us, but we deserve some peace while we are here. I just hope once we get home it stays that way.

...The end...but not.... This concludes Easton and Dylan's story.

Next up is Bentley and Amy's story: Remnants Of The Taken: Coming 2025.

If you want to know who Spade and Jameson are.

Start with Chaos: Kings of Chaos and Mayhem Book I on my website Ashlynnauthor.com

Acknowledgements

As always, thank you to my alphas & betas for all your help while writing this book. I'll forever be grateful for every one of you.

Thank you to my PA Jenny for taking care of everything so I could just write and not worry about all the things. I love you to the moon and back, baby.

Thank you to my groupies for all of your constant promoting and support. Ya'll are the real MVP's.

Thank you to my editor, Kelsey, for dealing with all my rogue changes, last-minute bullshit and getting this book done under a time crunch. Love you always.

To my readers, thank you for not giving up on me and I hope this book sucked you in and took you away from reality for a few hours. Remember, you are not alone. We are all in this shit together. Hop on my struggle bus and let's ride.

Sir Chaz.....Book 5 and still no list. Tsk, tsk.

ABOUT THE AUTHOR

Ashlynn is a wife and mother of 3. Hailing from Long Island, New York. She currently lives in Florida, spending her days working a full-time job and nights kicking it with her girls in her office closet, destroying souls. She is a Dark/ Horror Romance Author who is known as the Evil Mastermind, Edge Queen, Soul Destroyer, and Queen of Cliffies. She loves to tear your soul apart but also drench them panties. Her characters are dark, sultry and complex.

Made in the USA
Las Vegas, NV
06 April 2025

20607624R00236